SHE'LL NEVER LIVE

Books by Hunter Morgan

THE OTHER TWIN

SHE'LL NEVER TELL

SHE'LL NEVER KNOW

SHE'LL NEVER LIVE

SHE'LL NEVER LIVE

HUNTER MORGAN

ZEBRA BOOKS
KENSINGTON PUBLISHING CORP.

ZEBRA BOOKS are published by

Kensington Publishing Corp.
850 Third Avenue
New York, NY 10022

ISBN 0–7394–4576–6

Printed in the United States of America

Chapter One

The Bloodsucker sat on the bar stool and smiled and listened attentively as the blonde twirled a strand of overprocessed hair around her finger. She lowered her head next to his so that he could hear her above the blasting music and the voices of the Sunday night crowd. "I'm really better without him."

He nodded. He'd never come here before. Bubbles; the hip martini bar was new this summer in Albany Beach. He liked to go to bars, watch women. Let them watch him. But, tonight, he'd had no ulterior motives in coming; he just wanted to relax and have a look around. He hadn't been looking for Brandy; he usually put more planning into it. He liked to follow his special women. He liked to watch them, learn their habits, get to know them, but Brandy had approached him. Divine providence?

She'd told him she'd just moved into town after leaving her boyfriend. She started a job last week as a temp at the local community hospital. He'd seen her there the other day behind the main intake desk in the ER; her blond hair had caught his eye. Apparently she'd noticed him as well; he was like that. Women noticed him, liked him.

Brandy had now been talking about her ex-boyfriend nonstop for forty-five minutes and she was getting on the Bloodsucker's nerves. He was beginning to get antsy. He jiggled his leg on the bar stool. He wasn't the kind to sit; he needed to be moving. Thinking. Watching, all the time.

He sipped his club soda that looked like vodka to a girl who was polishing off her third martini on an empty stomach. Clear drinks. He'd learned that on TV somewhere. You can have the bartender keep bringing you another round, make it look like you're drinking alcohol right along with her, when really, you're not. Really, you're just watching her. Waiting.

"I know that," she continued, reaching with a slender hand to retrieve her drink. "And I know it's going to be hard, but once I start getting out more, you know, meeting more people with this new job . . ."

The Bloodsucker watched her tip the glass, her pouty lips brushing the edge as she drained the glass.

"I mean, I should have done it ages ago. Right? All my girlfriends told me so."

He nodded again, his eyes full of feigned understanding. He'd seen the "concerned boyfriend" or "concerned husband" look on the faces of men in made-for-TV movies and he'd practiced the expression in the mirror on the back of his bedroom door until he had it just right. Without drawing any attention to himself, he signaled to the bartender to bring another round of drinks.

"What do you think, Cory? Don't you think I should have dumped him long ago?" She swiveled on the bar stool to question the man seated on the other side of her. Her fingers, the nails painted an unnatural pink with white tips, trailed down his forearm.

The guy, a computer geek from Altoona, had come over and casually sat down and began talking to them. The Bloodsucker didn't usually work this way. He was a loner, but a little variation now and then to his routine wouldn't hurt. It added a modest excitement to the evening. A little thrill. Not that he was one of those cretins who wanted to get caught, the kind you read about in the papers who left easily traceable clues behind. He was too smart for that. Hadn't his IQ scores proved he could have been a MENSA if he'd wanted to? But there was no harm in having a little fun with the cops, with Chief Claire Bear, was there? And the women like the one on the bar stool beside him made it so easy. Like taking candy from a baby.

As for Cory, he might even come in handy.

The Bloodsucker sipped his club soda on the rocks with a twist of lime, and flexed the fingers of one hand. He was getting impatient, now that he could see options opening up to him. He didn't really like this girl that much now that he had talked to her. Brandy was her name. Brandy Jones... Smith... something common like that. She smelled like cigarette smoke... probably tasted like it. But she had come to him. Wasn't that a sign? Didn't that mean she was meant for him?

He swallowed, trying to ease the constriction in his throat. In his groin.

The need had been building in him for days...

no . . . longer. Ever since Jillian had gone. Maybe Brandy had sensed it.

When Jillian had gotten away from him, returned to Atlanta, something curious inside him had turned over, something unfamiliar that scared him a little. It was anger. He'd never felt this way before. Not about his women. He didn't take these women, do what he did, out of anger. He wasn't one of *them*. He did it out of need.

But the anger was there again tonight, lurking just beneath the surface of his calm, nice guy demeanor. He could feel it tight and suffocating in his chest. He could hear it, strangulating, in his voice. But Brandy couldn't sense it, silly girl. Those around him didn't see the rage that lurked beneath the surface of his skin.

"Oh, gosh, thanks," Brandy told the bartender as he delivered her drink. She clasped the slender stem of the fresh martini glass and raised it in a toast. "To us, my newfound friends." She giggled, looking at the Bloodsucker and then Cory on the other bar stool.

"To us," the Bloodsucker echoed. As he sipped the cold club soda, he made his decision. He would take Brandy home with him tonight. By the time he set his glass down and reached for a handful of cheese fish crackers on the bar, he'd already begun to set his plan in motion.

Brandy and Cory were now deep in conversation. She was running her finger along his knee as she spoke, flirting with him, which could definitely work to the Bloodsucker's advantage. After all, he certainly couldn't walk out of the bar with Brandy on his arm. Men did that, but he was too smart to make such a blinding error.

Shortly, the Bloodsucker finished his club soda and climbed off the stool.

"Where you going, John?" Brandy spun around on the stool as she pulled a tube of lip gloss from her purse and ran it over her lips. "Little boys' room?"

"Actually, it's getting late." Suppressing the urge to chuckle over the fact that he'd been clever enough to give a false name, he checked his watch. "Sunday night, I have to work day shift tomorrow."

"I know, but you don't have to go yet, do you?" She rose off the stool, but the minute her high heels hit the floor, she swayed and grabbed onto him to keep from falling. "It's early, baby."

The Bloodsucker tensed the moment her hand touched him. His first impulse was to slap her. Punch her. Dig her blue eyes out of their sockets with something handy. A toothpick from the bar, maybe?

His jaw tightened. She was drunk and it was not terribly flattering. Not for any woman, but certainly not a pretty blonde like her.

Granny said his mother had been a drunk.

"She's right, you should stay longer, man," Cory echoed, sipping his beer.

The Bloodsucker forced himself to relax and stepped toward the bar to pay his tab, effectively moving away from her without making it obvious. "It was great to meet you, Brandy. I'm sure I'll be seeing you around."

"Right." She backed against the bar stool to keep her balance. "Guess I will. Once I get a phone, maybe you can give me a call?"

"I'd like that." He smiled. "Well, good night."

She waved. Giggled. " 'Night."

With a casual nod in the direction of Cory, the Bloodsucker weaved his way through the loud, crowded bar and out the door into the humid night air where he could breathe better. Away from the crowd . . . all the people.

As he cut across the parking lot, he hummed confidently to himself. So what if this was impulse? April had been an impulse, too, and she had worked out just fine. He was too great a creature of habit. People were always telling him that. It was time he broadened his horizons and learned to be more spontaneous.

He got into his car, parked as far from any light as possible, and pushed the driver's seat back to get comfortable. Now all he had to do was wait.

And he didn't even have to wait too long. Half an hour later, Brandy stumbled out of the bar on the arm of Cory from Altoona. The Bloodsucker watched as the computer geek pushed her up against a car and covered her mouth with his.

What was wrong with this young woman? Didn't she know the dangers of getting drunk in a bar, far from home, with men you didn't know? Didn't she realize how unsafe it was?

He licked his dry lips. Flexed his hands. He already had the latex gloves on the seat beside him. Already had the baggie with the chloroform-soaked gauze he would need to subdue her. In the trunk were the other items he would need: tape, rope, the plastic sheeting. Even though he hadn't come here tonight for Brandy, he was prepared. He took pride in the fact that he was a man who was always prepared.

"Come on," he urged under his breath, absently fingering the photo in his pocket. "Tell him no. I don't have time for this tonight. I've got work to-morrow."

If Brandy went home with Cory, that would make the night longer. It was doable, but now that he had made his decision, chosen his next guest, he was anxious to get started. Anxious to feel. To taste . . .

Brandy suddenly gave Cory a little push back and the Bloodsucker smiled. It was dark, the parking lot wasn't well lit so he couldn't see exactly what had happened, but Cory must have done something to anger her.

"That's right," the Bloodsucker whispered. "He's not interested in you as a person, Brandy. Just a sex object. He ought to be ashamed of himself, treating a lady that way."

Cory tried to catch her, to push her against his car again, but she ducked under his arm. Brandy was athletic, apparently. Strong. Strong was good. Strong women lasted longer. They fought the inevitable longer.

"I'm out of here." She lifted her hand to Cory.

The Bloodsucker smiled.

"Brandy, wait!" Cory hollered.

"Good night." She stumbled through a row of parked cars, headed in the Bloodsucker's direction.

Perfect.

"Hey, you sure you can drive?" Cory asked.

The Bloodsucker scowled. Like he was going to show concern for her now after he'd tried to take advantage of her sexually right in the parking lot? What a jerk.

"I can give you a ride home," he said. "Come on. I'm sorry. I just got carried away."

She continued through the parking lot. Cory hesitated, and then climbed into his car.

The Bloodsucker watched him pull out of the parking lot and then searched for Brandy again. She was headed straight for him; apparently, she couldn't find her car.

The Bloodsucker popped the lever on his trunk, then opened his door, reaching for the gloves and the baggie. Timing; it was all about timing. One quick look to see that there was no one in the parking lot and then he called to her in his best "nice guy" voice. "Hey, Brandy, you okay?"

She halted, looking over the roof of a sports car.

"It's John," he said, closing his car door, shutting off the dome light.

"John?" She suddenly seemed a bit uneasy. "You're still here?"

"Yeah." He slid his hands smoothly into the gloves, the car between them blocking her view. "I ran into somebody I knew inside." He could see that his easygoing tone was making her relax a little. She could see she had nothing to fear from him. "What's the matter, can't find your car?"

"No...I..." She laughed and leaned on the hood of a pickup. "It's here somewhere. A white Toyota."

Cory was right. She was too drunk to drive. But that didn't matter now; the Bloodsucker had no intention of letting her drive. "Doesn't that make you crazy? I run into the grocery store to grab a few things, come out, and I can't remember where I parked. Let me help you find it." He moved toward her quickly, lifting his arm as if he were going to put it around her shoulder.

She turned her head toward him. Maybe his

sudden haste startled her, maybe it was that un-
nerving instinct women seemed to have. Even
drunk ones. "Hey—"

He closed his hand over her mouth and nose. To
his surprise, she lifted her knee and tried to kick
him. She missed him, but in the process, she
knocked his elbow, sliding the gauze off her mouth.

The Bloodsucker felt an instant of panic. If she
screamed. If anyone came out the bar door or
pulled into the parking lot—

She opened her mouth to scream and his reaction
was as instantaneous as it was brutal. He punched
her as hard as he could, right in the stomach.

Brandy grunted, and doubled over. He covered
her mouth and nose with the gauze and jerked her
against his body. She began to relax and then she
was deadweight in his arms. His arms shaking, he
carried her the couple of feet to his car, opened
the trunk and dropped her in. He slipped off his
gloves and threw them in on top of her as he
glanced around the dark parking lot. Not a soul to
be seen. He slammed the trunk. He needed to tie
her up, to gag her, but he'd pull over in a mile or
two and take care of that. The chloroform would
last that long.

Calmer now, feeling good about himself, the
Bloodsucker walked to the front of the car and
climbed in. Started the engine. He had never hit
anything before. Never harmed a fly. Certainly not
a woman.

It had felt surprisingly good.

The Bloodsucker pulled up beside the barn and
then backed his car up to the door. As he climbed

out, he spotted his dog on the back porch of the house, waiting faithfully. "It's okay, boy," he called, patting his knee. "Car's stopped moving. It's safe. Come on, boy!"

The well-trained dog flew off the old porch and barreled across the dark yard. Reaching his master, he barked and jumped until the Bloodsucker scratched behind his ears and told him what a good boy he was. Then, with a pat on his rump, he dismissed the dog. "Okay, boy, that's enough. We have a guest I need to attend to."

The dog backed down immediately, stepping aside to allow his master to pass.

The Bloodsucker had already popped the hatch before he got out of the car, so when he walked around to the rear, soft light glowed around the edges of the trunk. Laying his hand on the warm metal, he hesitated a moment, taking the time to enjoy the little trill of pleasure that shot through him. That was the problem with people today. He'd heard Dr. Phil say so on *Oprah*. No one took the time to enjoy the little delights in life, the small accomplishments.

Unable to resist a smile, the Bloodsucker slowly lifted the lid of the trunk. Soft light from the interior bulb illuminated Brandy's blond hair. He couldn't see her face, but that was all right. It was better this way, actually. Lying in the trunk, ankles and wrists tied together, hair falling over her face, she took his breath away. She looked like a sleeping angel.

The Bloodsucker lingered over the trunk another moment, then went into the barn. He found the lighter and a camp lantern right on the shelf inside the door. There was no electric in the barn, too old. But he liked it that way; it made it kind of cozy at night, just him and his guest and the glow of the Coleman lantern.

The Bloodsucker used the lighter to find the valve, turned on the gas, and lit the wick. He liked the little hiss the gas made as it flowed. He added the clear glass globe and then carried the lantern to the picnic table in the middle of the largest part of the barn. Everything was already there, already set up and waiting. Now all he needed was Brandy to join him.

"Why are you doing this?" Brandy whispered, her eyes wild with fear.

He stood beside the picnic table, snapping up the clear plastic suit he'd bought for the occasion. It was disposable, used by painters. Quite effective for blood splatter, especially when you added the shoe coverings, hat and face shield. It was amazing the things you could buy over the Internet.

The four vodka martinis Brandy had drunk at the bar had worn off and now she was sober. He'd taken the gag off when she'd promised not to scream. Not that it would matter. No one would hear her. The barn was insulated with bales of musty straw the Bloodsucker had stacked against the walls more than a story high; it had taken him days, but was quite effective at muffling any sounds inside the barn. Quite clever.

"Please. What is it you want?" she begged, tears running down her face, leaving ugly blue and black streaks of mascara and eye shadow. "Money? Sex? I'll give you whatever you want. If it's a blow—"

He reached out and slapped her hard across the

face. It startled her. It startled him. It also shut her up.

"That will be enough of that talk," he said sternly, looking down at his hand now spotted with blood. He stared at it for a moment in fascination. He hadn't expected blood yet.

A little added bonus.

He glanced up and saw that it came from her lip. Fortunately, he had already donned the surgical gloves. There would be no trace of her DNA left on his skin. Not that this little old Podunk town of Albany Beach had easy access to DNA testing, but he liked to be careful just the same.

The Bloodsucker returned to the task of snapping up the jumpsuit. "You ought to be ashamed of yourself, a pretty young woman talking trash like that."

"I'm sorry," she sobbed. "I'm sorry. Please. I feel sick." She let her head fall forward for a moment and she slumped in the chair he had tied her to.

"I'm sorry, it's the chloroform. The feeling will wear off," he told her. "Just give it a little time."

He ran his hand over his chest, and satisfied that he was properly covered, he turned to retrieve the tray of supplies he'd prepackaged at the house. He'd gotten fresh gauze and sterile water, and he'd boiled the scalpel in a pot to rid it of any of Kristen's blood cells. On impulse, he'd also picked up another tool in the kitchen that might be handy. Intriguing. Something he had watched late on TV the other night had given him the idea.

Hearing him start toward her, Brandy lifted her head. She struggled against the ropes that bound her in the plastic deck chair. This was a change; he had used a wooden one before but wood was porous and more likely to hold trace evidence. Even with all the plastic sheeting, it didn't hurt to be extra careful.

"Please don't hurt me anymore," she begged, turning her face away as if there were any way she could avoid him.

Her words made him feel bad. Ashamed. His gaze fell to the freshly spread sawdust at his feet. He *had* hurt her. He'd punched her back in the parking lot. Hit her and given her a bloody lip.

But she'd made him do it, hadn't she? Women were like that. They made you do things you didn't want to do.

The Bloodsucker lifted his head in determination. "Hold still and be quiet," he ordered, setting the tray aside on a small table. He didn't have a lot of time tonight. He needed to get a good night's sleep, go to work fresh and ready to do his job. He wouldn't do much tonight, just have a little fun. He reached for the scalpel.

Brandy screamed and, without thinking, he belted her so hard that her head flew back and her neck snapped with a satisfying crack. "I told you before that you had to be quiet," he barked, reaching impatiently for the tape to gag her again. "You're ruining everything," he said, barely able to contain his rage. "Now, just shut up."

It's what Granny had always said. You're ruining everything.

Chapter Two

"Five dead women! Five," Dorothy Truder shouted into the crackly microphone. "A madman is walking our streets, Chief Drummond." The sixty-something woman with blue-rinsed helmet hair pointed an accusing finger at Claire. "And what have you got to show for your *ongoing investigation?* Hmmm? Tell me that."

Men and women Claire called her friends rose out of their folding metal chairs in the elementary school gym and clapped their hands.

Claire, seated behind the makeshift dais comprised of a cafeteria table and miniature green plastic chairs, wished she could slide to the floor and crawl out on her hands and knees. That, or maybe pop Dorothy Truder in the snout.

"Now, Dottie," Mayor Tugman soothed from the principal's podium usually reserved for graduation day and Fire Prevention Essay Award Night. "The purpose of this meeting is not to make accusations. It is to update you on the murder investigation, and to address any concerns the fine folk of this town might have."

"Address our concerns," Dorothy bellowed.

The microphone screeched and the crowd of more than two hundred cringed in unison. Some covered their ears. A baby began to cry. Claire didn't flinch as she gazed out over the crowd. Every local in Albany Beach had turned out for the town meeting.

Three of her off-duty officers, Sergeant Marsh, Patrolman First Class McCormick and Patrolman Savage sat in folding chairs in the front row, stoic. Though she was taking the brunt of this assault, she could tell they were feeling the heat, too. She spotted the elderly gossip twins, Mary Lou Joseph and Betty Friegal, toward the front, their heads bowed as they both talked at the same time, mouths going a mile a minute. Then there was Mr. and Mrs. Atkins. Their faces were impassive, but Claire could feel their pain, their resentment. They had buried their niece Kristen the previous week, the latest victim of Albany Beach's serial killer. Like the others before her, the monster had purposefully bled her to death and then left her body beside a Dumpster like a bag of garbage.

Seth Watkins, a local realtor, talking with Billy Trotter, the first victim's ex-boyfriend, caught her eye. Or at least his lime green sports jacket did. Past criminal records had turned up during her investigation of both men. But she didn't know yet how heavily she should weigh that information in her investigation. Mayor Tugman had a conviction on his record as well. And a kinky one, at that.

"We are not here, Dottie," the mayor said into the microphone when the feedback faded, "to make accusations or to criticize our fine police force." He had dressed in his best Hawaiian shirt and flex-band polyester pants; huge green and orange parrots danced across his rotund middle as he spoke. He paused to mop his wide brow with a handkerchief and Claire's gaze shifted to the crowd again.

Or could it now be defined as a mob? The voices were getting louder. Angrier. Any minute, she expected someone to hurl a rotten tomato at her.

A group of doctors, nurses and assorted technicians from the hospital congregated behind the rows of folding chairs, beneath the basketball hoop, their stark white uniforms a beacon in the brightly colored sea of pastel polos and bold T-shirts. A handful of postal workers sat in chairs on the aisle, most of them still wearing their light blue uniform shirts.

Claire could hear people whispering her name. The really rude ones spoke right out loud, their voices echoing off the scuff-marked gym floor.

". . . Should never have hired her, even if her father was our chief for forty years . . ."

". . . Should have called the state police in immediately . . ."

"I knew from day one this was too big for her to handle . . ."

"That nice boy, you know, the detective who used to be her boyfriend. See his name in the paper all the time. He—"

Claire shifted her gaze back to Morris Tugman. The crowd of "concerned citizens" was getting unruly. People were standing up, shaking fists. One man, a redneck from the trailer park on the edge of town, shouted at another, a neighbor she knew for a fact he'd been arguing with over a loose dog for three months. For a moment Claire feared she was going to have to climb over the table to break up a fistfight.

All she could think of, as the chaos unfolded around her, was *thank God her parents had agreed to stay home.* They had wanted to come to "support" her, but her father, now on oxygen for his emphysema, would likely have been one of the first good old boys throwing a fist. He'd always been a volatile man, but as he aged, he seemed less able to distinguish between minor annoyances and fighting matters.

The mayor was losing control, and he knew it. He was breathing heavier than usual and the sweat stain beneath his armpits was spreading. Soon the parrots would be soaked as well. She hoped he wasn't about to have a heart attack. At least there were a couple of doctors and nurses present. There was a county EMT truck parked out back, too. A defibrillator readily available.

Dottie Truder took her seat and a teacher from the high school stepped up to the microphone in the aisle. "We keep hearing that our police force is doing its best, Mayor Tugman, but frankly, I feel as if we're getting a lot of talk and not seeing a lot of action." His gaze darted in Claire's direction, then back at Morris. "I have wife and a daughter to be concerned about, and, damn it, excuse my curse, but I don't want talk. I want results."

More clapping. Some slaps on the back as the Calculus teacher returned to his chair.

Claire took one look at John Carter's back as he retreated and decided enough was enough. She rose from her green plastic kiddy chair and the room instantly grew quiet. Faces all turned toward her. Morris, spouting some pointless political mumbo jumbo in reply to Carter's comment, halted midsentence.

No one expected Claire to speak in her own defense. She was here to merely decorate the mayor's dais, hold down one of the plastic chairs. Her friends and neighbors, the men and women she attended church with each Sunday, hadn't expected her to respond to their disparagement.

A few with good enough manners to be embarrassed now sat down. Someone coughed, cleared his throat. Jenna Talbot's baby was shushed with a pacifier.

Claire focused on the orange basketball hoop above Dr. George Larson's head as she walked slowly to the podium. A prominent physician in town, he'd become one of her greatest adversaries, or so she'd heard through the grapevine. She raised the height of the microphone six inches and leaned over it. "You know who I am, so we'll dispense with introductions and I'll get right to the point."

The gymnasium was so quiet, she could hear raindrops pattering against the glass of the west parking lot doors.

"While I can't go into the details of the investigation, for obvious reasons," she said calmly, "I want you to know that our police force has made progress and that the state is, as we speak, convening a task force to aid us in catching this killer." She gripped the podium as she met the gazes of several of her most obvious opponents. She relaxed a little. "And we will catch him. Now, in the meantime, there are some steps we can all take to . . ."

* * *

The Bloodsucker, surrounded by fellow citizens of Albany Beach, pretended to listen conscientiously to Chief Drummond as she reviewed the safety measures the women of the town needed to use. But his attention wavered.

He was delighted to be in the midst of the crowd and actually hear them all speak of him. *The killer. This monster.* Some were still even calling him "Bloody Bob," the silly name a newspaper reporter had given him. The Bloodsucker kept all the news articles he could find. He was even buying the national weekly newsmagazines at the local newsstand, just in case he was mentioned there.

Chief Drummond, his Claire Bear, said something the men and women surrounding him approved of and they clapped. Nodded. He clapped with them, even going so far as to meet the gaze of the lady who cashed his paycheck, and nodded. A woman he worked with spotted him and gave a little wave. The Bloodsucker waved back.

They thought they knew so much. But they were wrong. Dorothy Truder was wrong. It wasn't five. It was six. He smiled to himself at the secret he had in the barn. Well, it wouldn't be a secret any longer, once he finished with Brandy tonight and took out the trash . . .

The police chief continued to speak and he continued to clap, nod and acknowledge others around him in the metal chairs, as if he were one of them. They *believed in their hearts* that he *was* one of them. That's what made the whole event even more exciting.

The Bloodsucker was so glad he had decided to leave Brandy in the barn and come tonight. Granny had said he was stupid, but he wasn't, and this was proof once again. Right here on the gym floor. They were clapping *for him.* Conceding his superior intelligence.

Granny said he was an idiot, a nobody and a nothing. A speck of fly dirt on the wall. But she was wrong, and here was the proof. He had the citizens of his hometown all fooled, and not just the stupid ones who swept floors or pumped gas for a living. He had the doctors, the teachers, the business owners, even the cops, hoodwinked.

The Bloodsucker smiled to himself. And deceiving Police Chief Claire Bear was the best of all.

Claire heard the blaring rock music before her log cabin, at the end of the quarter mile of wooded lane, came into view. She didn't recognize the artist, but she was certain the band used only lowercase letters, and that there would be snakes and skulls on their CD covers. Her fifteen-year-old daughter Ashley had gone Goth in the spring, and that had been the end of rock and roll as Claire knew it, in their household.

"What do you think you're doing playing music that loud, Ashley Anne Drummond?" Claire muttered, guiding the police cruiser up the lane, through the dark woods. The rain had stopped, but the trees still hung heavy with moisture and the gravel road was muddy. "Thank God we haven't got any neighbors; they'd be calling the cops."

She chuckled at her bad joke. On a day like the one she'd had today, she'd take any joke she could get, no matter how weak.

Claire made the bend in the driveway, around

the grandfather oak tree she hadn't had the heart to cut down when she'd put in the new driveway, and the solar-heated log cabin came into sight. The cabin with music blasting, every light in the house lit. The cabin with eight to ten cars parked all over her lawn. Cars that only teenagers would dare drive.

"I'll kill her." Claire pulled up beside a dented Ford pickup she recognized as Ashley's boyfriend's and slammed on the brakes. "I'll close my hands around her neck and put her out of my misery," she mumbled as she climbed out of the car. "No jury of my peers, of parents of teenagers, would dare convict me."

"Cops are here!"

Claire heard someone sound the alarm before she reached the front porch. The door opened and two young men dressed alike in black pants and black T-shirts, their hair spiked and dyed black, nearly collided with her on the front steps.

"Chief Drummond," the braver of the two muttered.

"Joshua." She nodded, giving him her best *bad ass bitch cop eye.* "Your dad know you're here without an adult present"—she spotted a beer can in the other boy's hand—"drinking underage?" Josh's father was the Presbyterian minister in town. Great guy.

"Um . . . he knows I was out with Jimmy." He indicated the kid trying to figure out how to make a Pabst Blue Ribbon can he held behind his back disappear into thin air.

She reached around and plucked the beer from his hand. She tipped the can and watered her flower bed with the remainder of the contents. "You been drinking, Josh?"

He shook his head.

She leaned closer. "Breathe."

Obviously embarrassed, but unable to find a way out of his predicament, he exhaled.

Claire didn't smell beer on his breath. "You drive home," she ordered, pointing toward the cars. "You see Jimmy gets safely to his house and we forget this happened."

Josh kept his gaze downcast, further obscured by a mop of unnaturally inky hair. "Um, it's Jimmy's car and he has to be home by eleven-thirty."

"I don't car if it's the Apostle Paul's car." Claire gave him the eye again. "You drive him home. You put him to bed and then you figure out how to get home yourself." She settled her hand on her sidearm. "Or, I could call your dad and see if he'd like to meet us down at the station and—"

"I'll drive him home." Josh hustled down the steps, past her.

"Key's in the ignition," Jimmy said, right behind his buddy.

"Thanks, Chief," Josh hollered as he climbed into a late model sedan with an amateur two-tone paint job.

She raised the empty beer can in salute as she crossed the porch. She was just opening the front door when she saw a guy and two girls dart out from the shadows of the house and race for a car. "You better not get behind the wheel of that car if you've been drinking, Ryan Carlisle," she shouted, not even bothering to look over her shoulder at them.

"I haven't been, Chief Drummond. Good night, Chief Drummond."

She heard car doors slam and an engine sputter and start as she walked in the front door of her humble abode. Her living room, kitchen and dining room were littered with chip bags, water bottles and a few empty beer cans.

Someone had courteously turned down the music, but Claire reached around a young lady with a double nose ring to hit the power button on her stereo and then set down the beer can.

A dozen teens, all dressed in black with dyed black hair, stared at her.

"Shit," someone muttered. "I thought Jimmy was just dicking around about the cops again. She wasn't supposed to be home until late."

Claire's gaze fell on her daughter who was busy trying to ease an empty beer can under the couch with the heel of her black hightop Converse sneaker.

"I told you she *hasn't* been home before midnight this week," Ashley muttered under her breath.

"True," Claire admitted, gazing at the teens one by one, recognizing most of the faces. Ashley's boyfriend, "Chain," the person responsible for the shit comment was there, of course. Claire didn't know him well, but she didn't like him one bit. She didn't like the clothes he wore or the head shop he worked in at the boardwalk. She didn't care what his sad story was; raised by his grandmother who was now ill and in a nursing home or some such crap. She didn't care how many times a day Ashley said he visited her; the kid was no good. He couldn't be.

Shauna Clemson, daughter of a dentist in town, was there, too. She'd gone Goth with Ashley this spring. Claire knew for a fact that her parents were so thrilled with the change in their daughter that they were talking about sending her to boarding school in Connecticut. Then there was Ashley's new best friend, also an Ashley. They'd met through Chain. They called themselves the A twins.

Claire knew her veins had to be standing out on her forehead. "I suppose it would be silly for me to ask what's going on here," she said, barely controlling her temper. But she didn't yell; Ashley found it disrespectful when she yelled.

"Mom—"

"I think I'd keep my mouth shut right now, Ash," Claire interrupted sharply. "Something about just digging the hole deeper?"

The girl who had once worn pink acrylic Cinderella slippers for an entire year crossed her arms defiantly over her chest, obscuring the skull and bat graphics of her Marilyn Manson T-shirt. "We weren't doing anything wrong." She jutted out her hip for good measure.

"No?" Claire leaned over and plucked the beer can Ashley had been trying to hide, off the hardwood floor. "Underage drinking." She sniffed the air. "Smoking a little weed, maybe?"

"It's incense. No one was smoking weed!" Ashley almost shouted the sarcastic words at her mother.

Claire's hand ached to slap her across her mouth, but she kept it pinned to her side. She saw enough violence on the job to know there was no place for it among family members. No place for violence anywhere. Her gaze shifted to Chain.

Ashley swore he was sixteen, but he could have been twenty-seven or seven for all Claire knew.

The black hair and eyebrow piercing threw her off
completely. "You been drinking beer in my house,
Chain? Smoking a little weed?"

"No, ma'am."

"Some guy brought the beer," Ashley said. "I
told them I didn't want them drinking here, but
they only had a twelve-pack. They're gone, anyway."

"Only a twelve-pack?" Claire echoed, still eyeing Chain. "What kind of party is that? You want
to give me a breathalyzer reading?" she asked the
young man who she feared was more intimate
with her daughter than she wanted to even consider.

He hooked his thumbs through the belt loops
of his black jeans; the link chain around his waist,
usually used to tie out dogs or lock fences, not
hold up pants, jangled. Mr. Cool. "Sure, I'll blow
for you."

Claire held the teen's defiant, dark-eyed gaze. If
he wanted to play chicken with her, he was going
to lose. She'd stare him down all night. "Ash, run
out to my car and get me a couple of breathalyzer
cartridges and the unit."

Chain muttered something under his breath
and looked away.

"Mom, you can't make me—"

Claire glared at her daughter, and Ashley slunk
out of the living room.

"Now, get this crap cleaned up," Claire ordered,
indicating the trash. "Then you line up by the
door. All of you. I want your names. If you haven't
been drinking, or partaking of any other *recre-
ational substances*, then I'll let you go. But I catch

you here again without me being present, and I'll haul all of you into the station house."

Ashley returned to the living room a minute later and handed her mother a zip lock bag of disposable breathalyzer cartridges and the unit. "I can't believe you're doing this," she groaned under her breath. "No one will ever speak to me again."

"We can hope," Claire quipped with a feigned smile.

A couple of the girls carried the kitchen garbage can around, picking up trash. The boys were lined up at the door, shoulders hunched, bodies slumped.

"Come on, April," one with a spike through his eyebrow barked. "Let's go. You're not the Merry Maids."

One by one, Claire tested the teens. To her surprise, not a single one of them, not even Ashley or Chain, blew an alcohol reading. No one appeared or acted as if they were high, either. So maybe it was the incense she had smelled and not marijuana.

Who said they could burn that nasty smelling incense in her house, anyway?

"Okay, you can all go." Claire took down the final name on a pad of paper she carried in her uniform breast pocket, not sure if she was relieved or disappointed that none of the kids here now had been doing anything illegal. "But I'm not kidding. I better not see any of you here again without a personal invitation from me."

The teens, all dressed as if headed for a bizarre funeral, filed out of the house. Chain was last in line. He lifted one hand to Ashley. She slumped in the doorway between the kitchen and living room and nodded to him, arms still crossed over her chest.

"I'll call you tomorrow," Ashley said.

"She'll call you next year when she gets her phone privileges back," Claire hollered. She waved. "Good night."

"I can't believe you embarrassed me like this," Ashley intoned the minute the front door closed behind her boyfriend.

"And I can't believe you had a party here while I was working! While I was at a town meeting being torn to bits by people who were supposed to be my friends." Claire balled her fists at her sides. "Someone finds out I'm serving alcohol to teenagers and I'll lose my—"

"You weren't serving alcohol to teenagers," Ashley said in her nastiest, *I hate your guts* tone. "Look, I told those boys with the beer to leave and they did. What else do you expect from me?" She threw up her hands and flounced away.

"Where do you think you're going?" Claire followed her down the hall, hot on her heels.

"My room."

"Oh, no you don't. I want you to stand here and let me tell you how many ways this little party of yours could have gone wrong tonight. Alcohol poisoning, drug overdose, pregnancy."

Ashley halted in front of her bedroom door, but didn't turn around.

Claire hesitated. "No, on second thought, you better go to your room and hide because I'm so angry with you right now, Ashley, that I could throttle you."

The teen disappeared into her bedroom, slamming the door soundly behind her.

Claire closed her eyes and stood there alone in the hall for a moment. She breathed deeply and then went back to the front door to be sure all of Ashley's *guests* had vacated the premises. The yard was empty except for her tan and green police car and the deep, muddy ruts the kids had put in her wet lawn in their hurry to get away.

She closed the door, locked the dead bolt, and flipped the front porch light out. There would be no more partying teenagers at her door tonight.

She went to the kitchen, realizing how naïve she was to think a light out would spurn any kids who had heard there was a party here tonight. Like they were good little trick-or-treaters, checking porch lights. Yeah, right. She'd probably be up half the night turning kids away.

Claire opened the refrigerator door. She'd eaten nothing today but a bran muffin with coffee some-time around seven this morning. Suddenly she realized she was famished. Of course there wasn't much in the fridge; she hadn't had time to shop. A bag of coffee beans. Mustard. Ketchup. Plain yogurt. A couple of apples and a carton of orange juice. Some macaroni and cheese that was growing some-thing fuzzy around the edges. Oh . . . and a can of cheap beer. The boys' twelve-pack must have gone a long way.

She closed the refrigerator. Even if there had been anything there, she didn't have enough en-ergy to cook it. Microwave popcorn would do.

She pulled a bag from a box in the cupboard and put it in the microwave. While it popped, she poured herself a glass of orange juice. Maybe the sugar would give her a little energy. She had sev-eral folders of papers out in the car that she had to go through tonight. Notes she had taken on the murders and on a couple of men in town she had begun investigating as possible suspects.

Claire's gut instinct still told her that the killer was one of them. Someone who lived right here in town. A man who worked with the people at that meeting tonight, played with them, maybe even went to church with them. She had no hard evidence for sure. Little circumstantial. But sometimes a cop had to go with her gut.

She leaned on the counter, listening to the popcorn pop, smelling the buttery aroma. The public meeting tonight had been rough. She knew that people were upset, that they were afraid. But she'd had no idea they were all so angry with her. That they held her responsible.

Didn't they see she was trying her damnedest to figure out who the killer was? Didn't they realize she was working fifteen hour days and then coming home to lie awake all night in bed and go over and over each detail of each young woman's death in gruesome detail? Didn't they see she was neglecting her teenage daughter? Pawning her off on her grandparents because she worked such long hours and then Claire was too exhausted to deal with a fifteen-year-old?

She felt tears sting the backs of her lids and she squeezed her eyes shut, fighting the urge to cry. She was the chief of police of this town. She had a job to do. There would be no crying.

The microwave beeped and she pulled her bag of popcorn out and walked into the living room. As she went by the hall, she glanced in the direction of Ashley's closed door. Her daughter had turned on her stereo just loud enough to annoy

Claire, but not loud enough to bring her mother down the hallway screaming to turn it down.

Typical teenage response to a reprimand.

But Claire was worried about Ashley. She'd been trying hard to tolerate the whole Goth thing. She kept telling herself that the dyed hair, the clothes, it was all just a phase and it would pass if Claire would ignore it. After all, Ashley had remained a B student throughout the school year and she never missed a day at the greenhouse where she had found a summer job. Claire knew it had to be hard for her, a teenage child of divorce, living in the small town where your mother grew up. Where your mother now filled your grandfather's shoes as chief of police.

But Ashley was pushing the envelope of maternal tolerance now. She'd been late for curfew a few times. Been caught places in town with Chain when she had said she would be elsewhere. Now this party. Was Ashley headed for serious trouble, and Claire had been too busy on this case to recognize it?

Her father, Claire's ex, was pushing hard to have Ashley join him in Utah. He had a cute new wife, two cute little girls. Apparently, he thought a cute, blond-haired, blue-eyed teen would round out his new family.

Wouldn't Ashley look *cute* in the family photo right now?

It would almost be worth it to send her to her father's just to see the look on his face when he laid eyes on his darling daughter. The dyed hair. The black eye makeup and silver rings on her fingers embellished with bats and skulls. The disturbingly graphic T-shirts and baggy black jeans.

Almost.

The thing was, Claire didn't think, no matter what Tim said, that Ashley would be better off with him. Attending the church school where his wife taught. Having the male role model a young impressionable teenager needed. Ashley belonged here in Albany Beach with her mother. That girl in there right now, lying on her bed with her feet up on the wall, listening to the screeching heavy metal rock, was Claire's life. Dyed black hair, bat rings and all.

She set her glass of orange juice down on a twig style end table and went back to the kitchen. Behind a stack of cans of olives in the pantry—a place Ashley would never dare tread—she located a pint of vodka.

This was definitely a screwdriver kind of night, if ever there was one.

Back in the living room, she added some vodka to her orange juice. Then an extra splash for good measure. She kicked her shiny black uniform shoes off, removed her sidearm holster and hung the Beretta Cougar over the arm of the couch. Then she sat down to dine.

Half a bag of popcorn and most of a screwdriver later, Claire heard a car engine and saw the flash of headlights behind the closed drapes in the dining room. She slapped down the bag of popcorn, muttering to herself. A latecomer to the party, no doubt.

She was tempted to meet him or her at the door with her Beretta subcompact drawn. But that might be overkill. And after the meeting tonight, she didn't need some snotty-nosed teen accusing her of threatening a minor with a deadly weapon.

Claire unbolted the dead lock and jerked the door open, not bothering to flip on the porch light. "Sorry, man, party's over—"

"Party's over? I can't believe I missed it, man."

Surprised first by the voice, then by the fact that it was an adult male standing on her porch and not a Goth teen, Claire took half a step back. She couldn't identify the voice. What was wrong with her, opening the door to a stranger?

Chapter Three

"Claire, it's Graham—Graham Simpson." The man on her step's tone suddenly became serious.

"Graham." Claire couldn't resist touching her uniform shirt where her heart had nearly leaped from her chest. It was funny how someone who had been a cop as long as she had could still get jumpy. Good old adrenaline, she supposed. "What are you doing standing on my front porch in the dark at eleven o'clock at night?"

"What are you doing not inviting me to your party?" he teased, trying to lighten the moment. Obviously he realized he'd startled her.

She couldn't resist a chuckle. The vodka must have relaxed her, at least a little. "Long story. But I still don't know why you're here." She flipped on the porch lamp and he became visible in a circle of pale light.

Graham Simpson was tall the way Claire liked men. Slender, but not overly so. He didn't look like he was a runner or a gym rat, just a person who kept tabs on the Big Macs. He was clean-cut. He hadn't gone with the longer, shaggier hair a lot of men in their forties were wearing. Sandy brown hair, green or gray eyes. Nice eyes. He was a widower and owned a rather profitable office supplies store in town. He was also a member of the city council, the same city council that had called tonight's town meeting to "address" its citizens' concerns. That made Graham the enemy right now, if only by association.

Her guess was that Graham Simpson, like the other council members, had no idea just how concerned its citizens ought to be right now. Especially the blond-haired blue-eyed ones.

"I wanted to talk to you." He hesitated, looking up, and when he made eye contact, she realized this was more a personal call than she first thought. She wasn't sure how she felt about that. He was a nice guy and all. Maybe a little geeky, but the cool kind of geeky, à la Clark Kent, with contacts. He was smart and seemed well-grounded. She'd have to be blind not to notice how good-looking he was, but of all the problems she *didn't* need right now, a man was right at the top of the list.

"They were pretty rough on you tonight," he went on when she didn't respond.

She shrugged. "I can handle it."

"I didn't mean to say you couldn't." He chuckled, raising both hands, palms out as if he were under arrest. "No question in my mind, Chief Drummond can take on this town."

She studied him suspiciously under the porch light. "And you came all the way out here to tell me this? I mean, I appreciate your support, don't get me wrong. But you could have used the phone."

"Tried. For more than an hour. Busy. I know you have a teenager. I thought maybe she was surfing the Net or something."

"We have high speed Internet cable so that won't happen." She glanced over her shoulder into the house. "But I wonder if—" She spotted the cordless telephone on the floor near the TV armoire. "I bet it's off the hook." Annoyed, she turned around, waving Graham in. "Damned kids."

He followed her inside, closing the door behind him.

She picked up the phone and sure enough, it was on "talk." One of Ashley's friends must have used it and not hung it up correctly. So apparently Ashley wasn't the *only* kid in Albany Beach who didn't have her own cell phone.

Claire turned the phone off and looked up at Graham. He was checking out her bag of popcorn, the near empty glass and the bottle of vodka on the kitchen counter. She felt her cheeks grow warm.

"Hey," he said, raising both hands in the same gesture she'd seen on the porch. "I can't tell you how many nights I've made a meal of low-fat microwave popcorn and a gin and tonic. No judgment here."

She couldn't help smiling. How could you not like a guy who could have popcorn and gin for dinner? And she thought that was only a chick thing.

"Crappy day, huh?" He watched her, giving her his full attention the way someone did when they were truly interested in what the other person had to say.

"You're not kidding. That meeting, if you can

call it that, was just the icing on the cake." She pointed to a leather chair and fell back in her spot on the end of the couch.

Earlier, when Graham had been seated at the dais in the gym, he had been dressed in a conservative pinstripe gray suit, but he'd removed his tie and jacket and unbuttoned the collar of his oxford. On any other man, she would have thought the white dress shirt looked outdated, but it worked for him.

She noted with interest that he grasped both pant legs and tugged before sitting down, the way she had seen male characters do in old movies. Old movies were Claire's clandestine passion. She loved old movies, more accurately, she loved the leading men of old movies: Bogart, Stewart, Tracy. She'd always secretly wanted to be Katharine Hepburn.

"So you came all the way out here to tell me you felt bad everyone was so mean to me?" she asked, amused. She grabbed a handful of popcorn out of the bag and passed the bag to Graham.

"Yeah, I guess so. And I've been thinking about the information I've read in the paper and the things I've heard." He took a smaller handful of popcorn than hers and eased it into his mouth, a kernel at a time. "I've got a couple theories and I—"

Not another one, she thought with an internal groan. "Wait!" she interrupted, needing to hear no more. "I already know what you want. You want me to deputize you and make you part of the force so you can solve the crimes."

He chuckled. "Not hardly." His brow furrowed. "People actually ask you to *deputize* them?"

She took the popcorn bag back. "Oh, yes. I had two men, this week alone, come to my office saying they could help me find the killer if I would just give them a real badge. I think they watch those old westerns," she confided with amusement. "They think I need to wrestle up a posse or something." She threw a couple more kernels into her mouth. "Of course, that's not nearly as weird as the calls into our hotline by the woman who believes aliens are coming down from outer space, to Albany Beach, to do experiments on human women and killing them in the process."

He pointed. "Sounds like a friend of our buddy Ralph's."

"Could very well be. Of course, they won't be getting much time together to chat about these alien forces. Ralph's still is the county prison, but his extradition trial is in three weeks."

Ralph, the dishwasher at the local diner, had actually been a suspect in the murders. Claire had discovered, during her investigation, that he was wanted in New Jersey for the attempted murder of a young woman. Even without a confession, she had raised him to the top of her list as a possible suspect who had killed Patti Lorne, April Provost, Phoebe Matthews and Anne Hopkins. Then college student Kristen Addison had turned up dead, murdered while Ralph sat in the Sussex County Men's Correctional Facility, awaiting extradition. And now she was back to ground zero.

"Well, I don't want a gold badge shaped like a star," Graham said. "But I thought I might be able to help you out in some way."

His words immediately put her on the defense. "The way you helped me tonight at the meeting by jumping in and stating your support of me *and my keeping my job.*" She emphasized her last words.

He grimaced. "Just come right out and tell me how you feel, Claire."

"Sorry. I'm a little edgy. If you were in my position, you'd be, too."

"No need to apologize. I've always admired you for the fact that you *will* come out and say what you think. You're a lot like your dad in that respect."

His comment made her smile. After Katharine Hepburn, she'd always wanted to be her dad. Until two months ago, she thought she'd been on her way.

"Anyway, I apologize for not speaking up at the meeting." Done with his popcorn, he brushed his hands together. "It's just that in the last week, I've pissed off a lot people on the subject of how this investigation should be handled and by whom. I just thought it might be politic to keep my mouth shut tonight and keep *my* job."

She didn't say anything, but the look they exchanged set them on even ground again.

"So . . ." He put his hands together fingertips to fingertips. "The reason I came by was to tell you I supported you and to see if you'd like some help thinking through this whole thing. I know you've been working long hours and it's got to be frustrating, seeming to get nowhere. I wondered if maybe you'd like a fresh perspective."

Claire dropped the bag of popcorn on the end table, sliding forward to the edge of the couch. "You guys met after the town meeting, didn't you? The council. The mayor."

He nodded.

"They really want to fire me? It's not just gossip?"

He frowned. "You didn't hear this from me, of course."

"Of course."

"They weren't so much talking of firing you as not renewing your contract. A prominent citizen is really putting the pressure on them."

"Who?" she demanded.

He frowned. "You know I'm not at liberty to say."

"Isn't that discussion a little premature? My contract doesn't come up for renewal for another six months." She shot off the couch. "How dare they start talking about not renewing my contract now. *Now,* of all times." She opened her arms in frustration and let them fall to her sides, pacing in front of the coffee table. "What? They think I'm not trying to find this creep? They think this is easy? Do they have any idea how hard it is to find a killer who leaves no evidence behind?" She ticked off on her fingers, getting louder with each word. "No fibers, no fingerprints. Nothing in two months but one frigging umbrella!"

"Claire—"

"And no witnesses, of course. No one has seen a thing. It's like these women just disappear off the face of the earth. Zoop." She gestured, drawing her hand skyward. "Gone with one of Ralph's alien friends."

"Claire," he repeated calmly. "I didn't say I agreed with them."

"One week." She shook her finger at him and turned on the balls of her stocking feet to reverse directions. "I'd like to see any of them do my job for *one week*. Do they have any idea how hard it is to go to a woman's house, sit on the couch beside her, hold her hand, and tell her that we've found her daughter's body beside a Dumpster?"

"Claire—"

"It's Morris, isn't it?" She eyed Graham. "He wants me out. You know, he never wanted to hire me to begin with. Chauvinist pig. *Never hire a woman to do a man's job,*" she mimicked.

"Claire, they can't get rid of you right now, not without a breach of contract lawsuit and they know it."

"You're right." She sat down again and leaned forward, propping her elbows on her knees, resting her chin in her hands. Suddenly she felt overwhelmed and surprisingly close to tears. She'd had such plans for herself in this job, in this town. How could it all be going down the toilet like this?

"I think this man lives here," Graham said quietly. "He's one of us. We eat with him, chat with him in line at the drugstore. We sit by him in the movie theater."

Claire lifted her head, pulling herself out of her moment of self-pity. "What makes you say that?" She was immediately intrigued because she agreed with him. Everyone else, her detectives, the townspeople, even her father thought they needed to cast a wider net, looking for suspects. But she knew they were wrong. She knew it was someone close to her, to everyone in the town.

Then a crazy thought passed through her head. What if Graham was the killer?

Just last night she'd been reading about a case in Indiana. The serial killer/pedophile had actually taunted local police forces by making contact with investigators—placing phone calls and even going into the station houses. He had pretended to be offering help on cases of dead or missing children, just to prove he was smarter than everyone else.

Graham had appeared at her doorstep, uninvited, late at night. He was attractive. Friendly. Claire had done her homework on the Internet and through publications made available by the FBI for law enforcement agencies. Serial killers who took victims without leaving behind a sign of struggle almost always had charm. They lulled their victims into trusting them and then struck.

Claire looked at Graham, eyeing her Beretta in its holster on the edge of the couch. Then she almost laughed aloud. She was really losing it now. Graham Simpson a serial killer? Graham Simpson, the city councilman? The president of the chamber of commerce? Graham Simpson who dressed up each year in a Santa costume and rode on the Kiwanis's float in the town's Christmas parade?

There was gossip around town that he didn't even like women. That he was gay and that was why he had never remarried after the death of his wife. Claire didn't know if that was true or not, though she found it unlikely. What she did know was that this man was not a serial killer.

"What makes you say he's one of us?" she asked again quietly, sliding forward on edge of the couch. "Can I get you something to drink? Orange juice? Diet Pepsi? Gin, maybe?"

He laughed. "No. I'm fine, thanks." He, too, slid forward a little in his chair, closing the space between them. "I think this killer is someone from around here, someone we're familiar with, because no one has seen anything. We're used to this guy. We might have seen him, seen something, and we don't even know it."

"Kind of like not being able to find the mustard in the fridge because it's right there every time you open the door?"

He chuckled. "Something like that."

"Okay, he's one of us. A local, not a tourist. Not a drifter. I agree with you for just the reasons you stated." She nodded in his direction. "Now, tell me what else you think."

"All of the women were blondes with blue eyes. Young, but not girls. I think there's someone in his life, or *was* someone who these women he is kidnapping remind him of."

"Like?"

He shrugged. "I don't know. An old girlfriend? A woman who spurned him? His mother?"

"Mother is classic in cases like this. You'd be amazed at how many ways a mother can screw up a kid's head."

"Maybe this woman, his mother, sexually abused him."

"He doesn't seem to be touching these women in sexual ways. He ties them up to restrain them. Gags them to keep them quiet, but I don't think it's about sex."

"Oh, it's always about sex. Everything is, really."

Claire didn't know why, but that struck her as funny. She liked this man. She liked the way he thought.

"So how do you think I can catch him? Because I need to catch him, Graham, and I have to do it fast."

"Because the state task force that's supposed to be convening is going to take over your investigation."

"I don't even care about that." She gave a wave. "Well, I do, but for God's sake, he's going to kill again." She met his gaze. Green. His eyes were green. "And I'm afraid it will be soon."

"I hate to say it, but I agree. Now, I think you need to go over all your notes, trying to look at them from a new angle."

"*Your* angle, you mean."

He tilted his head in a cute, Clark Kent way. "If you'll let me help, I'd like to."

He sounded so sincere. So . . . without any ulterior motives.

But in Claire's line of work, she had learned not to trust anyone at face value. Not trusting anyone at all was sometimes easier. But then she had found that path to lead to a lonely life.

"Just tell me you'll think about it," Graham prodded when she didn't respond. He got to his feet. "Give it a day or two. Roll it around in your noodle."

Her noodle? This *was* Clark Kent.

Claire rose, realizing all of sudden that she was dead on her feet. "OK," she said, walking him to the front door. "I'll give it some thought."

He stepped out onto the porch. "I wish you would because this is the best excuse for coming by . . . for calling you, I've had in the last year."

She looked at him, frowning. "Your best excuse?"

"Truth is, I've wanted to ask you out for at least a year." He stuffed his hands in his pants' pockets, but he didn't look away. "Just too chicken."

He laughed and she found herself laughing with

him. Usually, the minute the word *date* came up in a conversation, she sent the would-be Romeo packing, but she couldn't bring herself to tell Graham to take a hike. He was just being way too damned cute about this.

She cut her eyes slyly at him. "Now, wait a minute. Does that mean you're really not interested in helping me out with this case?"

"No, no, no." He waved a hand. "I always wanted to be Sherlock Holmes, growing up. I'm actually pretty good at this kind of stuff. I always figure out who did it before the end of the book."

She leaned on the doorjamb. "This isn't a book, Graham. It's real," she said softly. "Real women are being murdered."

His voice reflected her tone of seriousness. "I know that, Claire. And I really do appreciate all your hard work. I know you'll catch this guy. I . . . I just want to help."

"*And* get me to agree to go out with you?" she teased.

"Okay, maybe that, too." He backed down the porch steps. "Think about it. I'll call you."

" 'Night."

His wave was more of a salute. He climbed into his Volvo sedan, backed around her cruiser, and disappeared into the darkness down the long, dark driveway.

Claire smiled to herself as she leaned on the doorjamb watching the headlights fade. So, Graham Simpson was interested in her. She didn't know why, but that tickled her. After her divorce, she'd dated a fellow state policeman, now at headquarters in Dover. He was older than she was, senior to her. No kids. No desire to have anything more from a woman than a bed partner and occasionally a sparring partner. It had been doomed from the start.

But she'd loved Kurt. And even though she had been the one to break up with him, she still missed him. Missed him enough not to have even been slightly interested in another man in the last year.

Until tonight when one appeared on her doorstep.

Still smiling, she went into the house, locked the door, set the security alarm, and returned to the living room to clean up the evidence of her meal selection. Fifteen minutes later she was in bed with the lights out. She had to get some sleep or she knew she wasn't going to be able to get through this.

But sleep didn't come easily. Not when she knew there was a man somewhere in her town preparing to kill again.

It was over, and the Bloodsucker was spent. He was tired and he had a nagging headache. He was hungry, too. Working his shift, then going to the town meeting, then coming back to the barn to finish here had made for a long day. Seated at the picnic table in front of Brandy, he leaned forward, letting his head fall to his hands on the rough boards. He knew he needed to get going if he was going to take care of the disposal tonight, but he wanted to rest for a minute. The women were all exhilarating, but tiring, too. That was something you never saw on TV—how tiring women could be.

He closed his eyes for a moment, thinking about Brandy, about her blood. He let the thought envelop him. Consume him. For him, blood was the elixir of life.

Max whined and the Bloodsucker opened his eyes. The brown mutt pushed his cool, wet nose into his master's limp hand and the Bloodsucker smiled. "You're right, boy. No time to rest. I've got work tomorrow."

With a sigh, he used his hands to push away from the table and climb off the bench. He gazed across the table to study Brandy in the light of the camp lantern. She looked so pale . . . so peaceful. Death truly did become her. More than life. In life, what had she been? A trashy, cigarette smoking, vodka drinking temp in a going-nowhere job? But in death . . . in death, she was—tears of joy filled his eyes at the thought of it—so lovely . . .

Unable to take his eyes off her, he reached for a fresh pair of latex gloves from the box on the end of the table. There was a stack of plastic drop cloths there, too. He'd use them for the transportation and then burn them along with the jumpsuit he wore and the bloody sawdust.

It was a lot of work, the disposal and cleanup. He tugged back his long sleeve under the plastic jumpsuit sleeve and checked his watch. One in the morning. Where had the night gotten to? If he disposed of her tonight, he'd barely have time to clean up his car, get a shower and get to work on time. He bit down on his lower lip in indecision. Once they were dead, they were dumped immediately, before they began to smell, before their lovely skin began to putrefy. It was the rule. But as long as he got rid of her in twenty-four hours he'd be all right, wouldn't he? And it wasn't as if anyone around here was looking for her. Shoot, it might be days before anyone even realized she was missing. So what if she didn't show up for work? She was just a temp. Temps were no-shows all the time. Chances were, her car, left in the bar parking lot, would draw more attention than her disappearance. No one would even realize she was missing until the plates were run, her family in Jersey was contacted.

The Bloodsucker had all the time in the world.

Taking one last look at Brandy, he grabbed the camp lantern. "Come on, Max," he called. "We're going to bed."

Chapter Four

"Morning, Chief," a young, dark-haired man sweeping cigarette butts off the sidewalk greeted.

"Morning, José." As Claire approached the diner, she put her cell phone on vibrate and hooked it onto her belt. She was waiting for a return phone call from her ex. Of course she'd been waiting a week for his return call. His child support payment was late. Again. So she'd just called him *again* this morning. His wife, Rochelle, said he was in the shower, but that he would call her right back. By Claire's calculation, the man either took a lot of showers these days, or they were rather long showers. That was what wife number two had said the last three times Claire had called.

"How you making out alone, José?"

José had lived with his grandmother on a run-down farm on the outside of town until she had died back at Christmastime. He had inherited the old house they lived in, but Claire was concerned he wouldn't be able to afford the upkeep in taxes, despite working two jobs—one here at Loretta's diner cleaning, and the other at the hospital where he was a night shift janitor.

"Good." He nodded, continuing to sweep. "I got myself a dog to keep me company."

"Did you?" She stopped at the door.

Through the glass José had just cleaned, she could see Seth Watkins at the cash register. He was one of those men she had to tell to take a hike at least once a week. He was also on her list of possible suspects. The good old, clean-cut football star had had a run-in with the police in Las Vegas a few years back. One involving a recording device and women unsuspectingly peeing for his entertainment. She still didn't know whether to be horrified or amused. The older she got, the less surprised she was about anything anyone did.

"And how are your classes at the college coming?" Claire asked José, stalling for time, hoping she could somehow avoid Seth. She seriously considered borrowing the janitor's Salisbury Shorebirds ball cap and grabbing his broom. If she kept her eyes averted, maybe the urine-fetish realtor wouldn't see her.

Fat chance. He had already spotted her and was barreling straight for her.

"Good, Chief. Taking economics and calculus." José looked up from beneath his ball cap with kind, dark eyes. "Nice of you to ask."

"Well, you have a good day."

Seth held the door open for her. She had no choice but to walk into the diner.

"Good morning, Claire."

She usually didn't mind people calling her by her first name, even when she was in uniform. It

was a small, close-knit town, especially in the winter when the vacationers went home, the boardwalk all but closed down, and they were left with
nothing but a cold, wet winter ahead and each other.
However, there were some people she would have
preferred to have not been on a first name basis
with, ever, and Seth was one of them.

"Good morning, Seth."

"Looks like it's going to be another hot one," he
said, slipping his knock-off designer sunglasses on.

"Looks like it."

"Hey, you need a pen?" He plucked one out of
the breast pocket of his yellow polo.

Claire made it a habit to never trust men who
wore polo shirts with pockets.

He waved the fluorescent pink pen in front of
her nose. "Just got a new shipment in."

She fully intended to decline, but then she
thought of a photograph of evidence she had back
at the station house. The third victim, Phoebe
Matthews, had had one of Seth's pens in her purse
when she was found dead. A lime green one.
Claire didn't know how the pen might come into
play with her investigation, but she knew it wouldn't
hurt to have it.

"Sure. I'd love one." She grabbed the pen and
hurried past him. "Thanks. You have a great day."

"You, too," he called after her as she let the door
go and it swung shut between them.

Inside the diner, she took a seat beside two of her
officers whose breakfasts had just arrived. "Quiet
night?" Claire asked. She didn't pick up a laminated
menu. She already knew what she wanted.

"Yeah, we got lucky," McCormick, the senior of
the two officers, said. He'd been on the force since

just before she was hired. He was a little straight-laced for her. A little too gung-ho at times, but he was an excellent officer who had stood by her through the last eight weeks of morbid crime scenes, and as of late, a lot of finger-pointing. McCormick also had lousy luck. He'd been the first on the scene in four of the five cases attributed to the town's serial killer.

Claire didn't know Savage well. He'd come with good references from a Podunk town in Arkansas where he'd been with the county sheriff's department. He was quiet. Did his job, though he was a little squeamish. And according to Ashley, he had the hots for her. Claire didn't know if she should count that for or against the man.

"A disturbing the peace. Drunk college kid on a balcony rail trying to do the hokey pokey." McCormick salted and peppered his eggs, hash browns and scrapple as he ticked off his night's calls. "A guy urinating in public." He elbowed Savage. "Hey, tell the chief about the kids in the ocean."

Savage picked up a bottle of Tabasco from beside the Heinz 57. "She can read the report," he mumbled, concentrating on his eggs. "Leave her alone, Ryan. Let her order her breakfast."

"I don't know how you can ruin perfectly good eggs with that stuff." McCormick waved his hand as the smell of the hot pepper sauce mingled with the scent of the freshly scrambled eggs.

Even through the neatly pressed long sleeve uniform shirt, Claire could make out the officer's serious pecs. She had once asked him why he wore long sleeves, even in the heat of the summer. Memorial Day to Labor Day, Albany Beach's police force was free to wear short sleeves, but McCormick had informed her that short sleeves didn't look professional. She could see his point, but decided that, personally, armpit stains were even less professional.

"Come on, tell her about the kids," McCormick repeated, refusing to let the subject drop.

Savage set down the bottle of hot sauce and slowly screwed the lid back on. "We picked up these college kids."

"Nine of them," McCormick injected.

"They were swimming in the ocean about two in the morning," Savage continued, obviously against his better judgment. "Apparently making enough noise to wake up some folks in a nearby condo."

McCormick spoke with a bite of scrapple in his mouth. "They were swimming buck naked."

"They were skinny-dipping," Savage confirmed.

"Guess what they were doing naked," Ryan almost cackled. He pointed with his fork. "Tell her."

Savage looked around. "Ryan," he said under his breath. "This place is packed."

"No one's listening. Come on."

Savage glanced at Claire. Hesitated.

"Fornicating," Ryan said, lifting a broad eyebrow. "All of them right in the surf. One big 'effin' orgy." He took a bite of egg. "Imagine that, Chief."

"Imagine that." She sighed, glancing up at Loretta who had come to take her order.

"Usual?" The hefty woman's hair so fire-engine red it couldn't possibly be natural.

"Please." Claire smiled.

"Coming up."

Claire got up off the stool. "You guys get some sleep. Have a good evening, if I miss you. Be safe," she called as she walked away.

Loretta met Claire at the register a minute later.

"Bran muffin. Two jelly doughnuts and two cups of coffee." She leaned forward to speak softly as she sealed the plastic lids on the coffees. "I just wanted you to know I was with you last night. At the meeting."

Claire met the older woman's gaze. Metallic blue eye shadow. "That's good to know." She offered a perfunctory smile.

"I couldn't speak up, of course." Loretta gazed out at the room of busy diners. "People are funny about that kind of thing. I can't afford to lose no one's business right now. What with tourist trade being so bad."

Tourism was down in the little beach town. Rental condos were left vacant for weeks at a time, for the first time in years. Revenue was down everywhere—restaurants, gifts shops, the movie theater and bowling alley. Vacationers were staying away from the town they no longer deemed safe for their families.

"I understand." Claire reached for the coffee and doughnuts. "How much do I owe you?"

"Four." Loretta averted her gaze.

It was the first time she had charged Claire for morning coffee and doughnuts since Claire had returned to Albany Beach to accept her father's job. She pulled the money out of her back pocket. She'd been reading accounts of law enforcement officers who had dealt with or were dealing with serial killer investigations. Every first-person account mentioned that their lives were never the same again.

Sadly, she guessed it was true.

* * *

Claire was stopped at a red light only a block from the station when her cell phone lying on the seat beside her rang. "Drummond," she said.

"Chief, it's Jewel."

The hair rose immediately on the back of Claire's neck. Jewel was her bubble gum–popping day shift dispatcher who also served as her secretary, clerk, whatever she needed. Normally, Claire was contacted by the station over the car radio, or the radio she wore on her uniform. Her cell phone was mostly for personal use, although it was listed on her contact sheet at the station. "What is it, Jewel?" she said tersely, pulling into an empty parking space. The town had way too many empty parking spaces this summer.

"Something going on over at the ER."

The familiar pop of a burst bubble of gum sounded in Claire's ear.

"A girl's being transported to the hospital by the EMTs," Jewel continued. "Detective Robinson is already on his way over, but he thought you might want to be there with him for the interview."

"Tell me what's going on." Claire signaled, whipped the car around in a one-handed U-turn, and headed for the hospital. She usually made it a policy not to talk on the cell phone while driving. While not illegal in the state yet, it was dangerous and she always liked to set a good example for the citizens of Albany Beach. This morning, good example be damned.

"Detective Robinson said he would fill you in on the particulars when you got there, but apparently, this chick was attacked by some guy she met in a bar."

"Attacked? As in raped?"

"No, like he tried to kidnap her and throw her in the trunk, only she got away."

"Holy shit," Claire murmured.

"Amen to that, Chief." Jewel popped another bubble in concurrence. "So, Detective Robinson said for you to meet him in the ER."

"I'm headed there now." Claire's mind was flying in a million directions. Could this be the single stroke of luck she'd been praying for? Someone who had seen the killer? Someone who could tell her something that would lead her in the right direction?

She hung up the phone without saying goodbye.

Claire parked her police cruiser in one of the spaces designated for emergency vehicles in the ER parking bay and hurried through the automatic sliding glass doors. She saw EMT Kevin James and his partner headed toward her in the brightly lit corridor where there were colored lines painted on the tile floor, meant to be used to guide patients to various areas of the hospital.

"Kevin."

"Hey, Chief."

"I'll grab the coffee and meet you at the bus," his partner said, hooking a thumb in the direction of the auxiliary coffee shop as he turned the corner. "Maybe Madge still has some blueberry muffins."

"What's up?" Kevin asked Claire. He was in his early thirties with sandy colored blond hair and killer blue eyes that gave him an all-American look. He knew how to wear the county's emergency medical technician uniform, too. His long sleeve light blue shirt was always pressed and immaculate, his navy pants creased. He'd grown up in the area; his parents had chicken farms all over the county. Nice guy.

"I was kind of hoping you could tell me." She lowered her voice as a nurse pushing an elderly patient in a wheelchair approached them.

" 'Morning, Chief Drummond." The nurse avoided eye contact as she passed. She'd been in the group of hostile hospital employees at the town meeting the previous night.

"Good morning, Kathy." Claire nodded, turning back to Kevin as the nurse continued on her way. "Did you treat this woman just brought in?" she asked quietly. "The one who was attacked?"

Kevin nodded. "Apparently, she managed to get away from the guy. Got back to the apartment she's sharing with some girlfriends for the summer. Clothes torn. Beat up. They convinced her to call 911."

Clothes torn. Beaten. Claire felt her blood pressure plunge in disappointment. This wasn't her guy. It didn't match the MO . . . unless the killer was changing, evolving. The possibility made her shudder. "So he tried to kidnap her?"

Kevin nodded. "He attacked her in a bar parking lot. Tuna's. Tried to throw her in the trunk."

"She was inside the bar? Underage?" She scowled.

"You know these kids, Chief. They've got fake IDs that look better than the real ones." His gaze shifted to the two lab techs from the phlebotomy lab approaching.

Dressed in scrubs, they carried plastic trays of glass vials to collect specimens. Alan Bradford and

Casey McCall. They'd both been at the meeting last night, too. Casey avoided eye contact as he walked by, but Alan had the guts to speak. "Good morning, Chief."

She nodded. "'Morning, Alan." In his early thirties, like Kevin, he, too, had lived his whole life in Albany Beach. She didn't know him well, but he was pleasant whenever she ran into him and she always let him take her blood when she needed tests run. Her veins were hard to hit, and he never had to make a second stab. When Ashley had required blood work over the winter when her doctor had suspected she might have mono, Alan had been the one to alleviate her daughter's trepidation, and get the sample without hurting her.

"Hope it's not more bad news that's brought you here," Alan said as he walked by.

She offered a grim smile. "I hope not, either." She met Kevin's gaze again as the lab techs disappeared into an elevator. "Was she sexually assaulted?"

"It wasn't clear. She was pretty out of it. They'll take blood in the back, run a tox screen, but she was still under the influence of alcohol when we arrived. Maybe something else."

"And how old?"

"Eighteen. College freshman."

Claire closed her eyes. Only three years older than Ashley and she was out drinking, probably raped, almost kidnapped. Claire's ex and his Mormon wife were looking good to her this morning, especially in light of Ashley party the previous night. "OK, listen, thanks." She brushed her hand down Kevin's arm. "You have a good day."

He headed for the doors leading out into the parking bay. "You, too, Chief. Good luck."

Claire found Detective Robinson speaking quietly with Dr. Larson in front of a closed door to an examining room. Through the window in the door, she could see a young blond girl, covered by a sheet, lying on her side on a hospital bed.

"Robinson." Claire nodded. "Dr. Larson."

Dr. George Larson seemed as permanent a fixture in Albany Beach as the diner . . . or the Atlantic Ocean. He'd been practicing medicine in the town since the sixties, both in private practice and as a doctor on staff in the hospital. A few years ago his wife had died of cancer and there had been talk of his moving to Florida to be near his sister, but nothing had come of it. Claire had been hearing for weeks that George had been telling anyone who would listen that he had known she should never have been hired as the police chief of the town. He was probably the "prominent citizen" who was putting pressure on the town council to get rid of her.

With Larson, it was personal. No one in town knew it, but he wasn't quite the good-natured country doctor he liked to portray. He had once had a roving eye with the ladies and a drinking problem. Years ago, as a state police officer, new on the job, she'd pulled him over up in Kent County for erratic driving and ended up arresting him on drunk driving charges. He'd begged her to just let him go, claimed that a conviction would ruin his reputation, his practice. She'd followed procedure and taken him in. The charges had ended up being dropped later, a mix-up in the lab with his blood test, supposedly, but he'd been holding a grudge against her ever since.

"So what's going on?" Claire asked her detective. "You think our killer tried to kidnap her and flubbed it?" If he did, this would be the first mistake he'd made as far as she knew. The man was very intelligent, and he was careful. The worst kind of serial killer.

"Too early to tell," Robinson said.

She could see by the look on the detective's face that he wasn't getting a lot of cooperation from the good doctor.

"I'll tell you what I told him," Dr. Larson said, making no attempt to be civil. "You don't interview her until she's been treated medically."

"I understand she was beat up and then her assailant attempted to force her into the trunk of his car. Was she raped?"

"We haven't gotten that far. She has a pretty serious laceration on the back of her head." Larson motioned with a clipboard. "I've ordered a head CT. Once brain injury has been ruled out, she'll need stitches."

"If she's been raped, I want a rape kit used."

"Of course." Larson sneered.

"By a trained female nurse, and not the day janitor," Claire snapped back. She didn't care what Larson thought of her. She was sick of his petty bullshit. "I've seen some piss poor work coming out of this ER, lately, Doc."

"Look who's talking about piss poor job performance," Larson fired back as he walked off. "I'll call you as soon the patient can be interviewed, *Detective*."

"Son of a—" Claire slapped the mint green painted wall.

"Hey, don't let him get to you." Robinson motioned with his head. "Go on to the office. I'll sit tight. Call you when we can go in."

She hesitated. Then nodded. Robinson was right. She needed to get over to the station, see what piles of manure were waiting for her there.

"Just as soon as he gives you the green light," she said, pointing to him as she walked away.

"You bet."

Claire walked out into the bright morning sun of the parking bay to find Chain leaning casually against her cruiser, smoking a cigarette. *Just who she wanted to see.* "You old enough to be smoking that thing?" she asked, checking out his eyebrow stud.

"Yup." He exhaled a puff of smoke and dropped the butt, grinding it out with a black combat boot, left unlaced.

"Look, Ashley's on restriction for that little stunt the other night. She's not going to the party Friday night, I don't care how many bands are playing or how many live bats they're eating, so there's no sense trying to dissuade me."

To her surprise, the teen dressed all in black, his hair dyed shoe-polish black, broke into a grin. So he had a sense of humor. "Actually, Chief Drummond, I saw that you were here and I just wanted to . . ." He lifted one shoulder. "You know."

"No, I don't know, but let me guess. You were cruising the ER parking lot, saw me and wanted to say hi?"

"I come by mornings to see my granny." He stuffed his hands into the pockets of his baggy jeans. "She's in the old folk's wing. Parking lot was full and I have to pay on the street." He lifted his chin in the direction of his beat-up car. "Free parking back here."

Claire set her jaw, determined not to be dragged

in by this kid's sad tale. "Actually it's illegal parking back here. Emergency vehicles only." She hooked her thumb in the direction of the large red metal sign at the entrance to the lot.

Chain exhaled. "Anyway, what I wanted to say was that I was sorry about the party. And no matter what you think, we weren't drinking or anything. Me and my friends, we don't drink or do drugs."

Claire stared at him drolly. "I can't tell you how hard I find that to believe."

"Look, you don't know me." He stared with hostile dark eyes, shaking his head. "Ashley told me not to say anything to you. That you wouldn't listen." He walked away.

Claire rested her hand on the door handle of the car, watching the boy slump his way to his car. She was tempted to call him back. Accept his apology, give him the benefit of the doubt. After all, she had no evidence that he drank or did drugs. But what he didn't understand was that even though she didn't know him, she certainly knew kids like him. She saw them arrested, booked, every summer.

She just let him go.

Chapter Five

At the station house, Claire let herself into the "fishbowl" with her passkey card, armed with the coffee and doughnuts she'd picked up earlier at the diner. Jewel was on her cell phone.

"I don't care what he says." the dispatcher insisted. "I'm not going out with him again. He's a freak."

Anyone who entered the building from the public entrance had to talk to Jewel through a speaker in the glass partition. No one got into the back without her expressed permission. Despite her little idiosyncrasies, Claire liked her and depended on her.

"Coffee with extra cream. Two jelly doughnuts." She set the coffee cup down in front of the young woman. "Sorry, coffee's probably pretty cold."

"Got to go." Jewel snapped the cell phone shut so fast that the person on the other end of the call couldn't have had time to respond.

"Thanks. I can heat it up in the microwave."

Jewel removed the lid on the cup and gazed into the white bag with interest. "Grape or strawberry jelly doughnuts this morning?"

She said nothing about the personal phone call that was not permitted inside the fishbowl. Claire didn't mention it either.

"Grape, I think. A gross thought this time of morning."

Jewel took a bite of the doughnut, leaving powdered sugar around her pink lipstick-painted mouth. Her makeup was seventies Jersey hooker, but she was pretty in spite of it.

"Not as gross as the thought of that bran muffin." Jewel pointed as Claire pulled her breakfast out of the bag and set it on a napkin that appeared to have been only slightly used by someone on the night shift.

"I'll be in my office."

"Okeydokey." Jewel rose with her coffee cup in hand, headed for the microwave.

"At the risk of sounding like Rodney Dangerfield, I could use a little respect around here," Claire said as she exited through the self-locking door.

"Who?"

"An old comedian. Never mind."

"I do respect you, Boss," Jewel hollered as the bulletproof door swung shut. "You should see how I talk to the people I don't respect."

Claire barely caught Jewel's last words as she headed down the hall.

"Need to speak with you later, Chief," Sergeant Marsh said as he passed Claire.

She turned around, walking backward, sipping her cold coffee while balancing her muffin. "Can you give me a half hour?"

"You bet."

Claire was assaulted by a ringing telephone when she walked into her office. The sound of the phone, the sight of her desk covered in mounds of paperwork made her want to turn around and walk right back out the door. It had to be quieter back at the ER.

The phone continued to ring as she circled her desk and sat down in her chair. It was the line directly from the fishbowl.

Claire groaned and hit the loudspeaker button. "I'm trying to get my daily allowance of fiber here."

"Incoming." Jewel popped her gum. "Flack jacket required. Ex on line three."

Claire groaned. She had completely forgotten about waiting for Tim's call. She hit the line three button, leaving the speakerphone on. He didn't deserve the effort it would take her to pick up the receiver. "Chief Drummond," she said to annoy him. He had always hated the fact that she never took his name when they married. Apparently, subconsciously, she'd known the union was doomed from the start.

"Claire, how are you?"

"You read the papers. You know how the hell I am." She bit into the muffin and caught crumbs before they hit her freshly dry-cleaned pants. "I've got a whack job killing women and leaving their bodies at Dumpsters. How good could I possibly be?"

"Actually, that's the reason I wanted to talk to you."

"The reason you wanted to talk to me?" Claire snapped the tab back on the lid of the coffee cup and took a sip. It was now cold *and* bitter. "Tim, I called you. About eight times in the last week. You're late on the child support payment. *Again.*"

"I understand completely—" He started in with that psychologist's singsong tone of his meant to placate, but also to manipulate.

"Understand completely?" she interrupted before he got on a roll. "Do you understand that fifteen-year-old girls have to eat? They have to have shoes on their feet. There are dental bills, tutoring bills, guitar lessons—"

"Which is why I wanted to talk to you," he continued in the same irritating tone. "Rochelle and I were wondering if you had given any more thought to Ashley coming out to stay with us for the coming school year."

"No. No, I haven't, Tim." She tossed the muffin onto her desk, hitting the napkin square in the middle. She'd lost her appetite. "In case you haven't figured it out, I'm a little busy right now."

"All the more reason why this might be an excellent opportunity for Ashley to come spend some time with her sisters and—"

"Tim . . .?" She tried to imitate the voice she knew he must use with his manic, depressed, deranged clients. "Did you mail the check?"

"No, I didn't—"

"Tim, we'll be back in court again," she patronized, "and I don't want to do that if I don't have to."

"Let me tell you what I was thinking," he continued evenly, ignoring the money issue. "Ashley could—"

"Mail the damned check or I'm calling my lawyer." Claire hit the disconnect button and then stared at the black desktop phone. "Now, wasn't that mature," she muttered.

The line from the fishbowl immediately blinked red again, buzzing like an angry bee.

Claire hit the black button above the light. "Yes, Jewel?"

"Line three again," she sang.

Claire picked up the phone. "If you don't send that check, I swear, I'll come there and get it out of you myself. Forget lawyers and judges, I'll just pound you into the ground until you starting spitting out child support checks."

"Ummm . . ." the masculine voice on the other end of the line intoned. "I'm guessing that wasn't directed at me."

"Graham?" Claire groaned, recognizing his voice immediately. "Ah, hell. I'm sorry. No, no, of course not. I thought you were my ex-husband. I mean, I didn't think *you* were my ex, I thought—"

"Claire, it's okay.

She closed her eyes and rolled her head back until it touched the headrest of her chair. "I was embarrassed last night, but now I'm truly embarrassed."

He chuckled. "If that's the worst thing you do today, you should count yourself lucky."

He made her smile. "What can I do for you, Councilman?"

"I was wondering if you'd considered what we talked about last night."

"Helping me out or going on a date?" Claire was surprised by the flirtation in her voice. A little shocked, too. There was a girl in the ER who might have been attacked by the serial killer; she might have a clue to lead Claire to him. She didn't have time to be playing footsies under the table, not even with a Clark Kent look-alike.

Again, the dry chuckle. "Well, eventually both, but I'm a patient man."

She fiddled with the lid to her coffee cup. "I would say so, considering how long it took you to show up on my doorstep."

"My help. Would you like it?"

She hesitated. There was the touchy issue of privacy to consider. It was being battled out in offices similar to her own, in courts, as well. Some might argue that the councilman had no right to view any information that was not available to the public. Then, of course, there was the issue of dead women to consider. Claire knew that this man would kill again, and he would continue to kill until he was caught. Were privacy issues really more important than solving crimes?

"I want to say yes, but you know I can't—"

"Don't just say no," he interrupted. "Why don't you come out to my place tonight? I'll make you dinner and we can talk about it?"

"Can't. I have a fifteen-year-old prisoner to guard. My daughter's on house restriction."

"For how long?"

"Until she's thirty-seven," Claire quipped.

She could tell he was smiling when he spoke again. "Fine. I'll bring dinner and make it for you at your place. You have a grill?"

"Stainless steel. Double propane tanks. Two additional burners on the side."

"A serious griller. You eat red meat, right?"

"Still mooing."

"See you at seven?"

"I shouldn't agree to this. I cannot bring a civilian into my investigation, no matter how many Sherlock Holmes novels he's read," she said opening a manila envelope on the desk in front of her.

"Fine. The dinner invitation still stands."

She pulled out a stack of crime scene photographs. The top picture was a close up of Anne Hopkins's upper torso. The tiny gold crucifix around her neck caught Claire's eye. She had returned the necklace to Anne's mother and when she had lifted it out of the evidence envelope, the gold had seemed hot to her touch.

"Thanks, Graham," she said quietly. "I think I could use a friendly dinner."

Claire picked up her desk phone with a sigh. "Yeah, Jewel?"

"Detective Robinson on two."

Claire hit the line two button. "Walt, she ready for our interview?"

"Actually"—the middle-aged man cleared his throat—"I'm not sure there's going to be much of an interview."

"What do you mean? What's wrong?" She was shuffling papers on her desk, trying to prioritize, but halted, memos in each hand. "Walt?"

"Her boyfriend is here, with flowers and big slobbering apologies."

She let go of both papers and watched them float to the desk. "You have got to be kidding me. The guy who tried to kidnap her was her boyfriend? I thought he beat her up."

"Yeah, well, you ought to see him. She didn't quite give her girlfriends or me the entire story. Looks like she took a tire iron to his face. Then she got home, started to sober up a little and got pissed. Wanted to get back at him, I guess. Now everything's peachy between them."

Claire tilted her head to rest it on the back of her chair and closed her eyes. "This was a lover's quarrel?"

"Apparently he really did try to stuff her into the trunk, but only after they had a knock-down drag-out in the parking lot because she tore her clothes off on the dance floor." He gave a dry chuckle. "The boy's missing his front tooth. Apparently she knocked it out in the scuffle."

Claire's eyes flew open. "This isn't funny, Detective. I was hoping—" She exhaled and started again. She couldn't make this personal. Not if she was going to catch this killer. Becoming emotionally involved would only hamper her investigation. It might even cloud her thinking. "If neither want to press charges against the other, you can let them both go. Then hightail it over to Tuna's and speak with the manager. I don't care what they have to do to keep underage drinkers out of there, but if they don't, I'm closing them down. Kids get killed this way."

"Right, Chief."

Claire hung up and lowered her head to her hands. She felt robbed. It hadn't been much, but it had been something.

She only gave herself a minute to feel sorry for herself and then she picked up her head and reached for a stack of notes on the murders. She'd chart every detail in every case so that she could more easily make comparisons. Surely there was something there she had missed. Something that would lead her closer to the killer.

* * *

That evening, Claire knocked on Ashley's bedroom door, then walked in.

"I thought you weren't supposed to just barge in." Ashley peered over the top of the magazine she'd been reading. She was stretched out on her bed, head propped on a pile of pillows. She wore large headphones, which she now slid back to let them hang around her neck.

"I knocked." Claire stepped over a huge pile of clothes in the middle of the floor to carry the TV tray to the bed. "Guess you couldn't hear with the loud music deafening you. I brought you dinner." She set the tray on the edge of the nightstand.

"Bread and water?"

"Close. Rosemary potatoes, field greens salad with ranch dressing, and fresh pineapple."

Ashley glanced at the tray. "That's it? That's dinner?"

"Graham brought New York strips. I'm sure he'd be happy to throw one on the grill for you."

Ashley turned up her nose. "I'm no longer eating red meat. Do you realize how those poor animals suffer before they're slaughtered?"

"I brought you cranberry apple juice, too." Claire backed toward the door, circumnavigating the clothes pile. "You need anything else, you can get it yourself, Miss Sourpuss. And maybe you could wash some of these clothes?"

"They're not dirty."

Claire started to say something, then bit her tongue.

The teen flipped a page in the magazine, her eyes downcast. "You dating that guy out there? The city councilman?"

"No."

"So he's just here to . . ." Ashley glanced up. "Make you a gourmet dinner?"

"I guess." She lifted her hand lamely. "It's hard to explain. It's just dinner. OK." She glanced away, then back at her daughter. "Did Chain tell you he and I spoke today?"

Ashley worked her jaw, staring at a page in the magazine. "Those weren't exactly his words."

"Look, I don't expect you to understand, you're just going to have to believe me when I tell you, I'm just trying to protect you. Keep you safe."

"Think what you want. You will anyway."

Ashley's tone was bordering on disrespectful, but Claire didn't say anything. She tried to pick her fights. "I'm going to clean up." She stopped at the door, glancing in the direction of the window. Was that the faint hint of cigarette smoke she smelled again? She and Ashley had had a go-round about this a few weeks ago. "I'm assuming you're not smoking in here anymore and that that window is locked."

"That would be the correct assumption." Ashley flipped another page.

There was that tone thing again. Biting her tongue, Claire closed the bedroom door behind her. She found Graham at the sink rinsing off the dirty dishes and loading them into the dishwasher.

"So tell me who your suspects are and why," Graham said. "I'll clean up. You take notes."

"I can't tell you who my suspects are." She thrust a small container of potatoes into the fridge. They'd make a perfect lunch the next day at work. "And I told you on the phone, I can't accept your help. The agreement was just dinner."

He glanced at her, then back at the plate he was rinsing off. "So, let's see. Ralph the dishwasher would have been at the top of the list. He had contact with all the women, had a record of abusing women."

Graham slid a plate into the dishwasher rack. He was dressed in a pair of khakis and a white oxford shirt, but he'd ditched the tie and rolled up his sleeves. He looked good in the fading light of the kitchen. "But you had to cross him off the list because Kristen was murdered while he was behind bars."

"Lucky guess." She stuck the steak sauce in the refrigerator door and walked to the sink to wash her hands.

"But I like your idea that our guy is using the diner as his jumping off place." Graham handed her a towel. "It's clever on his part, and yours."

She glanced at him, slowly rubbing her hands with the terry towel. "How did you know I was looking at the diner?"

He closed up the dishwasher and started it. Claire liked a man who could run a dishwasher.

"You've been there at least once, sometimes two and three times a day for the last week. Lingering over lunch, having that second cup of coffee." He leaned against the counter, taking the towel from her to dry his own hands. "Scribbling notes in that little notebook of yours."

"And how'd you know that? Loretta say something to you?"

"Nope." He hung the damp dish towel on a drawer pull. "ESP . . . that and the fact that I can see the diner parking lot from my office doesn't hurt."

She glanced away, feeling foolish that she hadn't remembered that his office supply store was on the same street as the diner. "I'm a hell of a detective, huh? It's a wonder I can catch a cold."

"You're being too hard on yourself. Now let me pour us both another glass of merlot and you get your notes, which I know, full well, you bring home with you." He reached for the half empty wine bottle. "You're probably one of those who sits up all night thinking about cases, going over and over them in your mind, trying to find some clue you think you might have missed before."

"You are not helping me with this case, Graham." She walked into the living room. "And as for taking my work home, sorry. That's what good cops do."

He met her at the couch. "I know, and you're a good cop." He offered her one of the glasses and then took the same chair he had sat in the other night. "Now, on to your suspects. It's a man. Someone we know. Someone who frequents the diner. Someone who probably knew the dead women pretty well, at least the local ones. Possibly a man with a record for battery, a minor sex crime, maybe." He sipped his wine, glancing over the rim. "You start interviewing our fellow citizens with criminal records?"

Seated on the end of the couch, Claire propped her feet on the birch twig coffee table. "Not that it's any of your business, but I haven't started interviews yet. In a small town like this, I have to be careful who I interview, how and why. People talk. Innocent people's reputations can be ruined."

"If I were going to chat with some people, it would be those men with records first: Billy Trotter, José Lopez, the mayor."

Claire looked up. "How did you—"

"Did I tell you my sister's a cop? Actually, she's an FBI agent at Quantico. A computer geek." He shook his head. "You'd be shocked what's available on the Internet."

"You can't get your sister to use her connections to—"

"Claire, I'm talking about public access to records, here. You just have to know where to look."

She eyed him. "Which is where your sister, the FBI agent slash computer geek, comes in handy."

He pointed. "Exactly."

She studied him for a moment. "Graham, I've known you for years. Spoken to you hundreds of times." She tipped her wineglass, watching the rich red liquid swirl. "I never realized you were so—"

"Witty. Charming?"

"Devious, is what I was going to say." She flashed a smile. "You mentioned José, who works for Loretta. I didn't know he'd been in trouble. I don't even think he started working at the diner until July."

"But he was around. He probably ate there."

She sipped her wine. "Out of curiosity, what was he arrested for?"

"Minor drug charge a few years back. Went through a first offenders program."

She stared into space for minute. "I don't see the killer as a druggy. This guy is too controlled. Too . . . meticulous."

"You still need to consider José. He works at the diner, for God's sake."

"Who else do you think I should look at?" She

lifted one shoulder. "You know, just out of curiosity. Seth Watkins?"

"Seth? You're kidding." He grimaced. "I hadn't caught that one yet. Talk about someone who will creep you out." He shuddered.

"Tell me about it. And his was actually a sex offense, of sorts." She studied a photograph taken of her and Ashley the previous summer, camping in the Appalachian Mountains. There had been no vacation this summer. She thought about Seth and the pen in the evidence envelope back at the station. About the pen he'd given her the day before.

She looked back at Graham. "And what about yourself? You have a record? Should I be checking? You eat at the diner all the time. Tuna on whole wheat, hold the chips, an extra pickle."

"I don't have a record."

"Actually" —she wrinkled her nose playfully—"I know that."

He lifted a brow. "You ran my record?"

"I've been trying to keep a list of every man who walks through Loretta's door. I run everyone's record on the list. I don't know how I missed José." She set down her glass and drew her knees up, wrapping her arms around them.

"You make a good point there, though."

"What's that?"

"You can't limit your suspects to only men who have records. As you pointed out, your killer is clever." He stroked his chin. "Maybe he's been clever enough not to get caught at anything, so far."

"You're serious? You want me to put your name down as a possible suspect?"

"Nah, because I'm not the killer." He leaned back in the leather chair, resting one ankle on his knee. "You're not going to like this, but I think you need to add McCormick to your list."

She'd been rubbing a smudge beside her on the leather couch, but she looked up. "Ryan McCormick? You've got to be kidding me. He's a police officer. One of the good guys."

"I know that."

"He's probably the best all-around cop I've got."

Graham continued to nod. "But there's something not right about him, Claire. I mean, all that time in the gym. Strutting up and down the boardwalk at night. And who wears long sleeves in August?"

She looked at him and the rolled-up sleeves of his white oxford.

"Ok, I do. But only because I think short sleeve dress shirts look silly. And I work in an air-conditioned office and store all day. He's in and out of his car, walking the boardwalk—"

"Ryan McCormick is not a killer," she said firmly.

"The ladies like him. He likes the ladies." He finished off his wine and set the glass down. "And did you know he likes it a little kinky?"

She frowned. "No I didn't know—how the hell do you know he *likes it kinky*?"

"The girls in the store talk. You know, in the break room. When the store's empty. Business is slow." He shrugged. "A guy can't help but hear sometimes."

"You eavesdrop on your employees?"

"Don't have to. They don't seem to care who

hears." He got up. "Guess I'm going to go now. Thanks for dinner."

She set down the pile of cards and followed him to the door. It seemed to her as if he were leaving a little abruptly. Truth was, she really wasn't ready to let him go. Having him here tonight reminded her of how lonely she was. How much she missed Kurt. "I'm the one who's supposed to be thanking you for dinner. You brought it. You cooked it. You even did the dishes."

He halted at the door, sliding one hand into his pants' pocket. Studying him, she wondered how tall he was. She was a hair under six feet and he was four or five inches taller than she was. Both her ex-husband and Kurt had been her height or shorter. Had that been the problem?

"You're welcome, then." He grinned. "Thanks for having me over. I'm glad I could help out."

"You did not help me out."

"I think I've got you thinking in a couple of different directions."

"McCormick."

He nodded.

She shook her head, sighing. "I'm telling you. McCormick is not our guy. I've worked with him day and night. He might get a little . . ." She searched for the right word. "Uptight sometimes, but—"

"What officer has been the first on every scene, except Kristen Addison?"

Claire's mouth went dry. She had been the one to find Kristen. "McCormick," she said quietly.

They were both quiet for a moment. "Look, I'm not saying it's him. I'm just saying you need to look at this with open eyes. This guy, when you catch him, you're going to know him, maybe better than you'd like to think."

She rested her hand on the smooth wall for support and closed her eyes. "You know how scary that is?"

She felt his hand on her waist.

"I have a good idea."

Claire opened her eyes to find him looking down at her. He smelled good.

"I was thinking about trying to kiss you," he said quietly. "What do you think?"

She wished he'd just done it because the same thought had crossed her mind. But now that he put it that way to her . . . She covered his hand with hers. "Graham. I've got a man killing women out there. I can't begin to think—"

"You're right. I'm sorry." He let go of her. Took a step back.

Claire considered crossing the short distance between them, throwing her arms around him and laying one on him. Instead, she opened the front door to let him out. "I might do a little snooping around tomorrow on my possible suspects. I'm not ready to bring anyone in for questioning, but I might have a friendly chat with a few people."

"I think that's smart."

"I'm going to keep my eye on the diner and . . ." She lifted one shoulder, letting it fall. "I guess keep my eyes and my mind open."

"'Night, Claire."

"Good night," she said a little more wistfully than she'd intended. She watched him turn around in the driveway and then she went back into the house. She knew it would be a while before she slept so she decided to start making a list of questions for the men on her suspect list.

As she walked back into the living room, she thought about what Graham had said about Mc-Cormick, about the fact that she needed to realize that this killer really was someone she knew. That meant that even though she thought she was a pretty good judge of character, she was wrong about someone. Could that someone be Ryan McCormick? Could she really have a man on the force who was also a killer?

Chapter Six

The phone beside Claire's bed jangled and she instinctively reached for it, even before she was fully awake. "Drummond," she said, squinting to read the digital clock beside her bed. It was 4:46.

"Chief. This is Jesse Perdue, night dispatcher." He hesitated.

She rubbed her eyes, trying to sit up and sound half intelligent. "Yes, Jesse."

"Sorry to wake you, but we got another dead girl."

Claire swore as she slid her bare legs over the side of the bed and turned the bedside lamp on. *Dear God, not another one,* was all she could think. "Where?"

"The elementary school."

She closed her eyes for a moment, rubbing both eyelids with her thumb and forefinger. "You've got to be kidding me."

"Night janitor found the body beside the Dumpster behind the gym. The call just came in. All available units have been dispatched. EMTs and an ambulance. Not that they'll be needed. They say she looks like she's been dead a little longer than the others were when they were found."

"I'll be there as quick as I can." Claire hung up the phone and dropped her face into her hands for a moment, letting her blond hair fall over her face. Maybe Dr. Larson, the mayor, the others were right. Maybe she was in over her head. Maybe it was her fault another woman had been murdered.

Wearily, she got to her feet and went to her closet for a clean uniform. At least two weeks ago she'd been told the attorney general was making noise about gathering a task force to take over the investigation. Maybe it was time for her to officially ask for assistance.

Claire walked the perimeter of the now familiar crime scene. The sun was just rising in the east, casting a golden yellow glow over the redbrick wall of the school, the green industrial-size Dumpster and the body sprawled on the dark pavement. Flashing blue ambulance lights and police car lights added a strange, ethereal sentiment to the early morning vista.

The young woman had been identified by the New Jersey driver's license in her purse as Brandy Thomas, aged twenty-three. Claire held the plastic coated license in her gloved hand, studying it. A pretty, heart-shaped face stared back. Five foot six inches, 135 pounds, blond hair, blue eyes. Of course Claire had known the girl would be a blonde before she got here.

"Chief." Detective Robinson approached. He'd

also been pulled out of bed. At least he'd taken the time to shower. His thinning hair was still damp and he smelled of shaving lotion. "Found some paperwork in her purse; looks like she just started working for a local temporary agency in town."

Claire handed him the driver's license to be bagged with the dead woman's other personal belongings. "Call the place as soon as it opens. Find out where she's living and where she's working."

"Will do."

"ME been here?"

"On her way," Robinson called over his shoulder as he walked away.

Claire turned toward the Dumpster and the dead girl beyond the yellow crime scene tape. There were people milling everywhere: cops, the EMTs, and an ambulance crew. Two men, one Hispanic, one Caucasian, dressed in custodial jumpsuits, stood near one of the town's police cars. Someone sat in the front seat of the car, asking questions. She couldn't see which officer it was.

She shifted her attention back to the body. Slowly, she blocked out the hushed, uneasy voices around her. She let the school's brick wall, the Dumpster and the distracting emergency vehicle lights fade into the background. This was just about Claire—Claire and Brandy. Claire sensed that the young woman had something to tell her; she just had to listen.

Trying to put every detail of the scene to memory, as she became aware of it, she ducked under the repulsive yellow tape and squatted beside the body.

Brandy, like the other women, had been dumped. She had been killed in another place, and then disposed of here. As Claire had been told over the phone, it was immediately obvious that she had been dead longer than the others, when they were found. Rigor mortis had already come and gone and Brandy's body was beginning to decompose. Though Claire couldn't yet see the breakdown of the flesh and organs, she could smell it.

Brandy Thomas was fully dressed in a pale yellow cotton top and a short jean skirt, sandals on her feet, her purse carefully placed over her shoulder. From what Claire had been reading about serial killers, the scene wasn't as bizarre as it appeared. Killers like this one did everything for a reason and to discover his motives could mean discovering him.

So, what was the killer telling about himself here, Claire wondered. That women were trash. That he was not a thief. That he liked order. Like the others, not only had he left her purse with her, cash untouched, but he had slipped the strap over her shoulder . . . where it belonged. As if she would need it. Like the umbrella he had left behind for the dead Anne Hopkins . . .

Claire continued to make her observations. Both of Brandy's wrists had been repeatedly slashed. Claire could now recognize the smears of blood where the killer had attempted to prevent the wounds from closing up, then cut her again when the blood coagulated. Once again, the death had been a slow one. It was the process of dying; that was how this killer got his rocks off.

Claire's stomach did a flip-flop and for a moment she feared she'd embarrass herself by barfing all over the crime scene. She closed her eyes and took deep, steady breaths through her mouth. Five thirty in the morning and it was already hot. Sweltering.

The sickening feeling passed and she opened her eyes. With a gloved hand, she brushed the young woman's hair off her face to get a better look at her. Thankfully, her eyes were closed. The chief ME, Martha, up in Wilmington, had told Claire that if it was any comfort, all these women had died relatively painless deaths. She said that when one bled to death, one just got sleepy, that everything faded into darkness and that was it.

A discoloration around Brandy's mouth caught Claire's eye and she pulled her flashlight from her belt. The sun was not fully up yet so there were still shadows cast against the building and the girl. Claire flipped on the light and aimed the beam on Brandy's face. She had a split lower lip. There was no blood. The wound looked as if it had been cleaned, but there was a definite bruising. This was a prior to death injury; she knew that much from her basic forensic training.

Had the killer done it?

Claire glanced in the direction of Kevin James who was standing around, talking with Patrolman McCormick. "Kevin," she called. She tilted her head, gesturing for him to approach. "Did you see this?"

"Looks like someone hit her, huh?" he said, walking over.

"So I'm right? This took place before she died?"

"Definitely." He was wearing latex gloves, too. Similar to hers, but his were blue. "See the bruising around here?" He brushed his fingertip around the corner of her mouth. "You can't get that post-mortem."

Claire lifted her gaze to stare at the green Dumpster. "You think the killer did this?"

The medical technician shrugged. "Hard to say. After the autopsy, they'll be able tell you how old the bruising is. You figure when he snatched her and—"

"I'll know if it was the killer or not." She looked at Kevin. "You know, we've seen no violence before." Realizing how ridiculous what she had said sounded, she laughed without humor. "You know what I mean. He didn't knock the others around. He tied them up, taped their mouths, slit their wrists, but he didn't hurt them. From the appearance of the other women's bodies, the ME thought he was actually pretty gentle with them," she continued, thinking aloud. "But if the killer hit her, that means something is changing. Violence is a result of anger or frustration."

"Something else new, too. Anyone tell you about this?" James brushed the dead woman's silky blond hair aside to reveal two angry red welts on the side of her neck.

"What the hell?" Claire leaned closer, directing her flashlight beam. "A bite?"

The technician stood up. "Who knows? I'm not good with dead ones, just the live ones. The ME upstate should be able to tell you after the autopsy, though."

He walked away and Claire got down on her knees for another look at Brandy's neck. It definitely wasn't a human bite mark; those she'd seen.

"You need the camera, Chief?" Officer Savage asked from behind her.

She stood up, still contemplating the two red marks. "Thanks." She took the camera bag and crouched on the ground again. She loaded a fresh roll of film and began to methodically take pictures from every angle.

Sometime in the middle of the night, when she hadn't been able to sleep, she'd decided she had to look at solving these murders as a mental exercise. Graham was right; this guy was smart. But so was she; she just had to be smarter.

So what could she learn from this particular crime scene? The similarities between Brandy's case and the others were pretty easy to pick up on. Young blond-haired, blue-eyed women. The abduction was non-violent, so they were somehow lured into the killer's confidence. They all died of blood loss. The bodies were all dumped next to some sort of trash receptacle.

So what was different here? The marks on the neck, obviously. What else? The camera shutter whirred as she snapped photo after photo, averting her eyes to keep from blinding herself with the flash. What was different? The fact that he had hit her, if Claire's guess was right. Did that mean he knew her more personally?

The actual location of the Dumpster was different, too. No two women had been dumped at the same place. She glanced up at the brick wall. Of all the places the bodies had been found, this one was the most easily accessible, and most public. Anyone could drive by on the street behind the school and see a car pull up and dump a dead girl's body. In every other case, the Dumpster was in an alley, or in an isolated spot like a construction site or a state park. Why the school?

Snapping the last photo, she stood up, staring at the redbrick wall of the gym. The gym . . .

"Son of a bitch," she whispered, turning away suddenly.

"What you got, Chief?" McCormick called, coming off the patrol car he was leaning on.

She glanced over her shoulder at the wall behind her. "He was here," she murmured.

"Who?"

"The killer," she said, shocked by her epiphany. "He was here at the town meeting the other night."

McCormick scowled. "How do you know that?"

She glanced at her officer and for the first time in her career, wished she hadn't shared information with one of her own. "I just do," she said.

At 4:30 that afternoon, Claire pulled into the gravel parking lot of Stewart's Lawn and Garden shop. She parked under a shady locust tree near the rear gated entrance that led to the greenhouses and cut the engine. Ashley didn't get off for another half an hour, but Claire needed some downtime. Some time to think through what she'd learned today.

The latest victim, Brandy Thomas, according to her tearful father who Claire spoke to around noon, had just moved to Albany Beach two weeks prior to her death. She had broken up with her boyfriend and left her hometown in New Jersey to make a clean break. She'd ended up in the southern Delaware beach town because she had worked here summers when she was in high school and an old friend had offered her a couch to sleep on until Brandy got settled. She'd gotten a job with a temp agency doing secretarial work at the hospital, her father explained, and she had been very excited. She had actually been talking to her parents about starting nursing classes in the fall. As far as the father was aware, Brandy knew no one except the girlfriend she'd been staying with.

Claire ran her pen down the side of the yellow legal-size notepad, going over the details she had so far. The roommate, Rachel Clause, had already been interviewed. She'd last seen Brandy at Bubbles martini bar Sunday night. It was a new place on the edge of town where the young crowd liked to hang out. According to Rachel, when she left the bar around nine-thirty, Brandy was still there. Rachel couldn't recall anyone in particular her friend had been talking with. The bar had been crowded and loud, the young woman had explained. Brandy's car had been located in the bar parking lot this morning. This time of year, beach goers looking for free parking used the lot all the time. No one had noticed the car hadn't moved in three days.

Claire had had the ex-boyfriend in New Jersey checked out immediately. He had an airtight alibi. After Brandy broke up with him, he'd apparently gone on a tear. Sunday night, he'd been sleeping off a drunk in a New Jersey municipal jail, after a bar fight.

So where did all this leave Claire's investigation? She removed her sunglasses and rubbed her aching eyes. The chief medical examiner for the state assured Claire she'd have an autopsy report for her by morning. In the meantime—

Motion out of the corner of Claire's eye caught her attention and she turned to look out the passenger-side window to see Ashley trudging toward the car from behind, dressed in her usually black on black, backpack on her shoulders. "Mom, what are you doing here so early?"

Claire glanced over her shoulder in the direction her daughter had come. "I wanted to be on time for once. You just get off work?" She looked at the open gates that led into the nursery in front of the car. Ashley usually came out through the gates.

"Mr. Stewart said I could go a few minutes early." She opened the car door. "Guess he saw you pull in." She tossed her backpack into the backseat and climbed in.

Claire watched as she sat down stiffly and reached for her seat belt. "You okay? Your back bothering you?"

The teen fiddled with the buckle on the seat belt. "Yeah, a little. I was carrying all these fifty pound bags of fertilizer today. We had to move them from one pallet to another because we had this one bag with a hole in it or something."

Claire tucked her notepad into her briefcase on the seat beside her and tossed it over the seat. The photos of Brandy Thomas's body were inside and she didn't want to risk Ashley seeing them. Being the daughter of a cop, she was already exposed to more of the realities in life than Claire liked. No fifteen-year-old needed to see pictures of a woman who had been purposefully bled to death.

"When we get home, take some ibuprofen. The heating pad's in the hall closet, if you need it."

"Okay."

Claire stared at Ashley. She'd been in the car a full two minutes and she'd not argued a single point with her mother. Not made a single *Mom, you're an idiot* face.

"What?" Ashley said.

"You're being awfully pleasant," Claire intoned suspiciously. "Are you in trouble?"

"Mom."

Ashley rolled her eyes, making Claire feel a little better. That was the fifteen-year-old daughter she knew.

"First you're pissed because you think I'm using the wrong tone of voice," Ashley groaned. "Then, when I try to be nice—"

"Okay, okay. You're right." Claire started the car and backed out. "But you're still on restriction."

"I know that."

Claire pulled onto the street. "I have to pick up my dry cleaning. Then I thought we'd get some Chinese take-out."

Ashley gazed out the window. "Whatever."

"So Grandma was there on time to pick you up this morning? You made work on time?"

"Yup." Ashley continued to gaze out the window. "I heard you found another dead girl."

Claire glanced at her daughter. Ashley had parted her shoulder-length black hair in a crazy zigzag and then used two black rubber bands to tie it up in what Claire had referred to as doggy ears, back in the days when Ashley's hair was still a beautiful blond and she wore butterfly clips. "Your roots are showing," she said.

Ashley ran her finger over the top of her head. "Yeah, I know. Need to hit the Miss Clairol aisle at the drugstore."

"You know, you could bleach it back to blond."

"Mom," the teen groaned. "I like it this way."

"Fine." Claire signaled and turned into the

parking lot of the strip mall where the dry cleaners was located.

"You think you're going to have to leave early again in the morning?" Ashley asked as Claire pulled into a parking spot.

"I hope not. Why?" She cut the engine and reached in the console for her wallet.

"I don't know. I was just thinking that if you were, I could spend the night at Grandma and Grandpa's tonight." She cut her blue eyes at her mother.

"You never like to spend the night. Last week you groused for an hour about having to stay over."

"I know. They watch stupid stuff on TV like FOX News." She fiddled with the air-conditioning vent on the dash. "But I do get to sleep in because Grandma doesn't have to drive all the way out of town to get me, then drive me all the way to the nursery."

"I see, so this is about sleep?" Claire hesitated. "I guess we can call and see if they'll take you off my hands."

"Cool. I'll get your dry cleaning." The teen snatched the twenty dollar bill from her mother's hand and climbed out of the car.

Claire just sat there shaking her head, thinking she'd never live long enough to understand that child.

The Bloodsucker set his glass of Coke down on the end table beside his favorite chair. On a coaster, of course. He picked up the remote, pointed it, turned the power on the TV and sat down. He liked TV. Now that he lived alone, it kept him company. When Granny had been here, TV had rarely been allowed and then she was either watching soaps or that crazy religious channel that featured women with running black eye makeup and pink hair piled on their heads like cotton candy. He didn't watch soaps or religious shows anymore. He liked movies, especially old ones. This week, TNT had been running all the old, classic black-and-white horror flicks.

Max laid down on the floor in front of the TV and the Bloodsucker smiled. He used to be lonely, but now that he and Max had settled into a routine, he wasn't lonely anymore. Especially not when he had his women to keep him company.

He clicked the channel button, surfing for something to watch.

They had found Brandy this morning. The whole town was talking about it, even Ashley, Claire Bear's daughter.

He liked Ashley. And he thought Ashley liked him. Some might say he was too old for her, but he didn't think so. And even though he preferred his women blond, he was actually getting used to it black.

The Bloodsucker had talked to Ashley today about her mother. Pretty clever, he thought. He'd asked how she was doing. Acted all concerned. He asked if she was sleeping at night and the teen had admitted her mother wasn't. That her job was keeping her awake . . . and making her bitchy. The Bloodsucker had chuckled at the bitchy remark, and Ashley had laughed with him.

It was amazing to him how easily people were deceived. How he could be anyone he wanted to be, to anyone, and they would fall for it. It was because he was so smart, because he had scored so high on those IQ tests you could take in the back of magazines. Granny had never realized how smart he was. A cooking show filled the TV screen and he watched for a moment. The chef was making lobster bisque.

As he watched how the lobster should be cut for soup, he scratched his forearm absently. The fabric of the long sleeve T-shirt was irritating him. His arms itched. Both of them. He set the remote control on his lap so that he could scratch both arms at once.

"Don't scratch!" Granny had shrieked time and time again, slapping his hands, his face, the back of his head, whatever she could reach. *"Don't scratch or you'll get an infection. You'll get gangrene and they'll have to cut your arms off at the shoulders,"* she had threatened.

He scratched harder. He could hear that buzzing in his head that got in there sometimes. That buzzing that was Granny.

His forearms were suddenly burning now. Like they were on fire. This always happened after he was with a woman.

He groaned in frustration, in pain, and finally jerked up the sleeve of his shirt so that he could scratch the hideous scars that ran the length of his forearm.

"Puncture wounds?" Claire repeated what the ME said, over the phone, as she scribbled it down on her legal pad. "Made from what?"

"Something smooth, metal," Martha said in her gravelly voice.

"Like an ice pick?" Claire jotted it down, circled it and put a big question mark next to it.

"That's my guess."

"Why?"

"Why?" the older woman snorted. "Why do these lunatics do half the things they do? Because they're lunatics!"

Claire sat back in her chair, setting down her pen so that she could think for a minute. "Did he bleed her from the neck wounds? I mean, I saw some blood on the T-shirt, but not a lot."

"He may have gotten some blood out of the wounds, but not much. If our boy was shooting for the jugular, he needs to go back to Anatomy and Physiology class, because his mark was way off."

Claire frowned. "And that's all you've got for me?"

"Sorry, sweetie," Martha said rather tenderly, considering the curmudgeon she could be. "Everything else you know. He's using a scalpel that he could buy anywhere, latex medical gloves. No fingerprints, no bite marks. No fibers on the body, except her own."

"So the only difference between Brandy's body and the others is the two puncture wounds." Claire reached out and touched the corner of the photo she'd gotten of the wound.

"Well, and the bloody lip. He did it, I'm sure. Or, at least, it occurred while she was with him."

"He hit her."

"Or she could have fallen. No way to be sure."

Claire heard the rustle of papers.

"Oh," the ME continued. "And there's some bruising on her abdomen."

Claire slid forward in her chair. "Bruising?"

"She was punched or, again, she fell," Martha said. "Can't say for sure, but my guess is that she was punched. If you think she disappeared Sunday night and I place the time of death between Monday midnight and Tuesday, three A.M., he's the one who hit her."

"Son of a bitch," Claire muttered.

"I'm sorry?"

Claire brushed the hair off the crown of her head. "You know what this means?"

"He's getting violent. It isn't just enough to kill them now. He has to hurt them," Martha said.

"Yes." Claire pressed the heel of her hand against her forehead. "It also means that the victim was alive Monday night."

Two-pack-a-day Martha coughed. "I'm not following."

Claire propped her elbow on her desk and rested her chin in her hand. "Monday night we had a so-called *town meeting*. Basically, every local in town filed into the gymnasium to tell me what a lousy job I was doing on this investigation. He had her by then, but he hadn't killed her," she said, thinking aloud.

"And she was found beside a Dumpster behind a school?" the ME asked. "The same school?"

"Yup."

"So now he's taunting you."

Claire had never realized just how old thirty-four could feel some days. "I think so."

"You think it's something personal against you?"

"I don't know," Claire groaned. She sat up. "You said you thought she'd been dead over twenty-four hours by the time we found her."

"It's in the report."

"Well, listen, if you could overnight the autopsy report and photos, I'd greatly appreciate it."

"You bet," Martha said. "And Claire . . ."

"Yeah?"

"Hang in there."

"Do I have any other choice?"

At five Claire left the office, headed to her parents for dinner and to pick up Ashley. She just couldn't stand being in the office another minute. She had to get away from the clanging phone, the revolving door in her office, and worst of all the photos of the dead women she was collecting in manila envelopes.

But instead of going straight to her parents' house, in the same neighborhood where she'd grown up, Claire found herself in the parking lot of Graham's office supply store. She just needed to see him. To say hi. To talk to someone about anything other than dead women, if only for five minutes.

Claire walked into the store and was greeted by a clerk.

"Chief Drummond." She was a pretty brunette.

"Hi, is Graham still in?"

"Um, yes, he's in his office, I believe." She started to step away from the cash register. "I can get him for—"

"No, that's quite all right. Down this hall, right?" Claire had already started down the aisle of paper and envelopes.

"Um, yes," the brunette called after her. "Second door on the left."

Claire went down the hall past the break room and knocked on the second door on the left.

"Yes?" Graham called from inside.

Claire felt foolish all of a sudden. What was she doing here? Was she flattered that Graham was interested in her? Yes. But did she have the time or energy for a relationship right now? No way.

"Come in," Graham said.

Claire made herself open the door. "Hi," she said, walking in, closing the door behind her.

"Claire." He rose from behind a big mahogany desk.

"I know, what am I doing here?" She opened her hands, still feeling foolish. "Truth is, I don't know. I was just driving by, headed over to my folks' to pick up Ashley and—"

"You don't need a reason to stop by," he said, coming around the desk. "I'm just glad you did."

"Yeah, well, I—" She looked away, her eyes suddenly stinging with tears. God, what was wrong with her? She was losing it.

To her surprise, Graham wrapped his arms around her and pulled her against his chest.

"Graham, I—" She pressed her face into his shoulder, squeezing her eyes shut. His arms felt so good around her. Just to be hugged by another person, to have that human contact.

"Bad day?" he whispered.

She nodded, not yet trusting herself to speak. All she could do was hang onto him for dear life.

"Then I'm really glad you came by," he said, pressing a kiss to the top of her head. "So, call your parents, tell them you'll be late and to feed the kid and chain her to the couch or something, whatever it takes. You and I will go get some dinner—"

"No, I can't," she said, sniffing. "I . . ." She leaned back, her arms still around him, and looked up. "I really can't. I just came by—" She wiped her eyes and laughed.

"For a hug?" he said quietly.

She pressed her lips together, not knowing what to say to him. "Graham, right now, I . . . It's not that I don't want . . ." She exhaled, giving up trying to say what she wanted to say. Maybe because she didn't know what she wanted to say.

"Claire, it's all right." He brushed a stray strand of hair off her cheek with his fingertips. "I can wait."

The way he said it made her smile. She lifted up on her toes and brushed her mouth against his. Just a quick kiss. More of promise than of passion. "I have to go," she said, turning away, walking out of his arms.

"I'll call you tomorrow. But come by any time. Hugs are us."

She was still smiling when she reached her patrol car.

The Bloodsucker sat in the diner parking lot slumped down in the seat of his car. He watched the front door to the office supply store wondering what Claire was doing in there. Surely she didn't have to buy her own paper clips, envelopes. There was someone in the police department who did that sort of thing.

Maybe she was there to see the councilman. The Bloodsucker had heard her job was in danger. Pity. He smiled. Scratched the inside of his arm.

It was also possible that Claire Bear had begun interviewing possible suspects. There were rumors floating around out there about that, too. She was asking a lot of questions. Where people were, who they'd seen, what they had seen.

The questions made the Bloodsucker nervous.

The door at the store across the street opened and Claire walked out. The Bloodsucker held perfectly still, watching her through the open window. If anyone saw him, they wouldn't think it was strange. He was just here to grab something to eat on his way home from work.

The Bloodsucker watched Claire climb into her police car, start the engine and pull through the parking lot, out onto the street. He wondered where she was going. He started his engine ... eased out of the parking lot. There was only one way to find out.

Chapter Seven

"Thanks for agreeing to have lunch with me," Graham said, setting his menu aside as the waitress walked away.

Claire glanced at him across the table. "It's the least I could do after the way I fell apart in your office the other day."

"You didn't fall apart."

She lifted an eyebrow.

He leaned back on the pleather bench seat, stretching out one arm. He was dressed in his usual dark dress slacks, light colored, long sleeved polo and a conservative tie. He looked good, which Claire was trying hard to ignore. She still felt silly about walking into his office, throwing herself into his arms and then walking out. She didn't want to make any promises she didn't know if she could keep and right now, she didn't see how she could make any promises in the personal life department.

"All you did was come in for a quick squeeze."
He gave her that Clark Kent smile.

"Graham." She leaned forward over the For-
mica table. "This place is packed. Someone's
going to hear you." She leaned back not nearly as
annoyed as she wanted him to think. "And what I
don't need right now is another reason for my fellow citizens to want to run me out of town."

"I don't think it's that bad yet."

"No?" She sipped her coffee. Ordinarily, she
didn't drink coffee at lunchtime in August, but she
definitely needed the caffeine today. The hours she
was keeping were killing her. She had been leaving
the house before six in the morning and often not
pulling in her driveway until ten at night. She was
just thankful her parents were around to help her
out.

All week, Ashley had been staying with them
and Grandma was running her back and forth to
work. Claire missed seeing her daughter, even if it
was just so they could bark at each other, but she
was relieved not to have to leave her alone at home
so much. Even with the expensive security system,
Ashley home alone at night made Claire uneasy.

Graham laced his long fingers together on the
table and leaned forward. "You look beat."

She raised the eyebrow again. It seemed the only
response she could offer.

"You can't keep this up," he said. "You'll be the
next one dead."

She set down her coffee cup, exhaling. "I just
need to get a hold on this case," she confided quietly as she glanced up to see who was coming in
the diner door. It was Madge who had a gift shop

on the boardwalk. Claire's gaze shifted to Graham again. "Something changed with Brandy's death, something that should be leading me closer to the killer." She made a fist. "But I just can't see it."

"You interview your possible suspects?"

She shrugged. "Nothing official. I didn't drag anyone in and throw them in the interrogation room. I did have a chat with Billy Trotter again out at Calloway's Bar."

"Patti's ex."

She nodded. "It's not him. He couldn't work up enough energy to kill anyone." She wavered. She knew she really shouldn't be talking about this with Graham, but who did she have to talk to? In the past, McCormick had always been a good sounding board when they had a tough case. But now she was hesitant. She didn't believe for a minute that Ryan could be the killer, but there was something about him that now made her uneasy. Distrustful. Maybe it was because she feared she couldn't trust herself or her own conclusions anymore. "And I ran into Seth yesterday showing a model home."

"As a real estate agent, he has access to a lot of properties." Graham kept his voice low. "Some unoccupied. I know the guy isn't killing these women right off the bat. You have to keep them somewhere."

"I thought of that, which could make Seth a good candidate. He lives alone and he would have the means to hide someone." She reached for her coffee, watching José clear up a stack of dirty dishes off the lunch counter and carry them into the back. "Did you know that José's uncle works at the elementary school as a custodian?"

Graham's dark brows knitted. "The custodian who found Brandy Thomas's body?"

"Coincidence, probably," she mused.

"But you looked into his background, anyway?"

She cupped her hands around the coffee mug. "Yeah. Other than the one pot charge we already knew about, he's clean. Hardworking, model citizen." She lifted her hands and let them fall on the white table speckled with gold flecks. "I'm just grasping at straws here, thinking maybe this is more than I'm seeing."

"Meaning . . ."

The bell over the diner's door jangled and Claire looked up again. It was her favorite Goth, Chain. She watched him, hands stuffed in the pockets of his black jeans, as he took the only empty stool at the lunch counter. He spoke to Al Collins sitting next to him reading the paper and the older man struck a friendly conversation with him, which she found interesting, considering Chain's appearance. She'd seen the teen at the post office yesterday and had noticed him chatting with a woman with a baby in a stroller in line. Despite the dyed hair, black clothes and stud through his brow, people seemed to like him. Everyone but her.

Claire returned her gaze to Graham. He was waiting patiently. "I'm sorry," she said. "Just got distracted."

The new waitress, Carol, lumbered over, all six foot, two hundred forty pounds of her, carrying their lunch. Loretta had told Claire the other day that she and Carol had agreed, with a laugh, that Carol would be safe waitressing at the diner. In her mid-fifties, overweight and a brunette, there was no chance the killer would be interested in her.

Claire brushed her fingertips through her blond hair that fell across her shoulders. Over the last weeks, she didn't recall ever feeling vulnerable, even though she fit the profile of the murdered women, but last night she had dreamed he had come after her. No identifiable features, but she had known it was him. She had awaked in a sweat, breathing hard. She wasn't really afraid, but she would be a fool not to take into consideration what kind of women he was looking for. This morning, she'd realized that despite her haranguing Ashley, she was actually glad her daughter's hair was as black as shoe polish right now.

Carol set the Greek salad in front of Claire and the tuna croissant, no chips, extra pickle platter, on the table and walked away.

"You were saying you thought this case could be more than you're seeing," Graham prodded, cutting his croissant in half. "What do you mean?"

She dumped the vinaigrette dressing over her salad. "I don't know. I just feel as if I need to think outside the box. I mean, what if there's more than one killer? Or what if *he's* a *she?*"

"Has there been any evidence to indicate either?"

She stabbed at a black olive with her fork. "No, but we don't have *any* evidence. We have nothing but a cheap umbrella, some silicone powder from inside disposable latex gloves, and two puncture marks on Brandy's neck. Other than six women who've been bled to death, that's all I've got."

Graham was sympathetically quiet for a moment. He took a bite of his sandwich, chewed. "Listen, I know you said you can't really use my help, but what about my sister's?"

"The FBI agent?"

"The FBI provides information to law enforcement agencies; it's their job. I was wondering if a profiler would help."

Claire popped a grape tomato into her mouth. "You didn't say she was a profiler."

"She's not, but she knows people who are."

When the door jangled yet again, Claire instinctively looked up. That was part of the reason why she had joined Graham for lunch, even after turning him down yesterday. Seated at this booth, with her back against the wall, she could watch everyone who came in or out of the diner.

To her surprise, it was Ashley who walked in and she was so glad to see her. She felt so damned guilty about neglecting her these last few weeks. She was sure that was why she was acting out—the party, the missed curfews, the smoking. Claire started to rise, and then realized Ashley hadn't even seen her. Her eyes were all for the boyfriend.

"Could you excuse me for a minute," Claire said, wiping her mouth with a paper napkin as she rose. "It looks like my prisoner has found a way to sneak under the fence."

Graham turned around to see Ashley.

"Go easy on her," he warned. "You kill your kid with a fork in plain sight and you're definitely out of a job."

"Smart-ass," she muttered as she walked away from their table. "Remind me not to have lunch with you or come to your office anymore."

Ashley threw her arms around Chain and they locked lips.

"Ashley," Claire called cheerfully, walking up to them, hand on her firearm.

Ashley tore herself out of the guy's arms. "M-Mom, I thought you had a meeting—"

"You're supposed to be at work," Claire interrupted.

Ashley glanced around them. "Mom, people are looking," she whispered. "You're going to make a scene and embarrass—"

"You're damned straight I'm going to make a scene. The agreement was that you would not be walking into town for lunch anymore."

"Chief Drummond," Chain piped in.

She turned and glared. "You probably don't want to get in the middle of this, *Chain.*"

Ashley snatched her backpack off the floor and flounced away.

"Where do you think you're going?" Claire called, following her. So what if everyone in the diner was staring. So what if they would gossip among themselves that the chief of police had lost control of her teenage daughter. They were all talking about her anyway.

"I can't believe you would do this," Ashley threw over her shoulder as she shoved the diner door open and stomped out.

Claire ignored Chain, who was right behind her. "Ashley Anne! You won't walk away when I'm speaking to you. I won't have it."

At the bottom of the steps, Ashley halted, arms crossed over her chest, hip thrust out, her back to her mother.

"You were supposed to be at work," Claire said, coming down the steps. "You were supposed to stay at work until your grandmother or I picked you up."

"You didn't tell her yet?" Chain circumnavigated Claire to get to Ashley. "Man, Ash—"

Claire felt the heat rise in her face. This was all she needed today. "Tell me what?"

"Mom . . ."

"Tell me what?" Claire repeated, barely able to control her anger. She pushed on the teen's shoulder, forcing her to turn and face her mother.

Ashley stared at the loose gravel at her feet.

"What is it you haven't told me?"

"I lost my job," Ashley said softly.

"*Lost* your job, as in you can't *find* it?"

"It wasn't her fault, Chief," Chain said.

Claire glanced up, hoping to bore holes in him with her gaze. "Your being here is probably not the best idea right now. I realize my daughter isn't an angel, but you know, we didn't have any smoking, any parties, and past curfews until you walked into the picture."

"This doesn't have anything to do with him," Ashley snapped, viciously.

"Doesn't have anything to do with him?" As Claire turned to her daughter, something on Chain's neck caught her attention. She turned back to get a better look, the realization of what it was slowly sinking in.

A tattoo. A fresh one, still red and welted. It was a vampire bite with two drops of ruby red blood flowing from the black marks. "What is that?" Claire demanded of Chain, her voice gruff to cover her emotion.

"What?" Realizing what she was staring at, he laid his hand on his neck. "A tattoo."

"You're not old enough to legally get a tattoo."

Claire couldn't stop staring at the boy's neck, trying to process the possible implications. All she
could think of was the wounds on Brandy's neck.
Two puncture wounds—like a vampire's bite.

"I turned eighteen this month," Chain said, now
obviously more than a little annoyed with her. "It's
perfectly legal."

"What is it?" Claire demanded of Ashley, pointing at the boyfriend's neck.

"What do you mean?" Her daughter looked at
her as if she were a babbling idiot. "It's a tattoo. Of
a vampire bite."

"Are you two involved in some kind of satanic
cult or something?"

Chain shook his head in disgust and walked
away, stuffing his hands into his pockets. "I'm out
of here, Ash. I got to get back to work. Talk to you
later."

Still staring at the young man as he cut across
the parking lot, shoulders hunched, Claire took
Ashley by the arm and led her toward the car.

"You can't do this," Ashley spat. "You don't have
a right to put your hands on me like this! You
don't have a right to—"

"Shut up, Ash. Shut up and get in the car before
I put you in the car. And you know I can do it." It
took all of Claire's emotional strength not to shove
her daughter as she willed her fingers to release
her arm.

Ashley stomped around the front of the cruiser,
jerked open the door and threw her backpack into
the backseat. "I was going to tell you."

"When did you lose your job?" Claire climbed
into the driver's seat. She was so upset that her hands

were trembling. What if Chain was the killer? Graham had warned he would be someone they all knew, someone she knew. The thought that she could have allowed her daughter to be near such a monster . . . it was more than she could consider.

"I didn't tell you because you've just been so busy with murder cases. I didn't want to be a problem—"

"How long ago did you lose your job, Ashley?" Claire repeated, grabbing her sunglasses from her pocket just below her badge.

Ashley crossed her arms over her black T-shirt, obscuring most of the bat graphic. She stared straight ahead through the windshield. "About a week ago."

"About?" Claire thrust the sunglasses onto her face. "You don't know? I need to call Mr. Stewart and further embarrass you?"

"Mom, it was stupid. It was my fault. I was going to let things blow over and call him and apologize and see if he would let me come back to work."

Claire started the engine, not even sure where she was going. She knew one thing; Ashley was not going home alone. She wasn't going anywhere that Chain could get to her until she looked into this. "Ashley, I don't understand." She looked at her. "You loved your job."

"I know." Tears filled her eyes and she rubbed at them, embarrassed.

"Why did he fire you?"

She sniffed. "I was late getting back from lunch a couple of times and I . . . I kind of skipped a day or two."

"To be with Chain, who I could have sworn you

told me was sixteen." Claire threw the car into reverse, backed out of the parking space and shot forward, throwing loose gravel all over the lot.

"What was I supposed to do?" Ashley stared ahead. "You don't want me going out with him. You don't want him at our house."

"Without me there."

Ashley's head snapped around. "And just when are you there?"

Claire was the one who broke eye contact this time. Ashley's accusation was like a punch in her stomach. Because she was right. Claire was thankful she had the sunglasses on so her daughter couldn't see the tears in her eyes. She waited until she had her emotions in check before she spoke again, and then it was calmly. "We'll talk about this tonight. I need to get to the station house. You may have to talk to one of the detectives."

"What for?"

"About Chain." Claire stopped at a red light and glanced at the car beside her. It was a couple of hospital employees who looked as if they were headed to the diner for lunch. Alan Bradford was driving; Kevin James was in the front passenger's seat; he waved. Claire hadn't realized the two men were friends. Though they were always friendly to her, they both struck her as loners. Of course it made sense that they knew each other. Both in the medical profession and Kevin was constantly in and out of the hospital. She nodded, half smiled. The light changed and she pulled ahead.

"I'm not talking to any cops about Chain," Ashley declared, tightening her arms around her stomach. "I don't care what you do to me. You can torture me if you want, I'm not talking."

"Spare me the dramatics," Claire said, feeling better in control of her emotions again. "And if Chain has nothing to hide, there's no reason why you should feel as if you need to protect him. All the detective will want to know is where he hangs out, who his friends are. Maybe where he's been certain nights."

"I'm not protecting him," Ashley sneered. "It's an invasion of privacy to ask those questions!" She dared a glance at Claire. "And why do you want to know that stuff anyway? Is this your way to pull us apart? You don't like him, so you're going to launch a criminal investigation against him? I pretty sure that's not legal."

"Nope, you're right, it's not. But you know what is legal?" Claire said, her dander up again.

"What?"

"Sending a girl to live with her father in Utah, that's what."

"You wouldn't dare."

Claire cut her eyes at Ashley as she pulled into her parking space behind the station. "Try me."

"I don't know. Sounds a little farfetched," Detective Robinson said from behind his desk in the tiny office he shared with the department's only other detective, Cal Parker, who was on vacation for two weeks.

Claire had left Ashley in her office, threatening to put her in a cell if she moved, and had come to speak to the detective privately. Walt was a good guy, late fifties, potbelly and receding gray hairline. He was a retired air force MP and had been with the Albany Beach police for almost fifteen years. He had served Claire's father well, and served her well. The only real problem with Robinson was that he wasn't a creative thinker. He hadn't been much help with the serial murders so far because without any evidence at all, he didn't know how to come up with various scenarios. He didn't know how to *guess* who might be killing these young women.

"Walt, think about it." Claire pulled the only other chair in the office, Cal's, over in front of the detective's desk. "A young man, tall, strong, personable."

"Yeah, I know the kid. Works in the head shop. Also volunteers over at the Boys' and Girls' Club with me during the school year. He dresses like he works in a funeral parlor," Walt scoffed.

"Yeah, but you have to admit, people like him." She waggled a finger. "I've been taking notice around town. He's chatty with people. People talk to him."

Robinson loosened his cheap tie. "You already considered him a suspect?"

"No." She glanced past the detective's head where he proudly displayed several awards he'd won in the military and with the Albany Beach police over the years. She looked back. "My daughter's sort of been dating him."

"Aha, I see." He leaned back and the desk chair squeaked under his shifting weight.

"No, you don't see. One has nothing to do with other. So, I don't like him. I don't like his hair stylist or his fashion consultant—"

"Chief, with all due respect, I have two daughters. My Katherine, she gave me a run for my money the years we were stationed in Germany. Hanging out with the wrong crowd, skipping school, staying out all night. I'd have done anything to steer her straight. Anything," he said meaningfully.

Claire rose, annoyed by his implication. At the same time, she couldn't help being proud of him. So what if he wasn't creative; he was good at his job, and part of his job was to keep them all on the straight and narrow, even the chief of police. "I'm not saying this kid is the killer. He probably isn't, but I know there are some interesting circumstances with his home situation and you can't help but see the connection between Brandy Thomas's wound and the tattoo. We'd be derelict in a duty if we didn't investigate the possibility."

He rested the heels of his hands on the gray metal desk and pushed himself up to standing. "I'll run his name through the system. Stop by and have a chat with him."

She struck the back of the chair she'd been sitting in. "I want him interviewed. Officially. It's time we started being more proactive. I'm bringing in a couple of the guys on our possible suspects lists. Top two or three."

"We haven't got much to go by, Chief. People are going to be pissed if we start hauling in their husbands, their neighbors, their employees."

She shrugged as she opened the door. "They're already pissed. Let me know what you come up with. My daughter will be with me the rest of the day, so you have anything for me, buzz me and I'll come to you."

He rubbed the bald spot on the top of his head the way she knew he did when he was nervous. "Will do, Chief."

Claire strode back down the hall toward her office. "Jewel!" she called as she passed the fishbowl.

The dispatcher got up from her chair at once, opened the door and stuck her head out. "Yeah, boss."

"I want an available car to pick up Billy Trotter."

"You're kidding?" She cracked her gum. "You think he's the killer? I went to school with Billy. Danced with him junior prom."

"I'm just running some interviews, that's all. Starting at the beginning again."

"I'll put the call in now," Jewel hollered down the hall.

Claire jerked her office door open, half afraid Ashley would be gone when she walked in. When Claire had parked her there, Ashley had been making halfhearted threats about running away. She said she wouldn't go to her father; they couldn't make her.

Claire hadn't intended to threaten Ashley with sending her away; ordinarily she wasn't that kind of parent. And it would break her heart to lose her only child. But what Walt had said about his own daughter had really struck home with Claire. She would do anything to set her back on the right path. Do anything to protect her life.

Thankfully, Ashley was there, seated in the same chair where Claire had left her.

Claire walked around the desk to her chair. "It's going to be a long day. You have anything to read in your bag?"

Ashley wouldn't look at her. "I don't want to read."

"Fine." Claire sat down and reached for a file of work unrelated to the killings that she needed to tend to. "I plan to work until six. Stop at the grocery store, and then head home. I don't want you out of my sight until we look into Chain's nifty tattoo."

"What is it about the tattoo that's got you so fired up?" Ashley demanded, gesturing with both hands.

Claire opened the folder in front of her and scanned the memo on top. "The last girl who was killed, Brandy Thomas . . ."

"*Yeah?*"

Claire glanced up. "She had what appears to be a vampire bite on her neck."

Ashley seemed to visibly pale. "No shit," she breathed after a second. "That wasn't in the paper."

"It's one of those details we're trying to keep under wraps until we investigate further." Claire watched Ashley for a moment, almost certain there was something the teen wasn't saying. She seemed pretty disturbed. Did she know something Claire didn't?

But Ashley just leaned back in the chair and closed her eyes and Claire decided not to push it; if there was anything to Chain being a suspect, she'd know soon enough.

At six, Claire dropped her pen on her desk and ran her fingers through her hair. Quitting time. She still had a ton of work to do, but she wasn't entirely sure she could stay awake much longer, much less remain coherent. And then there was the little issue with Ashley.

Claire pushed away from her desk, rising from her chair. A knock sounded at the door.

With a groan, she dropped into her seat. "Yes?"

The door opened and Graham stuck his head in the office.

She smiled, relieved it was him and not someone else out for blood. The pun was bad, but she didn't laugh. "Hey," she said.

He stepped in and closed the door behind him. "How'd you get in?"

"Bribed Jewel. She likes jelly doughnuts, you know."

Claire grinned, getting out of her chair again. "I know. Um, I was just headed out." She hooked her thumb. "Ashley's waiting for me in the break room."

"That was why I stopped by." He was wearing his suit jacket but had loosened his tie. He was obviously done with work for the day. "When you didn't come back into the diner—"

She grabbed her head. "Oh, the bill. I'm sorry, Graham."

"No." He waved her away. "It was a salad, Claire. Don't be silly. I just wanted to make sure you were OK. That Ashley was OK."

"If you mean did I throttle her yet—" Claire came around her desk and backed up to perch on the edge of it, a little afraid to get too close to him. Afraid that in a fit of passion, she might rip off her clothes and jump on his bones right here in her office. "—the answer is no. I still intend to, I just haven't decided how to dispose of the body, yet."

He moved closer, but took his time, as if she were a wild colt or something. Like he didn't want to startle her.

"That's good that you've still got your sense of humor. I'm not sure I would."

She shrugged. "Not a lot of choices in situations like this."

He nodded. "But you're okay?"

She closed her eyes for a moment. "I'm okay."

Claire felt his fingertips brush hers. With her eyes still closed, she opened her hand. He clasped it and pulled her to her feet, wrapping one arm around her.

"Graham, I can't," she whispered, afraid to open her eyes. "Not here. Not now."

"I know." He pulled her against him, brushing his lips against her cheek. "Just came to bring you your daily hug."

She laughed. She knew this was totally inappropriate, a public display of affection with her boyfriend, at work . . . while she was in uniform. Hell, he wasn't even her boyfriend. They'd yet to go on a date. But his arms felt so good around her . . .

"I have to go," she murmured.

"So go." He kissed her cheek. Her mouth.

"No, really," she breathed.

He nibbled on her lower lip. "Who's stopping you?"

She laughed, opening her eyes as she pressed her hand to Graham's chest. "I really do have to go."

"Come to my place, tonight."

"I can't. Ashley's going to be under house arrest." She rested her forehead on his shoulder. "I have to walk up and down the hall all night, my Beretta loaded and ready to fire."

"I love a woman with a Beretta." He kissed her again on the mouth, lingering a little longer this time, his tongue darting out to tease her lower lip. Then he let her go.

Claire's eyes flew open as she took a step back. She was actually dizzy. One kiss and she was dizzy. Did she ever need to get laid . . .   .

"The invitation's open."

"I can't have you at my house. Not with Ashley. Not at her age."

"I understand that. So come to my place." He laid his hand on the doorknob.

"Graham," she groaned. "I don't have time for a relationship right now."

"I understand that. But eventually you're going to catch this guy and then you are going to have time for a relationship. You're going to have time for me. In the meantime, that doesn't mean you can't slip over . . ."

She laughed with embarrassment. "And what? Have sex with you?" She pushed her hair out of her eyes. "I can't do that."

"Okay." He started to open the door.

She followed him. "Graham, I can't."

"That's fine." He stepped out into the hall.

With a groan she opened the door all the way and stuck her head out the door. "Okay, so maybe I can stop by sometime," she called after him. "But, I'm not making any promises."

Not turning back, he gave a wave.

Claire stepped back into her office, closed the door, and leaned against it. It took her a full five minutes to gain her composure before she was able to go down the hall for Ashley.

Chapter Eight

The Bloodsucker cut the headlights as he pulled his car onto a dirt road that had once been used for logging. He'd found it the other day when he'd gone for a drive to scout out the house.

Sliding out of the car, he grabbed his flashlight, hit the lock button and closed the door quietly. He'd pulled in far enough so that, in the dark, his car couldn't be seen from the paved road. Glancing over his shoulder to be certain he saw no headlights passing, he flipped on his flashlight and was rewarded with a strong, steady beam. He'd replaced the batteries before he left his house. After all, it would be dangerous to be caught in the dark without a flashlight; who knew what kind of person could be lurking out here at night?

Using the flashlight to guide him, the Bloodsucker followed the logging road deeper into the dark woods filled with insect song and the croak of frogs. Though by the size of the trees he could tell it was an old forest, it was typical for southern

Delaware. There were mostly pine trees, but a few hardwoods. On both sides of the logging road—that was more like a path with two ruts—was a wall of green briars.

The green briars were what made it difficult to get through the woods this time of year. It was what had prevented the English from being able to foxhunt in the middle colonies, he had once learned on a History Channel special. They shipped the red fox, not native to North America, from Great Britain, set them free to hunt them, and then had given up the sport eventually, leaving the red foxes to multiply.

He liked red foxes and hated to see them dead on the road so he had enjoyed the show. He didn't like to watch those kinds of nature programs often, but sometimes it was all he could find. One hundred thirty seven channels, and nothing on, that's what a coworker had commented the other day.

That History Channel special was the best thing he'd seen since he'd caught that show with the pretty blond investigative reporter who did the interviews with America's worst serial killers. Sad, confused people, all of them, clearly the result of inbreeding or chromosome mix-up or something. Either that, or they were very bright, smart enough to present themselves as victims of society. No, he doubted that they could create such personas and carry them off. They were just delusional butchers, without the creativity to seek out their needs without getting caught. The blond reporter wasn't much better. She pretended to understand, but he knew that she'd memorized questions that smarter people had written for her. And she pandered to the murderers, whored herself, really. Anything for the ratings. She had no true understanding of the needs some people such as himself had, needs they were forced to fulfill. Still, if she'd been a few years younger, he might have liked to have brought her to the barn. He imagined the conversation they would share would be quite interesting.

The Bloodsucker walked a little faster. It was hot and close in the woods and the mosquitoes were buzzing around his ears, humming. The buzzing reminded him of Granny and he swatted viciously in the air, startling a bird in a tree above him. The bird's wings made a flapping sound in the dark, startling him, but only for a moment. He had forgotten bug spray; he'd have to remember it next time he came this way.

Using the flashlight to guide him, he followed the path to the split and took the left fork. He didn't know where the right would lead him; didn't care. This was the way he needed to go.

His destination was less than a ten minute walk. He saw the lights from the house, even before he reached the edge of the woods. As soon as he spotted the lights through the trees, he switched off his flashlight and then crept closer. As he moved slowly through the woods, he felt a sense of excitement build inside him.

Most people didn't like the dark, but not the Bloodsucker. It didn't scare him. In fact, he liked the way the darkness enveloped, making him feel safe, cared for . . . almost like a mother's womb.

He knew the path led right into the backyard behind the shed where the lawn mower and assorted rakes and shovels were kept. He also knew he needed to be careful there, because where the path ended, there were piles of rotting leaves that must have been dumped in the spring. Piles of grass clippings, too. Only no grass had been added to the pile recently. Apparently the chief of police had been too busy to cut her lawn.

The Bloodsucker smiled in the darkness.

He crept around the shed, drawn to the light glowing in the windows. The curtains were drawn, of course. In front of the shed, he stopped to have a better look, to get the lay of the land. There was a screened-in porch and a nice deck where a barbecue and picnic table and some chairs sat. There were glass French doors that led from the back porch into the house. Of course, it was always locked. Always. He had checked.

The Bloodsucker guessed that the window to the left was the kitchen. People tended to put kitchens in the back of the house. The window was probably over the sink. The small window to the right of the porch was probably the bathroom. Locked, too.

And from what he had read on the stickers on the windows and the doors, there was an alarm system. Poor Claire Bear was not a trusting person. Which was smart because she was so beautiful. She was tall and willowy like a runway model, but with those all-American features that made you think she was from the midwest.

He walked out in front of the shed, taking care to stay in the shadows as he studied the house curiously . . . just in case. After all, the chief of police did carry a gun.

It was the two windows to the right of the bathroom window that intrigued him. What were they?

Bedroom windows? Probably. The important question was, whose?

A shadow passed in front of what he suspected was the kitchen window and the Bloodsucker froze. They were home, his Claire Bear and Ashley. It was hard to tell, sometimes, because they apparently left different lights on when away.

His guess was that they were home fighting . . . considering what he had heard today.

He watched with fascination as the shadow moved in front of the window again. Yes, it was definitely a female. He could make out the shoulders, the head. Someone doing dishes? It had to be Claire. What fifteen-year-old did dishes?

Making no quick motions, the Bloodsucker eased down into the soft, fragrant grass. He would only stay a minute or two, he promised himself, his pulse quickening at the thought of the two women inside alone, far from town, no neighbors nearby. If a person were smart, if he were careful and clever, he could get inside that house.

And then they wouldn't be alone anymore.

"I don't understand," Ashley groaned, bare feet planted on the kitchen floor. "How can you even suggest a thing? You don't even know him."

"And neither do you." At the kitchen sink, Claire rinsed off the plate in her hand and slipped it into the dishwasher. "Not really."

"I do know him and he would never harm anyone. He certainly wouldn't *kill* anyone."

"He's not the only one we're investigating." Claire placed the other plate in the dishwasher. She'd made a nice dinner for her and Ashley, pasta primavera, no meat. Ashley had eaten almost nothing. She was very upset, even more upset than she had been earlier in the day.

"We're questioning quite a few people, but if you know anything—" Claire turned to look over her shoulder.

"Haven't you been listening to me? I don't *know* anything," Ashley pleaded with her hands.

Her eyes were red from crying again; her face smudged with black eyeliner. After dinner, when Ashley had retreated to her bedroom, Claire had removed her phone to prevent her from secretly calling Chain and warning him of the police investigation. She swore that hadn't been why she wanted to call him, but Claire was not going to allow her daughter to impede Detective Robinson's inquiry in any way.

"This isn't right, judging someone by what they look like," the teen continued. "I mean, isn't that what you've always said? It's what's inside that counts?"

"You're naïve to think we always know what's really inside people." Claire wearily reached for the dish towel to dry her hands. All the fight was drained out of her; she was tired to the bone and just wanted to crawl into bed and pull the covers over her head. No, what she really wanted to do was crawl into Graham's bed. "We might think we know someone, but sometimes we're wrong."

Ashley glared at her mother. "You got that right."

Her insinuation that Claire was not who she appeared to be was obvious. Claire let it go. She was just too wrung out tonight to go another round. "Go to bed," she said. "Stay in your room."

Ashley spun around and stalked off. "So now I can't even go to the bathroom?"

"You know what I mean." Claire watched the teen stomp down the hall toward her room. "And don't you dare open one of those windows to smoke," she called after her.

The bedroom door slammed shut and Claire dropped into the nearest chair in the dark living room. She felt like having a good cry. She was just afraid if she started now, she wouldn't be able to stop.

"I don't understand why you're asking me these things again," Billy said. He was seated in front of Claire's desk, spinning a pencil he'd taken from a cup Ashley had made for her mother in art class years ago. The pencil spun evenly and then began to wobble as its speed slowed.

Claire didn't usually talk to suspects in her office, but the station really had only one room suitable for interviews and Robinson had Chain in there this morning. Besides, she thought that talking with the men on her list like Billy in her office might put them a little more at ease.

"I told you, Billy, we're starting all the way back in June with our investigation, reinterviewing witnesses, going over our notes, detail by detail. Patti was the first to be murdered."

Claire sat back in her chair, her yellow legal pad in front of her. She was anxious to get through these interviews. She'd intended to start the day before, but they'd been unable to locate Billy and because she wanted to start with him and follow the murders in sequence, she postponed until today. "Patti's the most logical place to start," she explained, studying him across her desk.

The dead girl's ex-boyfriend and sometimes roomie was six feet tall, thin with brown shoulder-length hair he always wore pulled back in a pony-tail. He looked older than his twenty-four years, which seemed kind of a shame. As usual, he needed a shave so a tuft of brown whiskers jutted from his chin. He was wearing a lime green Calloway's T-shirt sporting a flying marlin. He served as a bar back and occasional bartender at the local bar and restaurant on the bay that catered mostly to locals.

He dropped the pencil back into the container, sat back in the chair, and tucked his hands behind his head. "I told you from day one, I didn't kill her."

"Do you know who did?"

He made a face. "Hell, no. If I did, don't you think I would have told somebody? I mean, she and I, were, you know, done, but that doesn't mean I wanted her dead. Not like that. No one deserves to be slowly bled to death." He stared at her. "What makes you think I'm that kind of person?"

She hated to admit it, but Billy was right. She had no reason to think he was that kind of person. A bust on a minor marijuana charge a few years back, a couple of speeding tickets, and the fact that he had slept with the deceased didn't make him a killer. She was grasping at straws here. "OK, Billy. You can go. Thanks for coming in. We appreciate how cooperative you've been."

He got up, scratching his shaggy head of hair. "Yeah, right."

"Hey, Billy."

"Yeah?" He turned back.

"You weren't at work last night and no one there knew where you were. You mind telling me?"

He shrugged. "I might have a new job, but I was keeping it under wraps. Something, you know, better. Better money and benefits."

She nodded. "Great. Where?"

"The hospital. A janitor to start with, but I'm thinking, maybe, some kind of technician or something. When I was a kid, I wanted to be a doctor."

"I didn't even know they were hiring at the hospital."

"Well, they're not really, but I've got a good friend there. He put a word in for me. You know, it's who you know."

Claire gave a wave and Billy walked out. Robinson walked in and closed the door. "Your daughter around?" he asked.

Claire didn't like the look on his face. "In the break room." She rose out of her chair. "Why?"

He patted his perspiring forehead with a folded white handkerchief. "I need to talk with her."

She started around her desk. "You want me to—"

"Chief. I think it's better if I handle this." He met her gaze, his face unsmiling as he tucked the handkerchief into the back pocket of his stretch-fit polyester pants.

Claire's heart gave a little trip. She eased back into her chair. "She's in the break room. Walt, if she needs a lawyer—"

"Don't let your cart get ahead of your horse." He held up a meaty hand. "I just need to ask her a couple of questions. That's all."

"So Chain had something to say?"

"We talked."

Her heart was hammering in her chest. "You like him for this?"

He made a noncommittal shrug. "Too soon to tell. You said you wanted me to be thorough." He paused. "Hey, did you know he's been living alone for some time? He's eighteen now, just going to be a senior in high school next month, but he's on his own. I guess nobody at the school picked up on it. I know we didn't down at the Boys' and Girls' Club."

"I thought he had an older brother. That he was living with him in a trailer or old house on some chicken farm. That was what Ashley said."

"That may very well be what he told her, but he has no siblings. There was a cousin he was living with and the cousin took off more than a year ago. Before Grandma went into the nursing home, apparently."

Claire glanced at the clock on the wall given to her father when he retired. He had loaned it to her because he said it belonged in that office. The second hand seemed to have stopped. All time seemed suspended to her. "So he's been living alone?"

"Going to school, to work, volunteering on his own. That's what he says. Eats those little bags of Chinese noodle soup for breakfast, lunch and dinner so he can pay the electric bill. So he says. I'm still checking up on what he's told me so far, but I know he never missed a day at the Boys' and Girls' Club, because I see him there."

She frowned. "So he's a saint?"

"I didn't say that, Chief. I only said that, so far, he checks out."

She ran her hand over her forehead. "Go ahead and talk to Ashley. If you think there's a problem, you halt the questioning." She watched him turn to go. "Wait—"

He glanced over his shoulder.

"I'm trusting you with my daughter. I'm not asking you for any favors, just to keep her best interest at heart."

He nodded and went out the door and Claire glanced at the clock again. It was ticking, but slowly. She figured she'd give him ten minutes alone with Ashley and then she was breaking up the little party.

The second hand dragged around the face of the clock. The minute hand tick-ticked.

Three and a half minutes and a lifetime had passed when the phone rang, startling her. She picked up the receiver, thankful to have the distraction. Watching the clock was ridiculous, and she wasn't going to allow herself to contemplate why Walt needed to talk to Ashley. She wasn't going to make herself crazy by wondering if Chain had killed those women and her daughter knew something about it. She just wasn't going to go there. She'd know soon enough—in six and a half minutes—why he needed to speak with her.

"Captain Gallagher, line two," Jewel said.

Claire switched lines. Usually she took a minute before picking up when it was Kurt. After all this time, she still got a little light-headed when she heard his voice. She still missed him in her life.

"Kurt." She opened her desk drawer and reached for a bottle of antacid tablets.

"Claire." It was the same voice she had known . . .

maybe loved on some level. A little gruff, definitely
cynical.

"I won't ask you how you are," he said, "because I can guess you've got your stomach turned
inside out and you haven't slept in weeks. You've
probably bought out the stores in town of ant-
acids."

She dropped the bottle and slid the drawer
shut. "I'm okay." There was no way she was going
to tell him that at this very moment, Walt was
interviewing her daughter in possible connection
to the murders. "What can I do for you?"

"This is just a heads up."

She sighed, a certain resignation washing over
her. "The task force I've been hearing about for
weeks. The state is finally going to move on it?"
She crossed Billy Trotter's name off the top of her
list in front of her.

"Yeah."

When she heard the word come out of Kurt's
mouth, she wasn't sure if she was angry or relieved. If the attorney general sent a task force
down to run the investigation of the serial killer, as
they had been saying they would, the case would
no longer be her responsibility. It would be out of
her hands.

It would also mean she had failed. Failed in the
investigation. Failed those dead women.

She flipped the page on the legal pad in front of
her, studying Seth Watkins's name. She scanned
the list of details that made him a possible suspect.
They were so damned weak, she wasn't even sure
she could bring him in on them. She could get
away with bringing a guy like Billy Trotter in be-

cause no one cared about Billy Trotter. Waterfront Reality, the multimillion dollar company Seth worked for, just might care.

"So, when is this so-called task force supposed to convene?"

"Still don't know yet."

She lifted her hand and let it fall. "Still grappling over money?"

"That and some other issues."

She rubbed her temples with her thumb and forefinger and opened the desk drawer again, going for the over-the-counter migraine medicine bottle this time. "Well, I appreciate you calling." She glanced at the clock. Somehow ten minutes had passed since Walt left her office. "You hear anything else." she told Kurt, "and—"

"Claire," he interrupted. "They're asking me to head up the task force."

"You?" she ground out, immediately on the defensive. "You're going to take my job?"

"I'm not going to take your job. You would remain the chief of police of Albany Beach, of course. You wouldn't even be taken off the case; you'd just be a part of the team." He seemed to be struggling with what he wanted to say to her. "Claire, listen, I don't want to do this. I've got too many other things going on here, but—"

"You of all people, Kurt." She popped two pills into her mouth and washed it down with flat diet soda. "You who supported hiring women, not because they were filling a state-mandated quota, but because you thought they deserved to be hired. You who—"

"Claire, this has nothing to do with you being a

woman, so don't pull that sexist crap with me, because you know it won't fly."

She leaned forward, resting her forehead in her hand. "You're right. I'm sorry. That was uncalled for."

"What I was going to say was that I'm dragging my feet with the attorney general's office and the governor's office because of what I've seen of your reports. I think you're on the right track."

"You've seen my reports?"

"Claire, I'm trying to make them understand that you don't catch these assholes overnight. It's the nature of the beast. They're serial killers because they kill over and over again. They kill over and over again because they can. Because they're smart. But we're smart, too. You are, Claire. You're just on the learning curve, that's all."

She didn't know what to say. Having him bust in and take over was almost easier to deal with than him being supportive. She brushed her hair off the crown of her head. "I have to go, Kurt. Something's come up." She hesitated. "Thanks."

"Talk to you as soon as I know anything."

Claire hung up the phone and got out of her chair. She couldn't stand it any longer. She was going to see what Walt needed to talk to Ashley about. It was her right; she was her parent.

Walt met her halfway down the hall between his office and hers. "You need to hear this," he said without any preamble.

Claire didn't say anything; she just followed him down the hall. She didn't know what to say.

Inside his office, she was surprised to see Ashley and Chain sitting side by side. Drinking colas.

Walt walked back around to his chair behind

the gunmetal gray county-issued desk. He cleared his throat as he eased into the chair that didn't seem quite big enough for him. "I asked Gerald where he was Sunday night, the night Brandy Thomas disappeared."

She glanced at Chain, struggling with the impulse to reach out and punch him. So his name was Gerald? An eighteen-year-old named Gerald? It was no wonder he went by *Chain*. She let Walt continue.

"And he said . . ." Walt looked to Chain.

Chain reached out and covered Ashley's hand on her jiggling knee with his hand. It was the first time Claire realized the teens wore matching silver skull rings. Skulls with a rose entwined in the orifices.

"I was with Ashley," the young man said.

Claire looked at her daughter, then at Walt. "That's a lie! Ashley was with my parents Sunday night. She—" The sympathetic expression on Walt's face made her look at her daughter again. "Ash—" Claire groaned and turned away. *Calm,* she told herself as she flexed her hands at her sides. *You have to stay calm.* She took a deep, cleansing breath before she spoke. "From when to when were you with my daughter that night?"

"From about ten P.M. until four A.M."

The bottom seemed to fall out of Claire's stomach. She wanted to accuse him of being a liar, but the expression on Ashley's face made her realize that such an allegation would make her appear more foolish than she already did. "You snuck out of your grandparents' house to be with your boyfriend?"

Ashley's eyes were bright with tears. She nod-

ded. "Yes, but Mom, you have to believe when I tell
you—"

"And you wouldn't lie to me, lie to the police"—
she indicated Walt with her hand—"to cover for
your boyfriend?"

"Chief Drummond, I could have lied here, even
though you would have found out. Ashley could
have lied," Chain said.

"I don't want to hear anything out of you, all
right?" Claire snapped. She looked down at Ashley
who seemed small in the chair right now, even
though she was close to Claire's height already.
The pediatrician thought she might be six feet before she stopped growing. "Where were you? Did
you go back to his place?"

Ashley shook her head. "We went to this party at
the Dunes. You can ask people who were there."

Claire folded her arms over her chest. The
Dunes was a large, sprawling old apartment house
right on the beach that catered to college kids
there working for the summer. It was notorious for
parties. "There was underage drinking, I suppose?"

"We went to the party," Ashley continued. "And
we just walked on the beach until about four when
Chain walked me back to Grandma and Grandpa's
and I climbed back in the window."

Claire didn't know what to say, where to start.
The throbbing headache of ten minutes ago had
become blinding. She took a moment to collect
her thoughts before she spoke again. "And you're
sure this is the truth. You're absolutely sure, Ash,
because if—"

"Mom," Ashley cried. "I didn't tell you the truth

before because I knew how mad you would be."
Tears ran down her face, smudging the black eyeliner, making it run down her cheeks. "You wouldn't
have understood why we needed the time together. Chain's got a lot going on. He has some de-
cisions to make."

"This isn't about Chain right now, Ashley," Claire
intoned. "It's about you. What am I supposed to
do about you and your deliberate defiance of the
rules set down in our house?"

She gave the typical teenage shrug. "I guess
you're just going to have to believe me when I tell
you that I know I shouldn't have sneaked out of the
house like that, but I didn't drink any alcohol. I
didn't do any drugs and I did not have sex. I wasn't
doing anything wrong, Mom."

"Not doing anything wrong?" Claire flared.
"Ashley Anne—"

"Chief, can I see you outside?" The detective
started for the door, not waiting for Claire's assent.

Claire balled her hands into fists and walked out
the door. "I don't want her alone in there with
him," she said from between clenched teeth.

Robinson closed his office door and spoke
softly. The calm in the storm. "I'm sorry you had
to hear that this way, but I know you needed to
know. Now, I'm going to check out this kid's alibi,
but—"

"Don't you understand that's my daughter, Walt?"
Claire whispered, barely holding it together. "I
thought she was tucked safely away watching TV
with my parents while I tried to catch a serial killer,
when in reality—" She pointed to the door, her
voice catching in her throat.

"I know, Chief. Hurts like hell." He reached out and rested his hand on her shoulder. "But what I wanted to say is that I'm going to investigate his alibi from the other night. Look at what we have on the murders, see if any circumstances could apply to him—"

"His grandmother lives in the nursing home at the hospital. Ashley said he goes almost every day. A smart kid, he would have access to latex gloves, maybe even a scalpel—"

"Chief, whoever is doing this is probably buying that stuff off the Internet and you know it." Releasing her, he plucked the handkerchief from his pocket and began to dab at his forehead again. "Do you realize how many sites on the Internet sell latex gloves? Scalpels? Hundreds. I know; I've been looking at them, night after night."

Claire's shoulders slumped and she stared at the clean institutional tile at her feet. "What am I going to do, Walt?"

He shook his head. "I don't know what to tell you."

"Her father lives in Utah. He's offered to take her for the school year. Just for a change." She pushed the hair from her face, over the crown of her head. "It might be what she needs."

"It might be," he agreed quietly.

She sighed, sniffed and looked over at him. "You don't think she's involved, do you?"

"My gut tells me he isn't either, but we'll check it out." He squeezed her shoulder and turned to go back into his office. "I'm done here. You want me to send her to your office?"

She shook her head, wearily. "She can go back to the break room. I need to make some calls. If I speak to her now, I might kill her, and then there would be all those forms to fill out, questions to answer, blood to mop up."

He chuckled. "That's the spirit, Chief. You'll get through this. Parents always do."

Chapter Nine

"So that's where I am with my daughter right now," Claire said, sipping her vodka and OJ by candlelight.

A thunderstorm had blown in out of the west just after ten in the evening and the house had lost power. She'd called into the station and found that within city limits, there were no downed lines. It was only some of the outlying areas that had been affected and the electric co-op had assured the police department that power would be restored within two hours.

Satisfied that she needn't worry about what was happening in her jurisdiction, Claire had settled down to wait out the storm. She didn't mind going without the lights, the TV or the air-conditioning for a couple of hours, but the fact that her home's alarm system was down was what made her uneasy. Her dad had been telling her for a year that she needed to get a generator and tonight she had decided that maybe he was right.

"I don't know what to say, Claire," Graham said, his empathy obvious in his voice. He had called her half an hour ago on the premise that he just wanted to check on them and be sure everything was all right; he had heard about the power outage. She'd been thankful for his call, even this late. It wasn't as if she would be sleeping tonight anyway, not after today.

"Maybe just that being a parent is damned hard these days," he continued. "And I really think you're doing well with Ashley."

"Yeah, right." Curling her bare feet up beneath her on the couch, Claire pushed the drink away. She'd made it and now she didn't even want it. She didn't need the alcohol muddying her thoughts. "What a great parent I am. My daughter dyed her hair black and started dressing like she belongs on a haunted house tour. She loses her job, lies about it, deceives me, oh, and, did I mention that she's climbing out windows to meet her eighteen-year-old boyfriend? The one I was told was only sixteen?"

"Claire. She's also a B student. She visits her grandparents regularly. She likes gardening. The Goth thing is a phase. It's an identity right now, a way that she can feel as if she belongs somewhere."

"Oh, the direction she's headed, she's going to belong, all right." Claire threw her hand up and let it fall to her side. "She's going to belong in the unwed mother's program at school, that or in the terminal care ward at the hospital with AIDS."

"You said she said she wasn't having sex with him. That she said she was still a virgin."

Claire stared into the flickering candlelight. The living room smelled of cinnamon and spice;

she only had decorative candles, nothing utilitarian. "She also said she was going to work every day. Look where believing that got me."

He didn't answer and she cradled the phone between her head and shoulder and reached for a cracker from the plate she'd made for Ashley. When they got home from the police station at seven, Ashley had gone directly to her room, refusing to talk anymore. When Claire went in to check on her after the power failure, she hadn't eaten the cheese and fruit she had taken to her. She hadn't even touched the bottle of water.

"You think I'm overreacting." Claire sighed.

"Honestly, I don't know. I've never had children—Annie wanted them, but she couldn't—" He stopped and started again. "What I'm trying to say is that there's no way that I can fully understand what you're going through right now. There's no way I can understand your fear, and that is what your reaction is about here, Claire. You're angry, yes, you're hurt, certainly, but mostly you're just afraid for your daughter. In the world we live, who wouldn't be?"

Claire caught the phone with one hand and smoothed the old quilt thrown over the back of the leather couch. "I don't want to overreact. I really don't. But I don't want to stick my head in the sand either." She got up, suddenly feeling restless. She could still hear thunder and occasionally lightning illuminated the room for an instant, but the storm was moving southeast and out over the ocean. "I've seen too many parents do that," she told Graham.

"But, the fact that she admitted what she'd done

has to account for something. She could have lied about the whole night."

Claire walked to the double glass doors that led to the back porch and pulled back the drape. Her restlessness was turning to uneasiness. She didn't know why, but she felt strange all of a sudden.

Maybe it was just the change in barometric pressure with the storm, or maybe it was the stress of the day.

She gazed out onto the dark porch and beyond, into the yard. The woods line that ran the length of the property was barely visible in the darkness.

"I suppose you're right; she could have lied," Claire admitted. "Of course, we would have found out if she did. We always do." She continued to study the woods, unable to shake her unease. "Which leads us to the next logical question, which is, is she lying now about where she was Sunday night to cover for him?"

"I suppose it's possible," Graham said.

She fingered the tapestry drapes, still staring into the dark. The candlelight from behind danced off the glass, misshaping images as some reflection from the room superimposed over her view of the yard. "Yeah, and then I wonder if I'm thinking that because on some level I want—"

A streak of lightning lit up the sky and a formless shape near the shed appeared. It only lasted a second, only as long as the lighting illuminated the yard, but abruptly her heart was pounding in her chest.

What was out there? Who was out there?

"Claire?" Graham said. "You all right?"

"Yeah," she said slowly, as she stared in the direction of the shed, waiting for another zigzag of lightning. "Fine, I just—" She didn't finish her sentence.

"You just what?"

"I don't know." She blinked. Rubbed her eyes. Lightning flashed again and this time, she saw nothing out of the ordinary in the yard. There was nothing there. She was just tired. She let the drape fall and thunder rumbled. "I'm sorry, Graham," she said. "Listen, I've been thinking." She paced the living room floor, shifting her focus. This was silly, she wasn't the jumpy type. The doors and windows were locked. For heaven's sake, she had a Beretta semiautomatic pistol. No one was coming through the door.

"Your sister, the one with the FBI."

"Paige."

"Yeah. You said the other day that you thought she might be able to help me with some profiling on this guy."

"I could ask. Give her a call tomorrow and get right back to you."

Claire smiled. She was glad Graham had called. He'd made her feel better about Ashley, about herself. "That would be great. Listen, I better go. I should try to get some sleep."

"Sure, well, listen, I'm glad everything is fine out there. But if you need anything . . ."

She chuckled. "Graham. I'm a police officer. I carry a gun."

"Right." He laughed. "Well, if *I* need anything . . ."

"Be sure to call me."

They were both silent for a moment. She wanted to say something . . . personal. About how she was feeling about him right now. About how much she wanted to be with him. But it just didn't seem right. Not now, not with everything that was going on.

" 'Night," Claire said softly. She hung up the phone and tossed it on the couch. Then she grabbed one of the chunky candles and the vodka and orange juice glass off the end table. At the kitchen sink, she poured out the drink and watched it swirl down the drain. She glanced up at the closed curtain on the window.

She had the strangest feeling that she was being watched.

Agitated, the Bloodsucker paced the small living room he had filled with lit candles. The electricity had gone out almost an hour ago and he was missing the end of the movie he'd been watching about a woman who had given up her baby for adoption, then wanted it back.

He was upset that he didn't get to see the end of the movie. He knew how it should end, how it would end if he had written the screenplay. The mother shouldn't get the baby back; it should stay with the nice family in the white house with the picket fence. The mother should be sent to death row for giving up her child. Executed by lethal injection, maybe firing squad except that no one used a firing squad to execute anymore in the United States. Gary Gilmore had been the last to be executed by firing squad in Utah in 1977. He'd learned all about it on an A&E special.

The Bloodsucker reached the far wall of the living room, turned and started back again. He felt jumpy tonight, as if he'd had too much caffeine. Like he needed . . . needed . . .

He flexed his hands at his sides. He was angry again tonight, agitated, and he didn't know why. He kept thinking about his mother. The old photo in his breast pocket.

He was angry with her.

No. He shook his head vigorously, trying to rid himself of that thought. That terrible, awful thought. It was Granny who made him angry. Granny who had called him names. Who had punished him.

Lightning illuminated the dreary room and he flinched. He had never liked storms; they scared him. He counted the way he had learned as a kid. "One, one thousand, two, one thousand," he murmured, "three, one thousand, four, one thousand."

Thunder rumbled at last.

Four miles away. The storm was four miles away and moving southeast.

The Bloodsucker turned like a soldier and walked in the opposite direction again.

Max, good old Max, lifted his head from his paws, looked at his master with those big, soulful brown eyes of his and laid his head down again. Max wasn't afraid of storms. But then, he hadn't known Granny.

Feeling chilled, the Bloodsucker wrapped his arms around himself. He'd been thinking a lot about Ashley, the police chief's daughter. She was pretty. Strong. He admired her strength. She was smart, too. The dark eyeliner, the black hair, it didn't fool him for a minute.

He had a feeling Ashley wouldn't be like the other women. She would be different. Her mother just didn't appreciate her; didn't realize what a jewel she was. It was Ashley's strength, her determination that made her so different from other teenagers. Maybe it could make *him* different.

But Ashley would be tricky. She wasn't working any longer. She wouldn't be walking from the garden store to the diner anymore. Claire Bear had seen to that. And the house, it was locked airtight, windows and doors. Then there was the alarm to contend with.

The Bloodsucker began to relax, the tension easing in the back of his neck. Ashley would be a challenge. It would take some forethought. Not a task to be taken impulsively.

But his need was building. He could feel it deep inside. Feel it inside his pants.

Stupid. Worthless.

The words came out of nowhere and echoed in his head.

Insignificant. Dim-witted.

It was as if someone was shouting at him. He covered his ears. Ducked. It was Granny shouting at him. Accusing. Demeaning.

No. It was someone else's voice he heard. But whose?

He slid down into his chair, cradling his head. His forearms were beginning to burn.

"No," he sobbed as tears filled his eyes.

Max whined and got off the old carpet. He walked over to the Bloodsucker and rested his head on his master's knee—pushed with his cold nose.

The Bloodsucker could still hear the words being shouted at him. Swirling around him like a whirlwind of dry leaves and sticks, beating him, licking him. But they were getting softer, moving farther away, like the storm.

"That-a boy," the Bloodsucker crooned, rubbing Max's head. Scratching him behind his ears. "What a good boy you are."

Three days later, Claire found a "While You Were Out" pink slip on her desk when she returned from a meeting with the mayor.

Morris had wanted an update on her investigation and he had not been pleased to hear that she still did not have enough evidence to arrest anyone. He became even less pleased with her when she asked if it would be all right if she asked him a couple of questions concerning his own whereabouts the nights the dead women went missing. He'd practically thrown her out of his office, insisting he would answer no questions without her officially bringing him in for questioning and only then in the presence of his lawyer.

Claire doubted Morris was the killer. Considering his size and the fact that he appeared to be a heart attack waiting to happen, she didn't think he possessed the strength that would be necessary to subdue the women or lift them in and out of a vehicle. Still, his Peeping Tom arrest in Florida remained in the back of her mind. What if he had an accomplice?

On her way out of the mayor's office, he had warned her that whatever she thought she had on him, she was wrong. He didn't care what her sources were. He said he would slap her with a lawsuit if she so much as breathed her unfounded suspicions.

Morris knew she knew about the incident in

Florida and it had him scared. That still didn't make him the killer.

Paige Howard had also called, according to Jewel's note, penned in purple ink. A phone number with a Virginia area code, where she could be reached, had been included. It was Graham's sister, the FBI agent. Graham had contacted her the day after he and Claire talked about getting assistance from a profiler. Claire had then spoken briefly to Paige who had requested that copies of the files and photos be faxed to the FBI offices in Quantico for analysis.

Claire felt a little flutter of hope as she sat in her chair and reached for her notepad. She dialed the number, followed by the extension.

"Special Agent Howard," said the pleasant voice on the other end of the line. Paige sounded more like a receptionist in a doctor's office than an FBI agent.

"Special Agent Howard, it's Claire Drummond in Delaware."

"Please, call me Paige. Every time I hear someone call me Special Agent Howard I hear the *X-Files* theme song in my head," she said with a chuckle.

Claire smiled. She liked this young woman; Graham had said she would. "And I'm Claire." She fiddled with her pen, clicking the point in and out. "I wasn't expecting to hear from you so soon. You said a week."

"Well, after looking over the case myself, I passed it to one of our profilers right away. You've got one sick coconut there."

"Yeah, don't I know it." Claire sighed. "So you've got something for me?"

"I do. I'll fax the report to you, but I thought you might want to hear what Katie thinks."

"Katie?"

"Special Agent Katelyn Carmelle, the profiler."

Claire clicked her pen again, ready to take notes. "Go ahead, I'm listening."

"Well, your killer is very intelligent, possible genius IQ level. He's average-looking, attractive, but not movie-star good looks. He blends in well in a crowd so you're not hunting for the creepy guy who *looks* like he's a killer."

Claire wrote AVERAGE JOE in caps on the paper in front of her. Beneath it, she added SMART.

"Now this is pretty typical," Paige continued, "but you've got a loner here."

"Like most serial killers." Claire had done some reading herself, plus her years of experience just told her this guy didn't have a lot of pals or close family members. It made it easier for no one to be aware of his clandestine behavior.

"But, Katie notes that this guy is a little different. He's a loner, but he's not the obvious loner. He's not necessarily sitting by himself in a restaurant. People know him, or think they do. He knows people. He might belong to clubs, go to classes. He might be the guy who makes everyone laugh in the lunchroom," Paige said. "He's an outsider who definitely wants in. He wants to be a part of the group, of society, but something prevents it."

Claire drew a circle with an arrow pointing in. This was a line of reasoning she hadn't concluded on her own. "He wants a friend?" she asked, trying to establish the killer's personality in her mind.

"Exactly. And he wants female friends, according to Katie."

"How'd she come to that conclusion?"

"Well, now mind you, I'm not in the behavioral science department, I'm strictly a number cruncher, but from what she says here, it has something to do with him not killing the women right away."

"According to our estimated times of death, he's definitely keeping them alive for a while," Claire said, becoming more excited by the moment. The information the FBI was providing could very well be what could lead her to this guy. "The ME upstate says he's bleeding them slowly. That's why the cuts on the wrists are shallow. Why he cuts them again and again. To delay the death, but that also means he's prolonging their life."

"Exactly," Paige agreed. "Katie says there's no way to say for sure, but he's doing something with them before he kills them. Maybe he plays house with them, maybe he just sits and watches TV with them. It's about a fantasy with these guys. They have a fantasy they are trying to reenact again and again."

Claire halted, pen poised. "I don't understand. What do you mean play house?"

"Maybe he pretends the women are his girlfriend, wife, even mother," Paige explained. "Maybe he sets up a little faux household where she brings him his paper, pours him coffee. He, of course, has to force her, but that's a minor inconvenience to a man like this. You see, Claire, he's keeping them alive so that he can create some kind of bond with them, however temporary. He wants these women to be his friend. Love him, if you will, if only for a few minutes."

"It's his fantasy to be *loved* by these women?" Claire set her pen down, trying to process the information Paige was providing. Trying to understand. "But he's *bleeding* them to death while he's playing out this cozy little fantasy."

"That's the part Katie can't figure out. It's a little odd, even for a whack-job serial killer."

Claire paused for a moment, thinking. "Now, you saw that the last victim had two puncture wounds on her neck—like a vampire bite, right?" She halted, then started again, her mind going a mile a minute. "You think this could be a cult thing?"

"Very doubtful. Cult murders are weird, all right, but different than this."

Claire nodded. Chain still wasn't entirely off the hook with her, but she knew it was very likely he was not her man. "OK, here's a question for you. Has he killed before these women? Also, what about the violence? This is the first victim we think he's hit."

"Both good questions. Hard to say if he's *ever* killed; sometimes we find that these killers murdered once or twice in the past. But something triggered this string of murders. He's definitely running what we call *hot* right now. He's on a streak, for whatever reason."

Claire could hear Paige rustling through papers.

"The escalation of violence is pretty typical, although it's not typical that he didn't injure them at all, per se—"

"Except the cutting and bleeding them to death part," Claire cut in.

"I told you, you have a sick bastard here. Now, he probably hit this victim because something changed."

"You mean she was the first one to try to fight him? I find that hard to believe."

"So do I," Paige said thoughtfully. "No, I think something is changing within him. Something is pissing him off. Most likely, the killings aren't as satisfying as they first were. That's pretty typical. They, more or less, have to do more to get their thrill."

Claire stopped taking notes and leaned back in her chair. "Okay, one more question and then I'll let you go. I've already taken enough of your time."

"It's no problem, really. I'm just tickled my brother has shown some interest in . . . the case," she said quickly.

Claire smiled. "What does Katie think he's doing with the blood?"

Again, Claire heard the rustle of paper.

"She doesn't say."

"This is going to sound bizarre, but . . . could he possibly be drinking it? I mean, what else could be the significance of the bite on the neck?"

Paige was quiet for a second. "I guess that's a possibility. We see them cut off limbs and eat them; drinking blood isn't any weirder, I suppose. And if he's drinking their blood, that might account for the neatness," she added thoughtfully. "You said all the bodies were clean of blood spatter."

Claire's stomach gave an involuntary lurch. "Drinking their blood. That's a lot of blood, considering the volume the ME thinks the victims lost before dying."

"Pretty gross, huh?" Paige remarked. "But remember, the drinking of the blood could be symbolic. Maybe he's drinking a little and saving the rest."

Claire chuckled without humor. "Now look who's being gross."

"Well, what he's doing with the blood is just speculation. That's not really what our profilers do. What they do is take the information they've gleaned from hundreds, thousands of criminals, and compile it. Criminals follow certain patterns for certain reasons. By our providing this information to you, hopefully you can begin looking over your possible suspects and focus on one or two. Often, in these kinds of cases, local law enforcement have a good idea who the killer is, it's just a matter of getting enough circumstantial evidence together to warrant surveillance and search warrants for property."

Claire talked with Paige for another five minutes, thanked her and hung up to wait for the fax with the details of the information the FBI profiler had compiled. As she waited, she jotted down the names of her possible suspects: Mayor Tugman, Seth Watkins. Below their names, she added José and his uncle, listing them as one suspect, and Chain. As she thought about what Paige had said, she wondered if she needed to add another name to the list.

Ryan McCormick was an excellent police officer. He also lived alone outside of town in a rented house and was someone any woman in town would trust, simply because of his occupation. And women liked him. They liked the tight abs and bulging biceps. He could be a charmer, but there was something about him that was standoffish. As if he thought he was smarter than everyone else. He was also into kinky sex, or at least what Graham's store clerks considered kinky. And he had been the first on the scene when four of the six women had been discovered. Did he have bad luck or did he know the women were there?

Claire didn't want to consider her officer as a suspect. Not a man she had trusted, not just with her own life and the lives of the men and women she was responsible for, but Ashley's, too. On more than one occasion, she had allowed McCormick to pick her daughter up from school, drop her off at the dentist or at Claire's parents' house. Suspecting Chain had already forced her to consider that she might have allowed Ashley to ride in a car with a murderer, but the possibility that that murderer could be McCormick was somehow worse.

Claire hesitated, then quickly jotted Ryan's name down. Before she had time to cross it off, she got up from her desk to go check on Ashley in the break room that had become her daytime prison cell, and then to see if her fax had come in. She felt as if time was running out, maybe because of the impending task force; she didn't know. What she did know was that she had to find the killer, a man she sensed was watching her.

The Bloodsucker sat at the traffic light and observed the tourists moving in a herd at the crosswalk. Everyone said tourism was down this year, by as much as thirty percent. True or not, there still seemed to be plenty of strangers available to him.

As he watched the tourists cross the street, the word *lemmings* came to mind. Lemmings following one another off a cliff. He had recently read that the notion of lemmings committing suicide by hurling themselves off a cliff was a myth, a myth perpetuated by a Disney documentary in the fifties. But he liked the analogy anyway.

He returned his attention to the sunburned swarm. There were couples pushing beach buggies weighted down with coolers and beach chairs and boogie boards, dragging kids behind them. Pushing strollers. An old woman he knew from the grocery store slowly pedaled her big trike across the street in front of him, seemingly oblivious to the traffic, the sun or age creeping up on her. The plastic orange flag on the back of the bike snapped in the breeze.

There were teens in the crowd, too. Good-looking young men and girls wearing rash guards over their board shorts and bikinis. They wore sunglasses manufactured by companies like Dragon and Arnette and carried three-hundred-dollar boogie boards and chilled bottles of Evian water.

The pedestrian signs on both sides of the street flashed a warning and the beach-bound throng hurried the last few steps, moving as if of one mind. There were tall men, short men, fat ones and skinny ones. Chubby babies in strollers and sullen pre-teens. But none of them held his attention like the blonde he spotted on the far side of the crosswalk.

He liked his women between eighteen and twenty-five for the most part. His mother had only been nineteen when she had him. Marcy—no, *Phoebe,* he corrected himself—had been older, but she had been an exception.

He felt his pulse quicken as a woman in her mid-twenties wearing denim shorts and a pink bikini top ran the last few steps to the curb, her blond ponytail sailing behind her.

The Bloodsucker gripped the steering wheel.

Someone honked behind him. The light had turned green.

He lifted his foot off the brake and moved it slowly to the gas pedal, still watching, enthralled. She was wearing sunglasses, but he knew she had blue eyes. He had seen them up close yesterday. Eyes as blue as those in the picture in his wallet.

Another honk. An SUV behind him whipped around, passing on his left.

The Bloodsucker was tempted to flip him the bird, but he didn't. *Never draw attention to yourself.* It was one of the rules he had drawn up before he began this journey. In a town as small as Albany Beach, even flipping off a tourist would get around and he was foolish to risk that. Besides, it was just plain rude.

The Bloodsucker tore his gaze from the blonde. He had to concentrate on the road before he hit something. He had to release her.

Loosening his grip on the steering wheel, flexing his fingers, he took a deep breath and directed his attention to the street and the traffic buzzing around him.

He'd been thinking a lot about Ashley, but he wasn't ready for her yet. Ashley would take time, planning. He needed something quick. Something easy. Something that would quiet the buzzing, the voice in his head.

Just the thought of the blood . . . the imaginary scent of it, warm and metallic, filled his nostrils. He needed that young woman he had seen on the street.

A woman in a ball cap passed in a convertible VW bug and waved at him. He smiled. Waved back.

But she wasn't blond, so his smile wasn't genuine. She didn't make him feel the way the blondes did.

The Bloodsucker signaled, turned onto another street. He was thinking about the young woman he had seen in the crosswalk, again. She lived with a roommate in an apartment in a complex. On Tuesdays, after work, she did her laundry at the Laundromat on the corner of Spruce and Main. Marissa. That was her name. Marissa Spicer. Even at this distance, he could almost hear her calling his name.

Chapter Ten

"You talk to Dad?"

Ashley's voice startled Claire. Even though they were pretty much spending twenty-four hours a day together, the teen had barely spoken to her in the last week.

The investigation of Chain had gone nowhere. The same went for José and his uncle. The FBI profiler's report had been very interesting, much of the findings reiterating the conclusions Claire had already drawn about the killer's personality, but she still felt no closer to him. In the meantime, the pressure was on. She'd talked to Kurt twice in the last few days.

The arrival of the task force was imminent; this morning two workmen had arrived to add additional phone lines in the conference room in the basement where it had been decided the task force would operate. Sometime in the next few days, Claire's station would be inundated with state police and she would turn her investigation over to

Kurt. The idea left a sour taste in her mouth, but she really had no choice.

Claire realized Ashley was staring at her. Waiting.

"Um . . . no. No, I didn't talk to him. He's dodging my calls again. I think he thinks I'm calling to get more money out of him." Claire pulled her sunglasses off and slid them onto the dash of the cruiser. It was almost seven-thirty; her father would be having a fit because they were late. Claire had said she and Ashley would be there for dinner and bring chicken salad from the diner. It was her father's favorite.

"So . . . you still going to talk to him about me going to Utah to live with him?" Ashley asked cautiously.

Claire exhaled; she had so many things to think about that she felt as if her mind were going to explode. "I don't know, Ash."

"Because I don't want to go."

Claire signaled. Turned. "I think you've already established that."

"And you really don't have a reason to send me away, now. I mean, if you really thought Chain was killing people, you'd have arrested him by now."

Claire cut her eyes at her daughter. They were leaving the house so early in the morning that Ashley was barely getting time for a shower. The first couple of days she came into the office, she brought her makeup with her. Two days running now, though, she hadn't bothered with the black eyeliner or lipstick. Even with the black hair, she looked more like the old Ashley than Claire had seen in months.

"Arresting someone is not as easy as you might think," Claire told her daughter. "You have to have evidence that you think someone might have committed a crime. Physical evidence."

"So you're admitting that you know Chain isn't the killer."

"I'm not admitting anything." Claire pulled into the diner parking lot. "I'm going to grab Grampa's chicken salad. You want to stay here or are you coming in?" She reached into the glove compartment for her wallet.

"Actually, I was wondering." Ashley actually made eye contact with her mother. "Could I go across the street to the drugstore and get some stuff?"

"I said you weren't to go out of my sight."

"Mom, you can't see me in the break room at the station when you're at City Hall."

"That's different. I've got all the cops in Albany Beach watching you, then."

To Claire's surprise, Ashley smiled.

Claire couldn't help but smile back. Graham was right. Ashley really was, basically, a good kid. She'd just gotten a little sidetracked this summer and Claire knew very well that she had to take some of the blame. "What do you need?"

Ashley screwed up her face in typical teenage grimace. "You need particulars like whether I'm going for the juniors or the heavy flow?"

Claire pulled a twenty out of her wallet and tossed it on the seat between them. "Make it snappy. I can hear Grampa bellyaching from here."

Claire and Ashley got out of the car at the same time; Claire headed for the diner door and Ashley made a beeline across the parking lot.

"Chain better not be waiting for you in that store," Claire warned.

Ashley rolled her eyes and ran to cross the street before the light changed.

Seeing her run like a kid made Claire smile. And she was beginning to think she would never smile again.

At the step to the diner, Claire shifted her focus. She told her parents she'd be happy to bring the chicken salad for dinner, but not because it was important to her that her father get his weekly dose of chicken salad. She was here because it was Tuesday, two-for-one burger night, and she knew Ryan McCormick stopped for burgers every Tuesday night after a workout at the gym, if he wasn't working.

She was hoping to catch a glimpse of him outside the job; she wanted to see him the way others saw him. She still thought Graham was wrong about him; she didn't really see him as a suspect, but he did fit the profile provided by the FBI, in some ways, and she was determined to check out every possibility.

The place was busy and there was a line at the cash register where the new waitress was ringing diners up. Claire took a seat on one of the stools at the lunch counter. "Be right with you, Chief," Loretta hollered.

She was taking orders from a table of six. They were all realtors with Waterfront Realty and Seth Watkins—her *pee-vert*—was among them. He was seated between two women; both were laughing at something he had said and seemed to find him quite charming. She wondered if they would be laughing if they knew about the little stunt he had pulled in Vegas.

Behind that table was another group, this one larger. Hospital employees. They were at a table for six, but someone had squeezed in another two chrome and vinyl chairs. The women all wore white pants and colorful smocks. The two guys in the group were more subdued; Cam Putnam who worked in X-ray was wearing a pale green scrub top and matching bottoms. The other guy, Kevin James, wore his paramedic uniform. He was either just getting off or just going on shift. Everyone seemed to be having a good time at the table; it was apparently one of the women's birthdays.

Claire moved on. Mayor Tugman was there, too, in the booth behind the Gomez's. Fortunately, he hadn't spotted her yet. He was occupied with a conversation with Mary Tyler, city councilwoman, and the plate of meat loaf, mashed potatoes and green beans in front of him.

The bell over the diner's door jangled and out of the corner of her eye, she spotted Ryan walk in. *Bingo.* Another man and woman came in right behind him. Alan Bradford, from the hospital, and Laree Carmen, a librarian's assistant in the school district.

"Hey, Alan. You decide to join us after all?" one of the young women called from the table of hospital employees.

"Can't. Not tonight, but thanks." Alan waited at the cash register.

"Can you wait one sec, Chief?" Loretta laid her hand on Claire's shoulder as she went by. "Alan called in."

"Sure," Claire answered cheerfully. She didn't

know if McCormick had seen her before, but he certainly saw her now.

"Chief." He lifted his square chin in her direction.

She reciprocated. "Enjoy your day off?"

He shrugged. He was wearing a pair of light-colored cargo shorts, a tight black long sleeve T-shirt that showed off his work out at the gym, and flip-flops. He removed his sunglasses. "Wasn't bad. Had to take care of some things out at my parents' farm. But I got a chance to hit the beach for an hour. Picked up my dry cleaning. You know." He gestured with his glasses. "You eating in or on your way out?"

"I just stopped to pick up something to take to my parents'. Ashley's waiting for me."

He nodded. "Well, have a good night, Chief."

"You, too."

He walked behind her and she gave him a minute before turning her head to nonchalantly check out where he was headed. He spoke to someone at the realtor's table. Two young women Claire didn't know spoke to him and he leaned on their table, chatting for a moment.

"Sorry," Loretta huffed, leaning on the counter in front of Claire. "What can I get you?"

"A quart of chicken salad. Four croissants."

"You bet." She pressed her hand to the table and lifted it. "Something sticky," she muttered. "José!" When she got no immediate response from the back, she looked at Claire, shaking her head. "I'm run ragged without Ralph. I haven't got enough help and it's not like girls are lining up to take a waitressing job here. I just thank God I got Carol, there." She indicated the waitress behind the cash register.

"I know," Claire said, resting her hand sympathetically on Loretta's. "You're doing just fine. I can wait. We can all wait."

"You're a good egg, you know that, Claire?" Loretta turned away. "José! You back there or you takin' another smoke? Don't you know why they call them cancer sticks?"

When Claire saw Loretta reappear from the back with a plastic quart-size container and a bag, she got up off her stool and walked to the register. As she handed Loretta a twenty, she dared one more glance McCormick's way. He was at the birthday party now, talking to one of the cute nurses who worked in the ER.

"Nine's your change." Loretta counted out the bills.

"Thanks."

Claire walked out of the diner. So she'd gotten what she came for, a glimpse of McCormick off duty. But she really hadn't seen anything other than that he was friendly enough with people. Women liked him.

In the parking lot, Claire was thankful to see Ashley waiting in the car. She had the window down, leaning out to talk to Alan. As Claire approached, Alan said good-bye to Ashley, gave a wave in Claire's direction, and headed for his car.

"How do you know Alan?" Claire asked, glancing his way.

Ashley shrugged. "How do I know half the people in this town? I guess because I live here. He might have come to my biology class or something last year."

"So, you get what you needed?" Claire climbed into the car. She handed Ashley the white plastic bag with the chicken salad.

"Yup." Ashley pointed to the drugstore bag on the floor at her feet.

"Grandma called on your cell. You left it in the car. She says Grampa says he's eating without you."

Ashley cracked another smile and Claire chuckled with her as she pulled out of the parking lot. Maybe her daughter was right; maybe there was no need to send her to Utah. Maybe this was all going to blow over and they were going to be just fine.

The Bloodsucker sat on a hard plastic chair connected to a line of plastic chairs and looked at a newsmagazine on his lap. Only he wasn't really reading it, he just wanted people to think he was.

He liked the Laundromat. Even though he had his own washer and dryer at home, he liked to come here sometimes. Liked it even better now that he knew this was where Marissa washed her clothes. He glanced at the industrial-size machine directly in front of him. He was drying a couple of rugs; he'd come here on the pretense that they were too big and bulky to wash at home. Everyone knew there were certain items you didn't wash at home—quilts, blankets, rugs. No one would think it odd that he was here, so long as he didn't come too often.

He checked his watch. It was beginning to get late. He'd have to go soon. He'd left Max alone long enough tonight. Max was like him; he didn't like being alone.

The Bloodsucker glanced through the glass windows to the parking lot behind the Laundromat. It was well lit. If Marissa pulled up in her white Civic, he'd see her right away. He had learned early in life that humans were creatures of habit and he hoped she was. He'd been watching her for a week now and last Tuesday night she had done her laundry here.

He'd learned a lot about her in the last week, just by listening, watching, checking a file that was easy enough to gain access to if a person was clever. Marissa was a commercial artist at a sign shop in town. She painted huge cheeseburgers and businesses' names on road signs while dreaming of being an artist in California. Twenty-two years old and a community college drop-out, she had recently moved out of her parents' house on the western side of the county to live with a roommate she'd known from high school. She didn't have a boyfriend, which he found interesting because she was so pretty. The other thing interesting about her was that she was really into living a healthy lifestyle. She had food allergies so she ate whole grains, and organic vegetables and she exercised regularly.

The dryer tumbling his rugs buzzed and he closed his magazine, rising slowly from the chair. His legs were a little stiff today. He'd bumped up the weight with his leg presses and he was wondering now if maybe he'd gotten a little overenthusiastic.

Placing the magazine in his rectangular laundry basket, he set it in front of the dryer. There were only two people left in the Laundromat; a woman and her little boy. But she wasn't a blonde. She didn't interest him. She had two dryers running at once.

The Bloodsucker opened the dryer door and pulled out the first rug. He took his time folding it. Beside him was a dryer full of clothes that had buzzed and stopped some time ago. Now he could see that it was a woman's clothes.

Women did that sometimes. Especially young ones. They'd wash a load, throw it in the dryer, then run an errand and come back. Sometimes they were late and didn't make it before the dryer shut off.

He glanced at the clothes through the round window. Panties. A pink bra. A pale yellow night-shirt. He glanced at the woman with the boy. She was talking on her cell phone, pulling clothes out of the dryer. The little boy was fussing and she was arguing with the person on the phone. She wasn't paying any attention to the Bloodsucker. She didn't see him, which was the beauty of his existence. He moved in and out of their lives, watching them; everyone saw him and yet no one saw him.

The Bloodsucker folded his second rug and then, after a quick moment of vacillation, he opened the dryer beside him and reached in. He pulled out an armload of fluffy pastel clothes. His head swam and he closed his eyes for a moment, dizzy, lost in the pleasure of the warm, sweet-smelling underthings. He wanted to bury his face in them, but fought the urge.

He carried the clothes that smelled April fresh to the folding counter and dropped the pile. The first item he picked up was a pair of panties. He remembered the panties he had found in the trash can on the beach weeks ago. Marcy's panties. Red. But these were white. Very tiny. Thong. He licked his dry lips and folded them carefully.

The Bloodsucker's heart pounded as he reached into the pile and picked up a strappy tank top.

This was dangerous, folding some else's laundry. A stranger's. But it happened sometimes. A good Samaritan would fold a load of laundry that wasn't his or her own and leave it on the counter for the owner to discover when he or she returned. No one could get angry at a man doing a good deed.

He glanced up at the woman still on the phone as he reveled in the satin feel of the pale green bra in his hands. This delicate piece of lingerie was nothing like the ugly white armor Granny had worn. He pushed one cup into the other, the way he had watched women do on TV, folded in the strap and added it to the growing pile.

The woman on the phone still paid him no mind. She was carrying a basket of laundry she'd just pulled from the dryer out to her car. Didn't she realize how wrinkled they would be by the time she reached home? Clothes had to be folded fresh out of the dryer, still warm and soft and pliable.

The woman returned; the child was whining and stomping his foot now. It was past his bedtime and he was tired, poor tyke. She dumped the remainder of her clothes into another basket and called the little boy. He followed her out, leaving the Bloodsucker alone.

Marissa turned up the radio, tapping her hand on the dashboard as she waited for the light to turn green. It had ended up taking her longer at the gym than she'd anticipated, then she'd stopped at the health food store for some flax seed and organic peanut butter, and now, by the time she got back to the Laundromat, her clothes were going to be wrinkled. She flew down the street, ignoring the twenty-five mile per hour sign that flashed by, even though she knew very well that she didn't need another speeding ticket.

At a stoplight, she flipped down the visor to check out her face. It looked a lot better than it had a few days ago. The allergist she'd seen after her trip to the ER last week wasn't sure what had triggered the allergic reaction and the rash, but he set up an appointment to do some more testing in two weeks. For now, she'd just stay away from the salad bars. This was proof that just because you thought a salad bar was healthy, it wasn't necessarily true.

The light changed and Marissa turned the corner and zipped into the Laundromat parking lot. She pulled up beside the only other car there. Before she got out, she looked through the large storefront windows to check out who was there. A guy with his back to her, but he was clean-cut and wearing nice clothes. Safe enough.

There was a new Laundromat in town, over by the Big Mart. A lot of the girls liked it there better; they said they felt safer, but she felt secure enough. The parking lot was well-lit and there was a surveillance camera in the ceiling inside. Besides, loads were twenty-five cents a pop less here than at the new place. Free money, by her calculation.

The man inside turned around and realizing she knew him, she hopped out, leaving her car running. She'd just grab the clothes and head home. She could fold while she watched TV. Her roommate was out of town so she would have the remote all to herself. "Hey," she called, smiling. "Fancy meeting you here."

He smiled back. "Hey."

He was a nice guy; she'd bumped into him every

once in a while in town or in a bar. He'd been really nice to her last week with the whole allergic reaction thing.

Marissa strolled to the dryer where she'd left her clothes, but it was empty. She turned to around to say something, then realized they were folded and placed neatly in piles on the counter that ran through the center of the Laundromat. She looked at him slyly. "Did you . . ."

He grinned, a little bashfully, which she thought was pretty cute.

"I hope you don't mind," he said, a laundry basket in his arms. "I needed the dryer a little earlier and . . ." He shrugged. "I didn't see any problem, but then when I pulled the clothes out and started folding them, I realized it was a little weird, me folding some stranger's panties."

She laughed as she added the meticulously folded clothes to her basket. "So now you see, you weren't folding a stranger's panties. And hey, you do a better job than I do. Feel free to come over every Tuesday night and fold for me. I'm just sorry the other load is already in the car."

He chuckled with her. At the door, he held it open with his back so that she could pass through.

"Been to Calloway's lately?" she asked as they walked to their cars.

"Not lately. It's too crowded."

"I know. Tourists. But, hey, summer's almost over; they'll all go home soon." She slid the basket into the backseat and shut the door.

He had put his basket into his trunk and was now coming around the side of her car. She wondered if maybe he was going to ask her out; he'd seemed pretty interested last week.

"And I guess business isn't what it's been in previous years," she said. "You know, with people being afraid to come to town."

"Right." He approached her, his hands in his shorts' pockets. He definitely wanted to ask her out; she could see that look on his face. It was just taking him a minute to get up the nerve.

"So Marissa"—he glanced around, as if he were afraid someone was going to catch him talking to her—"I was wondering . . ." He lifted his arm as if he were going to put it around her and she turned to face him. But instead, he covered her mouth and nose with his hand . . . with something.

It took Marissa a split second too long to realize that this man who she thought she knew, was not what he seemed. She tried to scream, but he had both arms around her now, pinning her against him. The thing over her mouth and nose, the rag, it smelled awful.

Her head swam and she suddenly was nauseated. Everything spun out of focus and she felt her knees buckle.

"It's all right," he whispered in her ear as she sank into the spinning darkness. "Don't fight it, hon. That's it. Good girl . . ."

"Missing since when?" Claire asked, rising out of her chair.

"Not sure yet." Jewel stood in the doorway to Claire's office, holding a slip of paper she had taken notes on. "The call just came in from the mother in Laurel. She said the girl's boss called looking for her at ten. She didn't show up for work this morning at nine. The mother already called her apartment and her cell phone. No answer."

"The mother think she could just be playing hooky?" Claire asked, forcing herself to remain calm even though her heart was pounding in her chest. "How old is she? Twenty-two? It's a nice day out. Maybe she hit the beach?"

"Mother says not."

Claire came out of her chair. "And what was the woman's name again?"

"The young one is Marissa Spicer," Jewel said, reading off the paper in her hand. She cracked her gum. "Her mother is Valerie Spicer. I've got numbers and stuff."

"The mother talk to her roommate?"

"Lucy Carmine. A preschool teacher. She's in Florida with her family."

"Son of a bitch," Claire muttered, coming around her desk. "Son of a bitch." She looked up at Jewel. "I want a car sent to her apartment, and I want Detective Robinson to go see the mother for starters."

"She's already on her way here. She was pretty upset." Pop. "I took the info because I figured, you know, head start."

"No, that's fine. Robinson can talk to her." Claire's mind was racing. *Not another one, not another one,* was all she could think. "Did you get info on her car?"

"Just that it's a 2001 white Civic. I'll run it through motor V, if you want." Jewel stepped back to let Claire pass. "Where you going?"

"To talk to Robinson. The mother bringing a photo so we know who we're looking for?"

Jewel nodded.

"Okay, well, I'm going to talk to Robinson and then I'm going to the diner—"

Jewel's plucked and penciled brows lifted. "The diner? Now?"

"It'll take too long to explain. I want that information on the car now, and get a copy of the driver's license photo. Make copies for everyone out on the road right now." She checked her watch as she hurried down the hallway. First Robinson, then she'd check on Ashley, then she was going to the diner to find out when Marissa had last been there. "I want everyone here in an hour."

"You think he's got her?" Jewel called down the hallway.

Claire didn't respond.

Chapter Eleven

"The cameras were fake?" Claire exploded. She stood in the parking lot behind the police station. It was almost eleven and Ashley was lying in the backseat of her patrol car, pillow cradled in her arms as if she'd been to the drive in. She'd just been asleep in the break room.

"I'm afraid so, Chief," Patrolman Savage said. He and McCormick had just finished their shift. McCormick was inside turning in some paperwork; apparently Claire had missed him on her way out.

"How can that be? You can't put fake cameras up in a public place, can you?"

"No law against it. No city ordinance requiring surveillance cameras. According to the owner, some guy in Ohio, the real thing costs too much."

"But women go into that Laundromat"—Claire touched her forehead and gestured in frustration—"thinking they're safe because they see the cameras. They see that blinking red light that says they're being filmed."

"Red light runs on a battery. It just blinks. Owners put these fake cameras in as a deterrent against theft and vandalism. Thieves, kids, don't know the cameras aren't for real." Patrolman Savage lifted his shoulder in a shrug. "Owner says it works. Says that at that Laundromat, he had less than a hundred dollars worth of damage done last year and not a single jimmied coin box."

Claire leaned against her car, only half listening to what her officer was saying. She was just unable to believe their bad luck.

Marissa Spicer's white Honda Civic had been located in plain sight in the Laundromat parking lot before noon. Claire and Robinson had been able to trace her steps Tuesday from the time she left work at the sign shop until she finished her errands and ran back by the Laundromat to pick up her clothes she told a clerk in the health food store that she had left drying. Marissa's clothes were found folded neatly in a basket in the back of her unlocked car. The keys were still in the ignition, a couple hundred dollars of CDs in a case on the floor, and her purse was on the passenger's seat with sixty-three dollars in it.

Claire somehow found it ironic that they lived in a town where you could leave your car unlocked for more than twelve hours and no one would steal your purse or your CD collection, but six women had been murdered here.

From the Laundromat, Marissa's trail had gone cold. Like the other women, she was just gone.

McCormick walked out the back door, joining

them in the parking lot. "I can pull another shift if you need me, Chief," he said.

"Not me," Savage groaned, rubbing the back of his neck. "I'm beat."

Claire shook her head. "I want you both to go home and get some sleep. It's what I'm going to try to do." She glanced in the backseat of her cruiser. It looked like Ashley was asleep again. "A couple of guys came in on their day off and Robinson is going to stay on through the night."

"We patrolling Dumpsters again?" Savage said grimly.

" 'Fraid so." She slapped the hood of the car and opened the door. She needed to get Ashley home and in her own bed. This couldn't be good for a fifteen-year-old who was already confused enough—watching her mother slowly sabotage her career as she tried to catch a killer.

"Call us if you need us," McCormick called across the parking lot as he and his partner headed for their personal vehicles.

Claire gave a half wave and closed the door. She gripped the steering wheel, tears filling her eyes. Fighting her emotions, she started the car, wheeled out of the parking lot. She was shaking all over. The girl was dead. She already knew Marissa was dead.

Claire picked up her cell from the car seat and dialed her parents' number. Her father picked up on the first ring. "You still up?" she asked, hoping he couldn't tell she'd been crying.

"Watching the news," he said. "Fire in an apartment house in Baltimore City. They think some kids set it."

She pressed her lips together. "Dad, can I drop Ashley off I . . . I have some things I need to do."

" 'Course you can. I'll sit up. Keep an eye on her." He hesitated. "I really feel bad about—"

"Dad, listen, it wasn't your fault. I don't think she'll be sneaking anywhere tonight. She's already asleep and she hasn't talked to the boyfriend in days. I'll be back to get her before she's up in the morning."

"Something going on?" he intoned.

"I'll be there in a minute." She hung up and turned into her parents' development.

At her grandparents' house, Ashley put up no protest about spending the night. She was so tired, Claire doubted she had the energy.

Five minutes later, Claire was back in her car driving, but not for home.

She pulled into a driveway in front of a nice Cape Cod with cedar shakes only a block from the ocean. She walked up the sidewalk, her stride long and assured to make up for the fact that she wasn't sure about anything right now. She rang the doorbell, half hoping he'd already gone to bed.

The front porch light came on and the door opened.

"Claire."

She looked up at Graham, her lower lip trembling. "I'm sorry, it's late. I just—"

He grabbed her hand and pulled her inside. "You want to talk?" he asked in the shadowy front hallway that smelled of cinnamon and clove.

She shook her head.

"Just need another hug?" He wrapped his arms around her.

"I'm thinking I need a little more than that," she heard herself say.

He was smiling when he lowered his mouth over hers. She clung to him, parting her lips, welcoming his tongue and even a moment's reprieve from what was going on beyond the walls of the cozy house.

She slid her hands over his shoulders, kissed him again and again.

"You want to go upstairs?" he whispered, nuzzling her neck.

"Or here," she answered shakily, slipping her hand under his T-shirt. He was dressed entirely different than she ever remembered seeing him. Bare feet, surf shop tee, gym shorts. A Clark Kent who could go casual. It made him even more delicious.

"Come on." He tugged on her hand. "Let's go upstairs.

Claire knew she shouldn't. She knew she only wanted this right now because of what was going on. The killer, her problems with Ashley . . . poor Marissa who might already be dead and Claire with no idea where to look for her. Claire knew that by morning she would regret this.

But Graham led her up the carpeted stairs and she followed. His bedroom was like the cottage, cozy, masculine. There was a light on beside the bed. He'd been reading a Gore Vidal book when she rang his doorbell.

He pushed the book off the bed, onto the floor.

She unhooked the belt with her pistol holster and hung it on the back of a chair near the door.

"I've never undressed a cop before," he teased

as his fingers found the bottoms of her uniform, shirt.

She laughed. "Just be careful. Dry cleaning's expensive.

And he was. He removed her clothes, piece by piece as carefully as if she were a china doll. He kissed every inch of bare skin he revealed and still managed to hang her shirt and pants on the chair with her gun. When she was down to panties and a bra, he led her to bed, laid down and drew her into his arms.

"We don't have to—"

"I want to," she breathed, rolling over to face him. "I need to have something. Feel something good," she whispered desperately.

He covered her mouth with his and she closed her eyes, moaning as he caressed her breast, first over her bra, then slipping his hand inside.

She pulled off his T-shirt, then slipped off her bra. His hard, muscular chest, his crisp hair felt so good against her breasts.

He kissed her shoulders, her clavicle, slowly working his way downward until he took her nipple in his mouth. Claire moaned. It had been so long . . . too long.

Her heart pounding, she pushed his shorts down. His fingertips found the waistband of her panties, then moved lower, emitting another groan of pleasure. She was already wet. Already needing him.

"Please," she whispered, moving under him.

"We don't have to hurry."

She squeezed her eyes shut, on the verge of tears again and not even sure why. "I do."

"Ah, Claire," he whispered huskily in her ear as

he slid her panties down and lowered himself over her.

Claire parted her thighs, opening up to him, welcoming him. The first sensation of penetration was overwhelmingly sweet.

He kissed her closed eyes, her cheeks, the tip of her nose.

She began to move under him, grinding her hips against his. He matched her motion, lifting her higher . . . moving faster. For a long moment she felt as if she hung suspended in time, in pleasure. The world, the town, the killer, faded away and there was nothing but she and Graham and their breathing that came faster and faster.

When Claire came in a burst of light and sensation and muscle contractions, she cried out, sinking her nails into Graham's shoulders. She held tightly to him as she rode the last waves of the orgasm. He slowly then picked up the pace again. Another three strokes and he groaned, collapsing over her.

Graham kissed her damp skin behind her ear and slid off her, onto his side, drawing her into his arms. Claire clung to him and burst into tears.

It was close to one in the morning the next night when the Bloodsucker pulled out of his driveway and headed into town, taking Marissa with him. She hadn't been as satisfying as he had hoped and he was disappointed. Agitated. There was something in him tonight that still went unfulfilled. His hands trembled on the steering wheel and he felt chilled despite the hot, humid evening.

He punched a button on the console, cutting the air-conditioning back, and rubbed his tired eyes.

The whole plan had gone so well in the beginning. It had been so satisfying, then. Patti, April, even Phoebe who he had taken mistaking her for her sister. But something wasn't right now. He slapped his hand on the steering wheel in frustration. *Nothing* seemed right. Not even the blood. Least of all, the blood.

He massaged the back of his neck where the muscles were tight. He was getting a headache, one of those kind that hummed. Buzzed, making room for Granny.

Maybe it was just that he was tired. He was working too many hours, burning the candle at both ends, as Granny used to say.

The Bloodsucker took a back road that cut east to Route One and then headed south. The first thing he noticed after he passed the "Welcome to Albany Beach" sign was a green and tan police car. Then another. Two blocks later, a third cruiser passed him in the right-hand lane. He smiled to himself. You never saw three cars on a weeknight. But, of course, Claire Bear had extra cars on the road. She was looking for *him.*

The idea made him proud, but at the same time, it concerned him. She seemed to be stepping up the investigation. It probably just had to do with the task force that would be arriving soon, but the Bloodsucker wasn't sure. This was beginning to feel personal. It was as if she felt that each time he took a woman home, it was a personal affront to her. As if it was all about her. Never about him.

Granny had been like that.

He pulled into an all-night mini-mart gas station and used his credit card to fill up. He leaned on the trunk as he listened to the gas pump into the tank and breathed in the fumes. He stroked the warm, smooth metal thinking about who was inside. Contemplating where he would leave her.

A pickup with Maryland plates pulled into the gas station, blasting country and western music. The Bloodsucker hated country and western music and he thought it was rude for people to drive around with their windows down, polluting the air with that southern *my dog and my truck* drivel.

The guy, dressed in blue jeans and a tank top, got out. He nodded in the Bloodsucker's direction as he removed his fuel cap.

"Hi," the Bloodsucker said. He didn't let on like he hated the Dixie Chicks. He even tapped his foot to the music.

A tan and green police car whizzed by, catching both men's attention.

The stranger turned his head, watching the lights disappear. "Wonder what's up. The cops have been crawling all over this town tonight."

"Another missing woman, I heard," the Bloodsucker remarked. The pump clicked off, the tank full, but he took his time. "I think they're looking for her."

The man shook his head. "Unbelievable, huh?" He leaned against his truck. "You know, when they catch this guy, I think they ought to skip the due process crap and kill the bastard."

"You think so?" The Bloodsucker settled the nozzle into the pump and turned back to screw the cap securely on the tank.

"I sure as hell do." He threw back his shoulders. "But I think they ought to torture him first, the same way he tortured those women. They always ask in those commentaries in the paper if those who believe in the death penalty would be willing to do it. I would. Hell, I'd volunteer. Only it wouldn't be his wrists I'd cut, it would be his jugular." He made a motion, drawing his hand across his neck.

The Bloodsucker closed the little door on the gas tank, annoyed. He thought about the pistol under the seat in the car. He just kept it for protection, but he wondered what this redneck would think if he pulled it on him. Shot him right in the face. Wouldn't be so macho arrogant then, would he?

But the Bloodsucker didn't have time for the redneck tonight. He had to take care of Marissa. Besides, shooting the guy would be dangerous. He'd have to kill the clerk inside the mini-mart, too. Then what if someone drove by, or if someone remembered later seeing him pull into the station? Only idiots did impulsive things like that.

He heard a voice in his head. Twitched.

"I'm not an idiot," he whispered under his breath.

"What's that?" The redneck had completed his gas purchase and was now hiking across the blacktop toward the mini-mart, probably to buy cigarettes or something equally stupid.

"I said, have a good evening," the Bloodsucker called cheerfully with a wave.

"You, too."

The Bloodsucker pulled back onto the highway and just drove. Usually he had a plan as to where he would go, where he would leave her, but not tonight. He stopped at a traffic light and watched with interest as one of the tan and green police cars ahead of him signaled and turned into an alley that ran between two restaurants. It was Patrolman Rumsfeld. What was he doing down there?

Then, the Bloodsucker smiled. He knew just what Rumsfeld was doing. The same thing Claire Bear had been doing the night she'd almost caught him dropping Anne off.

That was when he got the idea. The brilliant idea. Because *he* was a brilliant man.

He made a U-turn, a left turn, and then a right.

This would be riskier than the other times, but that was what it made it fun. Okay, Claire Bear wanted to make this personal? She wanted to buzz around in his head?

He'd make it personal.

"Ah, Jesus," Claire breathed. She ran her hand over her mouth. "I'm sorry, Robinson. That was uncalled for." Her detective was a religious man and she knew he took offense at her using the Lord's name in vain. It had actually come up at one of the shift meetings a couple of weeks ago.

"It's all right, Chief," he said quietly.

"No. No, it's not." She swung her legs over the bed and ran her fingers through her dirty hair. She felt as if she'd only been asleep a few minutes but her clock said 6:05. She'd slept in and it was already light outside.

"It is if you're asking for His help," the detective said quietly.

Claire didn't speak for a moment; she just closed her eyes. She couldn't pray; she was too scared. Too angry. But the silence, with Walt on the other end of the line, was somehow comforting. "Okay," she said, opening them a minute later. "I have to take a shower, then I'll be in. And I have to get Ashley up. It will be forty minutes before I get there."

"Not a problem, Chief."

Claire hung up the phone and padded barefoot down the hall, stopping at Ashley's door. "Ash, you need to get up. I'm getting in the shower now so you can have—" She halted in mid-sentence.

Ashley was sprawled on the bed, dressed in boxers and a T-shirt, her blond hair spilling over her pillowcase. Her *blond* hair.

"What did you do?" Claire cried, flipping on the overhead light.

The teen groaned and rolled over, covering her face with her arms. "What?" she moaned sleepily.

"What did you do, Ashley?" Claire covered the distance between the door and the bed in a second. She reached out and brushed her daughter's blond hair, stark against the black pillowcase. She was almost hysterical. "Your hair."

Ashley rolled onto her back, lowering her arms, squinting. "I did what you said. I made it blond again."

Claire sank down to sit on the edge of the bed, afraid she was going to burst into tears. Her hands were shaking. She knew her fears were unfounded. She was keeping her daughter with her every moment of the day, but seeing her blond hair spilling over the pillow made her think of the dead women, their hair fanned out on the dark pavement.

"I thought that was what you wanted me to do, Mom."

Claire ran her hand over her daughter's head, over the silky tresses, trying to get ahold of herself.

Ashley jerked her head from her mother's reach and pushed up on her elbows. "Mom, why are you crying?"

Claire looked away, her gaze falling to the huge pile of clothes on Ashley's floor that she had, supposedly, been putting away. "I need you to get up and get ready," she said, taking a deep breath and rising off the bed.

"No. Just let me stay here," the teen moaned, pulling the sheet over her head. "I swear, I won't go anywhere. I won't talk to anyone. I won't move from this spot."

"We're leaving here in twenty minutes." Claire walked to the door, willing herself not to fall apart. "Shower if you like, or don't shower. Dress or don't dress. Twenty minutes," she called as she headed for the bathroom.

It took Claire almost an hour to get to the station. While she was in the shower, Ashley had gone back to sleep and when Claire woke her again, the teen had dug her heels in. She said she wasn't going with her mother, not if she carried her out of the house. It had almost come down to that.

As Claire pulled into the parking lot behind the station, Ashley sat in the backseat, hugging her pillow, her eyes closed despite the fact that she wasn't asleep.

The scene in the parking lot was a dreadful repeat of all the previous homicide scenes that summer. Men and women in police and medical uniforms

milling around. The first of the reporters beginning to pull up in their minivans, having to be
forced back behind orange barriers. There were
police cars everywhere, and not pulled neatly into
their parking spaces like most mornings. They were
parked catty-corner, some even on the grass with
personal vehicles thrown in between. There were
emergency medical team trucks, and the ME's car,
too. Only there were no flashing lights this morning and the lack of them was almost eerier. There
was no pulsing blue police car lights because the
crime scene was in their own backyard.

"I need you to go inside," Claire ordered Ashley
as she opened the car door.

In the rearview mirror, Claire saw her daughter
open her eyes as she lowered her pillow and
brushed the tangled blond hair from her face.
"What's going on?"

"Chief." Robinson approached the car. She
knew he'd been up all night; he looked like it. It
was the first time she ever recalled seeing him
without one of his polyester sports jackets. His tie
was loose around his neck and his light blue shirt
wrinkled with a stain on his belly. Coffee, maybe.

Claire thought it was funny the things you noticed at times like this. How acute your senses became. And how they could so easily be confused.
Like right now, while she couldn't yet see the
body, she could smell the blood. Or the lack of it.

"Something happened." Ashley craned her neck,
looking out the window. "What happened, Mom?"

Ashley's voice penetrated Claire's disjointed
thoughts. "Detective, would you mind escorting my
daughter inside? Then you and I can talk. And have
someone get the news vans off the front lawn. Do

they know what it cost us to reseed that lawn last fall?"

"No problem, Chief." He opened the rear door. "C'mon, Ashley. I think we've got OJ in the break room."

Ashley left her pillow in the backseat and climbed out, still trying to see what all the commotion was about. The detective put his arm out to steer her in the opposite direction of the yellow crime scene tape, but he was a split second too late.

Ashley halted, and stared.

Claire turned to look in the same direction and then cursed under her breath. The killer had changed his MO again. Marissa Spicer was not on the ground beside the Dumpster. "Ah, Walt. You left her like that?" She turned to her daughter, caught between wanting to pull her police chief hat on and wanting to be the mother who could protect her child from such a horrifying sight.

Ashley's beautiful blue eyes, devoid of even a hint of black eyeliner, filled with tears. "He left her here?" she murmured, her voice filled with a mixture of shock and disbelief. "At the station?"

Claire didn't know what to say. What to do. The motherly instinct that filled her the moment Ashley had entered this world wanted to pull her daughter into her arms and shield her from the terrible sight of the dead woman hanging partially out of the large Dumpster, her long blond hair pale and shimmering against the green metal. But a part of her knew that Ashley needed to understand why Claire enforced the rules she did. Why Ashley had to be so careful where she went, who she spoke to, who she became friends with.

Marissa had obviously made friends with the wrong person.

Claire reached out and squeezed Ashley's shoulder, knowing that if she took her in her arms right now, she herself might break down. She couldn't let that happen because she had a job to do. "Go inside, hon."

The teen pressed her lips together, her voice trembling but in control as she spoke. "It's OK, Detective Robinson. I can go myself. You stay here and help my mother."

The detective glanced at Claire and she nodded to let her go. Then Claire took a deep breath and approached the Dumpster. "What time did—"

"Six A.M. Jacob found her when he dumped the trash."

Claire ducked under the yellow tape. "And what time do we know she—" A pair of familiar shoulders caught her eye and she turned. "Kurt, what the hell are you doing here?"

He ducked under the yellow tape. "Easy there, girl."

Robinson lifted his hands, palms out, making it plain he had nothing to do with Kurt's arrival."

"Don't you *easy girl* me," Claire ground out under her breath. "Who called you and how the hell did you get here before I did?"

"I was already up when the call came in. And no one from here called me. Someone at headquarters picked it up on a radio frequency or something."

"You guys are eavesdropping on our radio communication." As she spoke, her gaze strayed to the body. Unlike Brandy, Marissa didn't just have a split lip; she had a black eye as well.

"Claire, let's not turn this into a grassy knoll. I'll be taking over within the week. I should be here."

She stared at the dark pavement. A beige trash can lay on its side, probably just where the custodian had dropped it when he saw the body. "So as of right now, you've not officially taken over."

"No," Kurt said.

She set her jaw. "Then step back and let me do my job. Robinson!"

The detective was at her side.

"I want the photographing complete." She pointed at Marissa, grinding out each angry word. "And I want you to get her the hell down from there."

Mid-morning, the phone call Claire had been dreading almost as badly as having to speak with Marissa's parents came in. She'd spent the entire previous day dodging his phone calls. Expecting to see him any second in her office or at her front door.

"Claire," Graham said. "I tried to come in, but one of your patrolmen turned me away."

"We found Marissa," she said quietly, brushing the hair out of her eyes, resting her head on the heel of her hand, her elbow on her desk.

"I know, I heard. You okay?"

"Yeah. Her parents are coming in so—"

"I mean about us. About the other night. I'm sorry about Marissa Spicer, but I know you can't talk to me about that right now. I know you shouldn't."

She exhaled slowly. "I'm all right."

"You're sure?"

The backs of her eyes stung. She felt like such a

ninny. A weak, girly ninny. "Graham, I can't do this right now. I had a dead girl in the station house Dumpster this morning."

"I understand," he intoned. "I just—"

"Listen. I came to you of my own free will. I don't want you feeling guilty about anything. You hear me? We're not teenagers and this is definitely not prom week."

"It's just that you've been under so much stress," he said. "You—"

"Graham, I came to you because I needed to get laid." She was quiet for a second, knowing how awful that must have sounded. "What I mean is that I needed you to make love to me. If anything, I took advantage of you, of my situation. I used it as an excuse."

"Well, I just wanted you to know that I'm thinking about you. That my door's always open."

She half smiled. "And your bed?"

She could hear him smiling back. "You bet."

Claire lifted her head, surprised to realize she felt a little better. "I've got to go."

"I won't bug you. Call me when you can."

"Thanks, Graham," she whispered and then hung up.

Three days later, Claire sat at her desk wishing she was anywhere on earth right now, but there. She ran her pen over the list of questions on her legal pad, trying to be sure she'd covered everything. This was the second time she had sat down and talked with Mr. and Mrs. Spicer and she didn't want to have to put them through this again, if she didn't have to.

"Well, I think that's everything I needed to know." Claire looked up at the teary-eyed couple who sat across from her desk.

Mr. and Mrs. Spicer were in their late fifties. He was a bank manager; she was a homemaker. Marissa had been their youngest daughter. They had another daughter waiting for them at home; she'd just had a new baby the week before.

All Claire had been able to think of since they told her about the new grandbaby was that Marissa would never make Marty and Valerie Spicer grandparents.

"I really appreciate you coming in and talking with me," Claire continued. "I know this must have been very hard for you to do."

"Anything to help you catch this animal," the mother said, patting her mouth with a damp, balled-up tissue. "Anything to keep it from happening again."

Marissa's father nervously retrieved bits of the tissue that fell on his wife's skirt. After their appointment with Claire, they would be going to the funeral home to make arrangements. Marissa's body would be released by the state's medical examiner by the end of the day.

Claire glanced down at her notes and then up again. "One more thing," she said hesitantly. "And I know this is going to sound silly, but, do you know how often your daughter ate at the local diner? Did she go a particular day each week, or maybe she liked to have breakfast, lunch?"

Mrs. Spicer glanced over at her husband, then looked to Claire. "Marissa wouldn't have eaten at a diner."

There it was, that free-falling feeling again.

Claire held her breath. "Never? You're certain?" She leaned forward on her desk.

Mrs. Spicer shook her head. "Ask anyone who knows her. It was very important to her that she eat healthy. She preferred organic food and shopped at the little store down near the post office."

"Adam's Apple?"

The older woman nodded. "You see, Marissa had serious food allergies. Eating organic seemed to alleviate most of those allergies."

Claire pressed both hands to the desk. All along, she'd been sure the killer was picking his victims from the diner. Every single other woman had been from there, but if Mrs. Spicer was right, if Marissa didn't eat at the diner, that meant that either he had changed a strategy he had used from the beginning . . . or the women were linked in a different way. In a way that she had missed. "You don't think she might have come in just once in the last week or so? Maybe for a cup of coffee? A bagel?"

Mrs. Spicer shook her head firmly. "Absolutely not. In fact, she just had an allergic reaction last week and had to go to the emergency room for treatment. After an episode, she was always extra careful."

Claire scribbled down a note to check with the emergency room and then laid down her pen, rising to her feet. "I think we're done here, Mr. and Mrs. Spicer. Please, let me walk you out front." She opened the door and glanced over her shoulder at her father's retirement clock on the wall. All through the interview it had appeared as if it were barely ticking. Now, in her mind, the clock's second hand was moving faster.

Chapter Twelve

"Kurt, listen to me. I'm telling you, he's not singling out these women at the diner."

She slapped her hand on her desk with an enthusiasm she hadn't felt in a long time. This whole case was so grim that enthusiasm was probably too strong a word. Hope. *Hope* was what she felt.

"I thought the diner was the key," she continued. "And I've wasted days, weeks, staking the place out, watching every male who came and went, but I was wrong." Resting both hands on the desk, she gazed at him over piles of paperwork and file folders. "Now I know that. I can feel it."

"How? How do you know that?" Kurt stood in front of her desk. He didn't appear to be catching any more sleep than she was. And right now, he was getting pressure from two sides. There was pressure from the governor's office to get this task force off the ground, and she wasn't cutting him a break. Not for a moment. If you threw in the news media and all the speculation in papers and magazines, it seemed as if all of America had an opinion on how the killer needed to be caught.

"How do you know?" he repeated, his impatience bordering on resentment. He perched on the end of the chair across her desk from her.

"Because Marissa was never there. Her mother said she would never have eaten at a diner."

"Maybe Marissa Spicer went into the diner without her mother knowing it." He gestured emphatically with one hand. "Most twenty-two-year-olds don't tell their parents everywhere they go, especially not when they've just moved out of the house."

"I asked her friends here in town, too. They said it was big joke with them. They all wanted meat loaf and mashed potatoes but Marissa would never go to the diner because the food wasn't healthy. And Loretta, the woman who owns the place, who is there sunup to sundown, swears Marissa was never there. The waitress, the new dishwasher." She counted off on her fingers. "No one ever saw her there because she never stepped foot in the place."

"Okay, if it isn't the diner, why not a bar?" He crossed his arms over his chest. "All these women could have been in any bar in this town."

She shook her head, refusing to give in. She didn't know how she knew what she knew, she just did. "April Provost didn't go to any bars."

"April Provost?"

"The woman on vacation, walking her mother-in-law's dog when she disappeared. Victim number two," she said testily, annoyed that he couldn't remember her name. She'd gone over every scrap of information she had on the victims so many times that she felt as if she knew each one intimately, even the women she had never met. "*April* and her husband didn't go to any bars while they were here."

"Okay, so I'm not as familiar with the victims as you are, Claire. That doesn't mean I don't know what I'm talking about."

"You're not listening to me. Look at my chart." She grabbed her legal pad and spun it around for him to see. She'd made a chart comparing each victim and the places they'd been in Albany Beach in the two weeks prior to their abduction. She'd reinterviewed friends and family members, co-workers, retracing each woman's steps.

"You only started with the places the tourist had been?" He didn't look up from the chart.

"She was in town the shortest period of time. It makes sense to start there."

"So what if he just picked her up?" Kurt scoffed. "Maybe he hadn't stalked her like the others. Maybe he just came upon her and on impulse, threw her in his car."

"That's not the way this guy works." She tapped her pen in a column. "Look at this. This is when it came to me—when Marissa's mother told me that she had been in the hospital emergency room the week before for an allergic reaction to something she'd eaten."

Kurt frowned as he studied the heading in the box followed by seven check marks below. "The hospital?" he mocked. "You think one of your doctors is killing these women?"

"Could be. Scalpel. Surgical gloves. Bleeding them to death. He's subduing them with some kind of chemical—most likely an anesthesia of some sort, according to the ME. How else would he have gotten them into his car without leaving any physical marks?" She threw up her hands. "I just don't know why I didn't think of this sooner."

"You said he knocked the last two around."

She sat back in her chair. She wasn't going to back down on this; she knew she was right. "That's different. I sense he's hitting them now for a different reason."

"And why might that be?" Kurt lifted a dark eyebrow.

He was mocking her and she wondered how she could have ever fancied herself in love with him. He could be mean when he wanted to be. "Because he's pissed off about something. Something isn't going right. He . . ." She thought aloud, keeping in mind her conversation with Graham's sister. "He's not being satisfied as he once was."

"This is all speculation, Claire." Kurt shoved the notepad back at her.

"Speculation? A couple of weeks ago when I talked to you, you told me you thought I was right on track. A couple of weeks ago, I was getting *atta boys* from you all over the place."

"That was before you started making this personal." He met her gaze across the desk, his dark eyes fixed on hers. "Before you started using words like you can *feel* this or you *sense* that."

Claire wanted to cite the training they had both had on the differences between men and women in the workforce, in law enforcement in particular, but she could tell by the tone of his voice that, right now, it would be a waste of breath.

"I'm telling you," she said, pointing her finger

at him, knowing how much he hated that. Not caring. "The first time he sees them, it's at the hospital." She tapped her temple. "That's where they catch his eye."

He didn't say anything, so she went on. "It makes sense, Kurt. Think about it. Three weeks before her murder, Patti had a cyst on her breast biopsied. April was in two mornings before her death; a reaction to a wasp sting. Anne Hopkins had blood tests and a chest X-ray ordered by her family physician as part of an annual physical, while she was home from college. Two weeks before her death. Kristen Addison had a blood test, eleven days before she disappeared. Brandy Thomas had a pregnancy test." She stared at Kurt across the desk. "Six days before Marissa Spicer disappeared from the Laundromat parking lot, she'd been in the ER with an allergic reaction to a food she'd eaten at a salad bar in town."

"I'm not convinced." As he rose, he grabbed his suit jacket off the back of the chair and started for the door. "I'm just not convinced, Claire."

"When are you moving in?"

The task force's takeover was imminent, but the powers that be were still arguing over what pile of money the project would be funded by. Who would pay the overtime? Who would pay for the additional equipment, cars, surveillance?

"I don't know. Next week, probably."

"So, until next week"—she began to busy herself shuffling papers that really didn't need shuffling—"my keeping you up to date is just a courtesy?"

He opened the door. "You could say that, but . . ."

He paused. "Damn it, Claire, don't put yourself in a worse position than you're already in. Cooperate with—"

He sounded so damned arrogant, so condescending.

"Cooperate with you," she interrupted. "And you'll help me keep my job?" She glanced up thinking that if she had anything breakable within reach, she might have thrown it at him. That's what Katharine Hepburn would have done in one of her movies. "Is that what you were going to say?"

"No." He threw his suit jacket over his shoulder. "What I was going to say, was that if you cooperate with me, with the task force, maybe we can help you catch this guy. At the risk of sounding like a bad line from a song, we can do it together."

"It won't go down that way and you know it. This little old Podunk town police force will be overrun with suits. The next thing we know, our budget will be scrutinized, personnel files will be dug through. Someone from the state will start counting beans, trying to figure if we've got enough kidney and lima on the force, making sure we didn't overlook any chick peas, even if they scored low on the admittance tests."

"I'm not going to talk to you when you're like this. I'm just not." He lifted both hands in surrender. "I'll call you tomorrow. Earlier if there's any news from the attorney general or the governor's office."

He walked out before she could form a clever retort. It was just as well, because she didn't have one. Katharine always had writers to provide her with snappy rejoinders.

Almost immediately following Kurt's exodus, there was a knock on her doorjamb. "Claire?" Graham peered around the door.

"Graham." She smiled, relieved to see a friendly face, despite her embarrassment about the night Marissa had gone missing. "How'd you get past the front desk? I told Jewel not to let anyone by."

"Anyone but Humphrey Bogart, according to Jewel." He walked in, carrying a white plastic bag from the diner.

"You convinced my receptionist that you were Humphrey Bogart?" She dropped into her chair. It was one-thirty, and she'd only been in the office since seven, but she felt as if she'd been here at least two days.

"Actually, I'm not sure she knows who Humphrey Bogart was." He pulled a Styrofoam container from the bag and slid it across her desk. "But I brought her lunch and she let me slip by. I took Ashley something, too." He glanced up. "I know I said I wouldn't call. I really meant to stay away, give you some breathing space."

Claire decided just to ignore the whole subject of her going to his place, throwing herself into his arms. She popped open the Styrofoam lid to find a cheeseburger, a pickle and chips and grimaced. "Did you bring Ashley red meat?"

"Nope. A chef's salad with cheese and egg, no meat to sully the mix." He held up one finger. "On a paper plate, mind you. No Styrofoam for Ashley, I can assure you."

Claire chuckled. "Red meat is perfect for me. Bless you. I haven't eaten since . . ." She exhaled as she picked up the burger made on a whole wheat bun, with mushrooms and Swiss cheese. This was a guy who paid attention to details. "I don't know . . . sometime yesterday."

"I figured as much." He sat back in the chair in front of her desk and rested his ankle on his knee. "So was that him?" He hooked his thumb in the direction of the door.

"Who?"

"The blustery one who passed me in the hall. He the old cop boyfriend?"

She took a bite of the burger that was still warm and frowned. "How do you know about Kurt?"

"The gossip twins, Mary Lou Joseph and Betty Friegal. They were in the store yesterday. Buying envelopes."

She lifted a brow and took another bite. She knew she shouldn't talk with her mouth full, but she really was starving. "And they found it necessary to discuss my love life, or lack thereof, with you, while purchasing a box of envelopes? Envelopes, I might add, that would be much cheaper at the Big Mart than an office supply store." She grabbed a chip. "You let them talk about me?"

He shrugged, pulled a pile of napkins from the bag, and pushed them across the desk at her. "I take my inside info where I can get it. And they didn't buy a box. They wanted two envelopes." He tapped the corner of her mouth.

Claire grabbed a napkin and wiped away a smear of mustard. Mustard, not ketchup. She never ate ketchup on her burger and apparently he had noticed that, too.

"Yup, that was the ex-boyfriend. Captain Kurt Gallagher of the Delaware State Police. He's been appointed head of the task force that's about to boot me out of my chair."

"Now, the gossip twins did *not* tell me that."

"Probably saving it for their trip next week to buy a pen to address the two envelopes."

He laughed. "Actually, you'd be surprised how many senior citizen customers I have who come weekly for little things like that." He shrugged. "Keeps them busy." He leaned back in the chair. "Hey, I talked to my sister the other night. She said she talked to you. She or her colleagues any help?"

"I think so." Claire set the burger down. She'd eaten only half of it, but she was full. Six murdered girls in three months time would do that to you— take away your appetite. "But the most help I've gotten this week was from Marissa Spicer."

He gave a slight *do tell* nod.

She pointed to the door and he reached over the back of his chair and closed it. "You didn't hear this from me."

"Claire." He leaned forward, studying her with those honest blue eyes of his. "You don't have to tell me anything. I wouldn't want you to put your job or your integrity on the line for me. I was wrong to have come to you in the first place, offering my help."

"Save it." She gave a wave. "I think we're a little beyond that kind of stuff, don't you? Truth is, you're the first decent person who's paid any attention to me in a very long time. As for the job, screw it *and* my integrity. No one will listen to me, but I know where my killer is. Kurt thinks I'm crazy, that I'm on a wild goose chase, but all along when I thought he was choosing his victims in the diner, I was wrong." She grabbed a chip from the Styrofoam box. "It's not the diner, it's an even better place to blend into the crowd, to make friends, to find young women to kill . . ."

He waited. He was a great audience.

"The hospital," she whispered. "He's at the hospital. He works there, or he has a job that takes him there regularly."

Claire could see by Graham's expression that he was already considering the possibilities.

"I mean, think about it," she continued. "Doctors, male nurses, aides, technicians, office workers."

"Ambulance and EMT crews, volunteers, firemen," he added. "Even policemen."

She frowned. "I told you. It's not Ryan McCormick."

He sat back, opening his arms. "I'm just saying."

"Well, don't." She glanced at the lunch he had had been so kind to bring her. Not to mention the fact that he had fed her finicky daughter and her receptionist. "Sorry, I'm a little touchy. I can also include people who don't work at the hospital, but go there regularly. Like my buddy Chain, who visits his grandmother in the nursing home."

"You don't really think Ashley's boyfriend is the killer, do you?" he asked. He was quiet for a minute. "I mean, a part of you, maybe, might like it to be him. Then you could send him to the electric chair."

"The State of Delaware executes by lethal injection," she said drolly. Then, against her will, she smiled. "You're right." She slid back in her chair and tipped her head to stare at the ceiling panels overhead. "It's not him."

"So now what?"

She stared at the ceiling for a long moment, then looked at him again. "I think I'll wander on over to the hospital. Chat with a couple of people, get the lay of the land."

He smiled as he got up. "You know, I like you a lot better this way."

She tried not to think about how she'd been that night when she showed up at his door. Pretty close to a nervous breakdown. "What way?" She rose and gathered a file and several notepads.

"Confident. All kick-ass."

She laughed, mostly because the words sounded so funny coming from such a straight-laced guy. She laughed, too, out of relief, tickled he was such a nice guy not to mention what a mess she had been the other night.

"Hey, you want me to take Ashley back to the store with me? Put her to work in the storeroom or something? She seems pretty bored."

Claire considered his offer for a moment. She knew he was right; Ashley was bored to tears spending twelve hours a day in the police station with her mother. Not even the TV and DVD player that Robinson had hooked up for the teen could keep her occupied that long every day. And Claire knew she couldn't keep her with her forever, but . . . "Nah," she said after a moment. "Thanks, but she can just stay here. I'll be back in an hour or so to get her. Maybe I'll kick out of here early and we'll go for a walk on the boardwalk. Take in a movie."

He stood in the doorway. "You're sure? I can bring her to you later. Meet you."

She knew what he was getting at. He'd let Ashley hang out for a few hours with him at the store and then they'd hook up for dinner. Maybe the movie.

If he took her daughter off her hands for a few
hours, she certainly couldn't *not* invite him to go
out with them. And it was tempting. She liked him
so much; he was good for her. Good in bed, too.

She almost smiled.

But she still meant what she had told him weeks
ago. She couldn't do this thing right now. She
couldn't possibly have a relationship and make it
work.

"Thanks, but she'll be fine." She looked up
from her desk as she grabbed a pen. "And, hey,
thanks for the lunch, too. You're the best."

"I want you to remember when this is all over
that you said that." He gave her a look that was so
sexy, it could have made a woman police chief forget where she was, at least for a moment.

"Leave now," she said, pointing to the door.

"Or what?" he asked quietly. "You'll throw yourself into my arms again." He lifted a brow.

"Out!"

She was still smiling when she walked out into
the bright sunshine of the afternoon, past the
Dumpster where they had found Marissa's body,
and got into her police car.

That night, the Bloodsucker tried to concen-
trate on the movie on TV. It was bank robbery
week on TNT, and he was watching a movie about
Patty Hearst and the Symbionese Liberation Army.
As he watched the recreation of the Hibernia
Bank holdup in San Francisco, he jiggled his leg.

"You should have worn a mask, stupid bitch," he
said, watching "Patty" walk into the bank with a
machine gun in her hand. "What? You didn't know

banks had security cameras?" He threw himself back in his favorite chair and snatched up the remote control.

"Idiots," he declared. "The world is full of them."

Max, who lay asleep on the rug in front of the TV, lifted his head to look at his master.

The Bloodsucker punched the channel button. "If they'd worn masks, maybe they wouldn't have gotten caught. You see what I'm saying, Max?"

The dog whined.

Disgusted, the Bloodsucker flipped through the channels, but nothing caught his fancy. It was late. He knew he should just go to bed. It was a workday tomorrow. But he knew he wouldn't be able to sleep. Not after what had happened this afternoon.

He hadn't actually seen Claire Bear at the hospital. Hadn't talked to her, but he heard she was nosing around the emergency room. He heard from several sources that she had been asking questions about the dead women. He knew she already knew when they'd been to the hospital. She'd been in the records office days ago with releases from the families, granting her permission to look over their medical records. But just knowing they had been there wasn't enough for her. She'd come back, sniffing around, talking all friendly like, laughing with employees as if she were one of them. Only she wasn't.

Claire Bear was one of those people who was nice to you when she wanted something from you. Granny had been like that. Crazy old bitch. Granny was as nice as you please to the butcher when she wanted a little extra ground meat. She was as sweet as honey when she needed another day to pay her bill before they shut off the electric. But was she ever nice to him? Her own grandson? Was she nice to him ever?

"Never!" the Bloodsucker shouted, slapping the remote control down so hard on the end table that the little plastic door flew off the back and the batteries rolled across the table.

Max jumped up and raced out of the living room. He knew his master's moods. Better, maybe, than the Bloodsucker himself knew them.

Where was all this rage coming from? All these years, all the pain, the tears, he had never felt this rage before.

He got up and began to pace. He was wearing a long sleeve T-shirt with an oxford over it to prevent himself from scratching. He'd used calamine lotion twice tonight since he'd gotten home from work. His shirt would be ruined with the pink chalky stuff.

But, still, his forearms itched. They burned.

He passed the TV. There was a commercial on advertising floor cleaner. If only his floor could be that clean and shiny, everything would be fine. He'd be happy and loved. He would have a perfect beautiful wife. Two point two beautiful children

"I don't know what you think you're doing, Claire," he murmured under his breath. "You think you're smart, but you're not." At the curtained window, he spun on his heels and went the other way, ignoring his burning arms and the almost unbearable desire to scratch them.

"You think you're smarter than I am, but you're not." He grabbed a needlepoint pillow off the old couch and viciously sent it sailing across the room.

"You should have minded your own business, you know that? Done what your old boyfriend told you to do. You should have sat there and been quiet and waited for the state police to come in and take over."

That was what the Bloodsucker had been counting on. Depending on. He knew this *so-called* task force wouldn't be able to catch him. Not Captain Kurt of the State Police or Captain Kirk of the *Starship Enterprise.* Not in a million years.

But Claire . . . she had him worried. She had that woman's sixth sense that he had never understood. That eerie intuition that had warned Patti, and April, and Phoebe and all the others, just a split second too late, that they should not have trusted him.

The question was, what to do about Claire. Did he wait her out? Everyone said the suits would be taking over any day. Next week at the latest, right? Surely she wouldn't figure out who he was by next week. How could she? She had no evidence against him.

There was the barn, or course, the things in his car. They could all be very incriminating, but only if she got close enough to him to convince a judge to issue a search warrant. And on what basis would that be? She could speculate all she wanted, her woman's intuition was not going to get her a search warrant.

But Claire Bear was like a dog with a bone, all of a sudden. She was reading over the evidence again and again. She was re-interviewing friends and family members. What if she came upon something in the women's autopsies or the details of the crime scenes where he had left the women? He had been very careful, very smart, but what if he had overlooked something?

The Bloodsucker hated second-guessing himself like this. Questioning his own intelligence. He hated Claire Bear for making him question himself.

He rubbed his forearm with the heel of his hand, fighting the burning pain.

He couldn't have Claire Bear ruining everything. Not even a pretty, smart blonde such as her.

He passed the TV again. The Three Stooges. He stopped to watch for a moment. He liked the Three Stooges. Most people didn't realize that there had actually been four and that three of them had been brothers. He watched as they waddled into an old-fashioned bank, pretending to hold it up, napkins tied around their noses and mouths. How stupid was Patty Hearst? Even the Three Stooges knew you had to wear a mask when you robbed a bank!

The Bloodsucker began to pace again because his arms were itching so bad that he wanted to claw the fabric of the sleeves of the shirts to get to the bare skin.

He tried hard not to think about the pain. About the fear. About the bedroom door opening and Granny standing there with the straight razor in her hand.

A sweat broke out on his forehead as he forced one foot in front of the other, willing himself to think of something else. Anything.

His thoughts shifted to Claire Bear, again. He considered how stupid she was being with Ashley. Didn't she know that all teens acted out? Didn't she realize that all teens opened their bedroom windows once in a while and sneaked a smoke? Did she know how lucky she was to have such a smart, beautiful daughter?

Parents needed to be more appreciative of their children. They needed to realize what a precious gift they were. How imperative their job as a parent was, not just to the child, but to society in general.

He thought about Ashley, pretty Ashley with her hair blond again, and those piecing blue eyes. Claire was making noise about sending Ashley to her father. She was threatening to put her on a plane and ship her to Utah where the poor girl didn't know anyone. Didn't have any friends.

The Bloodsucker pressed his lips together and shuddered, remembering the pain of separation from his mother. The loneliness.

"You don't deserve her," he whispered angrily.

It was that moment that he realized what he had to do. What was his destiny.

He'd been thinking about Ashley for some time now. Thinking about how strong she was, how tough and determined. He had been thinking about how much he wanted to spend some time with her alone. He'd been thinking about her blood.

The Bloodsucker was tempted to take Claire Bear. He knew he could do it. That would certainly end her investigation, wouldn't it? She'd not be poking around anymore if she ended up in the trash, where she belonged. Where they all belonged, *blond bitches* like her.

But the better idea was to cripple her. To reduce her to a sobbing mass of spineless jelly.

The more imaginative idea was to invite Ashley to be his guest. To intercede before Ashley grew up to become what all women became. Before she reduced a good man to what he had been reduced to.

Now that was a clever idea.

Chapter Thirteen

"Back off?" Claire said into the phone as she reached for a wooden spoon to stir her home-made marinara sauce. "Hell no, Kurt, I'm not backing off."

She was standing in front of the stove in gym shorts, an ancient police academy T-shirt and bare feet. It was the first Sunday she'd taken off since summer began and she was pretty annoyed that Kurt would call her at home. Especially since, as of tomorrow, he would be in charge of her serial killer investigation and she would be working *with* him.

She'd pretty much resigned herself to shift of power, but that didn't mean she had to like it. And it didn't mean he had a right to call her at home this evening, when he could talk to her tomorrow at their first task force meeting at eight A.M.

"Claire, I'm not saying you can't look into the backgrounds of the employees, have a look around, but—"

"Kurt, don't you see— Hey, did the mayor say who was complaining about me being there?" She lifted the spoon out of the sauce.

"What?" Kurt asked irritably.

He had not taken the day off. He was in his office up in Dover trying to put out several fires at the same time. Her pissing off the mayor of Albany Beach was just one and apparently not even the largest.

"Did Tugman say who complained about me? I wonder if it was Dr. Larson." She tasted the sauce on the end of the spoon. It was so hot she flinched as it burned her tongue. "He's old for the profile, but he does live alone and he certainly has access to surgical equipment." She went to the sink for a drink of water.

Actually, there was another man she suspected. She knew it couldn't be him. She hadn't even interviewed him yet, but twice she'd caught him watching her. On the dining room table she had all her notes in a stack of manila folders. She'd marked one man's name in one of those folders with an ominous red question mark.

"Claire, listen to yourself. You're seeing ghosts around every corner. You're losing perspective, which is why, in the long run, you're going to see that the governor's office, for once, might be right about this. A task force is the way to go. A small hometown police force like yours, you just don't have the experience to go it alone."

"Oh, and like anyone else in the state has much more experience?" She looked out the open window as she sipped the cold water in the glass to ease her burning tongue. The shadows outside had lengthened with the setting sun and it was almost dark out. "The last serial killer in Delaware was the I-40 Corridor killer in the late eighties. What was his name? Pernell? How many people who worked that gig are still around?"

"Claire—"

"Don't you see, Kurt? Looking at everyone in the hospital, seeing each one as our possible killer is the way we're going to catch him." Setting down the water glass, she reached into the spice cabinet to her left and grabbed a container of red pepper. She shook it over the bubbling sauce. She didn't want to tell him about the man with the red question mark next to his name. Not yet. He wouldn't listen to her, anyway. Just as he wasn't listening to her now. "You know why?"

"No, tell me," he groaned.

"Because that's going to put the pressure on him. You should be doing your reading. Those behavior scientists with the FBI know these sickos. You put pressure on them and that's when they make a mistake. That's when even the smarter ones take a misstep. The misstep is when you catch them."

"We'll talk about this more tomorrow. Eight A.M. in the conference room."

"I'll be there." She gave a humorless chuckle. "Like I have a choice."

"There's one more thing."

"Yeah?" She pulled out a pot from under the counter.

"There's been some talk about the hate and discontent between you and the City Council and your boyfriend trying to smooth things over."

At the mention of Graham, her hackles went up. She was beginning to think she was in love with him, even though they'd yet to have a real date. "He's not my boyfriend."

"I just wanted to give you a heads up. The mayor is concerned that there could be a—"

"Kurt—did you hear what I said? Graham is not my boyfriend." She tossed the wooden spoon on the counter, not caring that it splattered sauce on the wallpaper. "What the hell is this? High school?"

"I'm just—"

"Well, don't," she said curtly. "Look, we're not dating, mostly because when the hell would I have time to date?" She ran her fingers through her hair, brushing it over the crown of her head. "I barely have time to pee."

"I'll talk to you in the morning."

She started to say something more, then stopped herself. "Sure. Okay. See you in the morning."

Claire turned the phone off and opened the cupboard to get the pasta. She had fettuccine and bow ties. Ashley always liked bow ties, but they had discussed fettuccine. She went down the hallway, headed for her daughter's room, but when she heard the shower running she opened the door without thinking.

"Hey, Ash—" Claire halted mid-step, mid-word. She had walked in on Ashley naked, just stepping into the shower, but it wasn't her teenage daughter's bare butt that made her cover her mouth with her hand in horror. It was the tattoo of a rose with blood dripping from it, the size of her hand, etched above Ashley's tailbone.

"Mom!" Ashley shrieked, grabbing a towel off the toilet lid to cover herself. "Get out!"

"What the hell is that?" Claire made no move to back out of the bathroom. "Ashley, what the hell is that on your back?" She felt as if she couldn't breathe. As if she were going to pass out. "Tell me that's not a tattoo of dripping blood," she begged, almost hysterically. "Tell me you didn't let that boy make you get a tattoo!"

"Chain didn't make me do anything," Ashley flung. "I wanted to do it. It's a symbol of our love!"

Claire closed her eyes for a minute. *A symbol of our love?* She didn't know if she wanted to laugh hysterically . . . or cry hysterically. As bizarre as it sounded, a line from an old Jimmy Buffett song ran through her head. *Permanent reminder . . . of a temporary feeling . . .*

"Shut the water off," Claire said quietly, eyes still closed. When Ashley didn't move, she shouted at her. "Damn it! Shut the water off."

She heard the sound of Ashley reaching past the shower curtain and turning off the faucet. The sound of spraying water ceased.

"Now." Claire opened her eyes as she breathed deeply. "Is it permanent?"

"Of course," Ashley sneered. "It's a tattoo. That's the point."

Claire fought the urge to smack her daughter across the mouth. "So you've seen him again since I forbid you to. When? How?"

"No, I haven't seen him." Tears filled Ashley's blue eyes as she tried to tuck the edge of the bath sheet in so that it would remain wrapped around her naked body. She looked so young undressed, blond hair falling past her shoulders, devoid of any makeup. *Surprisingly innocent for a girl with blood droplets tattooed on her ass.*

Claire folded her arms over her chest, waiting for the explanation.

"So fine, don't believe me." Ashley tried to get past her to escape to her room, but Claire wouldn't let her.

"The same day Chain got his, okay?" Ashley thrust out her hip.

"You mean the night you sneaked out of your grandparents' house?" *There was just no end to the joy with this child.* "You told Detective Robinson that you went to a party and then you just walked up and down the beach. You didn't say a thing about stopping by a tattoo parlor."

"Not that night. The day you came to pick me up at work. When I came through the parking lot."

Claire thought for a moment, not even sure what day she meant. Then she remembered Ashley saying her back hurt from hauling bags of fertilizer.

Claire didn't know what to say. What to do. The tattoo was permanent . . . at least until she paid a plastic surgeon a hefty sum to remove it. She knew she could go after the business owner for tattooing a minor, but as far as she was concerned, that was only misdirecting who was responsible here. And that was Ashley. Ashley knew very well she was not allowed to get a tattoo. That was why she had been hiding it for two weeks. And quite effectively, it turned out.

Claire glanced away, so angry she felt as if she were looking through a haze of red. "Well, that's it," she said, throwing up her hands and walking out of the bathroom.

Ashley didn't follow her at once, but Claire

wasn't halfway to the kitchen before her daughter was running barefoot down the hall after her, towel clutched around her.

"That's what?"

Claire could hear the fear in Ashley's voice. But there was still defiance there.

"You're going to Utah. You're going on the next plane I can put you on." Claire reached the stove and snapped off the burner under the sauce. Obviously there would be no cozy family dinner this evening. It was definitely a popcorn and vodka night.

"I'm not going to Dad's."

"Oh, yes you are. You're going as far from Chain and those friends of yours with the eyebrow piercings as I can get you." She spun around. "I'm— Jesus, Ashley, a tattoo? *A tattoo?* Of dripping blood, no less."

"It's a rose!"

"A rose with *blood!*" Claire's voice caught in her throat and her eyes teared up. In her mind, the blood drops on Ashley's back represented the blood of the women who had been killed in Albany Beach this summer. The women she'd been unable to protect.

"I don't care what you say. You can't make me go!" Ashley turned and ran down the hall.

Claire knew she should go after her, but she just couldn't. Not right now. Instead, she backed up to lean against the counter, grabbed a paper towel to wipe her eyes and reached for the phone.

Ashley slammed her bedroom door so hard that the wall shook. She would have locked it, too, ex-

cept that the lock had broken more than a year
ago and her mother had *conveniently* not gotten
around to installing a new doorknob that worked
properly.

She flung the bath towel onto the growing pile
of clothes on the floor and grabbed the T-shirt and
shorts she'd worn to bed the previous night. She
yanked the T-shirt over her head, not bothering
with a bra. "I don't care what she says," she muttered under her breath as she stepped into gray
gym shorts. "I'm not going to live with that ass-
hole. He's not my father. He's nothing but a sperm
bank as far as I'm concerned."

She turned her head toward the door. "I'm not
going," she screamed as loud as she could.

"You're going," her mother hollered back from
somewhere in the house.

Ashley flipped her the bird. It should have made
her feel better, but it didn't. She wiped at her eyes,
feeling silly for crying. Then she rubbed her ten-
der back where the tattoo was still healing.

She'd realized before she'd gotten up off the
table that it had been a stupid thing to do. Chain
had warned her that it wasn't a smart move. But by
then, it was done. Her idea had been to earn the
money herself to pay to have it removed. She knew
it could be done. She saw it on TV.

So getting a tattoo was a stupid thing to do. So
what! Didn't her mother know that fifteen-year-old
girls did stupid things? And there were so many
stupider things she could have done . . . such as
smoke crack or have sex with a bunch of guys.

She jerked open her bottom dresser drawer and
fished around for the pack of cigarettes she knew
was still there. She hadn't been smoking that

much lately, but she needed a cigarette, if nothing else, just to do it in defiance of *Mother Cop* in the other room. Her fingertips brushed the smooth, hard side of the box and she snatched it out from under some sweaters. She had a lighter in the drawer beside her bed. For candles, *Mom*.

Talk about stupid things a teenager could do! Ashley could have gotten pregnant. That's what Tiffany Lane had done. Going into the tenth grade and pregnant. Tiffany wasn't even sure who the father was. How would Chief Drummond have liked *that*?

Ashley walked around the heap of clothes to the double windows beside her bed and took her time opening the curtains. She unlocked a window and lifted it up in rebellion against her mother's no smoking, no open windows at night rules. She grabbed the lighter from the drawer and flicked her Bic.

The Bloodsucker had been studying the open kitchen window from the shadows of the woods line when he'd heard the muffled shouts from inside the house. He couldn't make out exactly what was being said, but Claire was very angry. She was screaming at Ashley in the bathroom. He'd been able to make out their silhouettes in the tiny, curtained window. Claire had screamed at Ashley the way Granny had screamed at him and it pissed him off.

He flexed his fingers, fighting the resentment bubbling up inside him. Didn't people know that wasn't the way you talked to kids?

But he knew he needed to keep his anger in

check. He needed to stay in control. Of all his jaunts this summer, this one would be the trickiest. The most dangerous. He had to be able to get in, get her out and escape into the woods, carrying her. It was farther than he usually carried the women. And he still wasn't sure how he was going to get Ashley out of the house without Claire knowing it. That was key; taking her beneath her nose. Showing her how she had failed her daughter. He wasn't even sure tonight was the night, although the timing would be sweet. To take Ashley on the eve of Claire Bear's capitulation to her failure.

Now, looking at the open window over the kitchen sink, forgotten in the fight he suspected, he couldn't help thinking that it might be providence. Ashley was meant to be his.

"Tim, it's Claire," she said angrily into the phone when the answering machine on the other end of the line beeped. "Tim, if you're there, would you please pick up?"

She exhaled, trying to hide her annoyance with him. She knew they were monitoring their calls. "Rochelle? Tim? I really need to talk to you. Not about the money." She turned around in front of the kitchen sink and gazed out into the dark yard. "It's about Ashley. About her coming to stay with you for the school year."

She hesitated, afraid she was making a mistake. Afraid she might be making a bigger one if she didn't get her daughter out of this town. "Tim, would you please—"

Beeeeep. The answering machine cut her off and she cursed as she hung up.

* * *

The Bloodsucker parted the branches of the tree he stood behind and stared in wonder as the curtains to the far right of the house parted and one of the double windows lifted. Like an angel in a dream, Ashley appeared.

His breath caught in his throat, in awe of her beauty. She really wasn't *that* young. His mother had only been a few years older than Ashley when he was born and girls really did mature sooner, these days.

He slid his hand over his breast pocket and the felt ridge of the old photo inside. He didn't have to pull it out to compare the two women. His mother's lovely face was forever etched in his mind . . . and soon, Ashley's would be, as well.

He stepped boldly out of the sanctuary of the woods. It was dark in the yard now, and would remain so as long as he stayed out of line of the electric eye of the two lights on the back porch. It would be at least another hour before the moon began to rise in the sky and then it would only be a quarter moon. Not so bright.

He watched as Ashley lit up a cigarette and he *tisk-tisked* under his breath. He would have to speak to her about the dangers of smoking. It was so unhealthy, and not terribly attractive on such a pretty young woman, either.

The Bloodsucker stood for another full moment, watching Ashley, then realizing he couldn't waste time, he pulled the ski mask from his back pocket. If Patty had worn one of these, maybe she wouldn't have gotten caught. Maybe she'd still be robbing banks today. He pulled the mask over his head, liking the feel of it on his skin despite the heat of the August evening. He didn't plan to keep the mask on all night. It would be important to him that he and Ashley be able to see each other as they got to know one another better, but he thought this might add to the fun.

The mask secure, he shifted the backpack on his back and cut across the yard to the phone utility box.

In the kitchen, Claire poured the still hot marinara sauce into a storage container and carried the dirty pot to the sink. A warm breeze blew in through the window, teasing the hair on her shoulders as she turned on the hot water. She leaned down to open the cupboard below the sink to grab the dish soap and several squirt bottles of assorted cleaning fluids fell out. The window cleaner struck her bare toe and she yelped.

"Am I the only person in the house who can put something away correctly?" she muttered. Tears sprang in her eyes and she wiped at them as she tried to shove the bottles back under the sink. As fast as she shoved them, more tumbled out.

"Damn it," she groaned. She shut the hot water off and went down on her knees, opening both cabinet doors. She began to pull out bathroom cleaners, furniture polish, rug deodorizer, a bottle of Windex, a second bottle. She found the dish soap at last . . . and another bottle of Windex, this one lemon fresh scent. She didn't know why two people living in an eighteen hundred square foot house needed three bottles, all half full, of window cleaner.

Claire got up, grabbed the trash can from the

corner of the kitchen and returned to the task at hand. So her daughter had a tattoo and she was going to have to send her out of state. So there was a serial killer murdering women in her town. So she was probably going to end up losing the job she had dreamed of her whole life. At least the cabinet under her sink was going to be neat and orderly.

Ashley ground out the cigarette in the flowerpot on the windowsill, then grimaced. "Sorry," she whispered, brushing her fingertips over the African violet. She dug the butt out of the potting soil and pitched it through the open window. That was one of the conveniences of having a paranoid cop mother. There were no screens on the windows because they were never allowed to leave the windows open.

"Now what?" Ashley wondered aloud. Did she go out into the kitchen and try to reason with her mother?

Like she was ever reasonable . . .

Did she pack her backpack, climb out the window and head for her friend Ashley's place? Maybe even Chain's? She'd never been to Chain's trailer, but she knew where it was.

Of course, with her luck, her mother would come after her, flashing blue lights and all.

She wandered away from the window and stopped to stare at the pile of clothes on the floor. She could start putting some of them away. Some of the clothes were supposed to go to the church yard sale—too old or they didn't fit anymore. Others had never made it to her winter drawer. If she was going to Utah, she thought morosely, she'd need them.

But she wasn't going to Utah.

She leaned over her desk and hit "play" on her CD player. KORN blasted through the speakers. The song was really obnoxious; she didn't really like it, but her mother hated it. She turned it up a notch and wandered over to her closet.

She knew her mother wasn't really going to send her to live with her father and Rochelle and those twit half sisters of hers. Her mother might threaten. She might scream and holler and put Ashley on double secret probation, but she wouldn't really send her away. They were a team and had been since the divorce. She loved her.

Against her will, tears filled her eyes again. She really was sorry about the tattoo and losing her job. Both were stupid mistakes. She was even sorry about sneaking out of her grandparents' house that night. It was just that she wanted so bad to be with Chain. And they really hadn't done anything wrong together ever . . . well, except for the tattoo, maybe.

Ashley tugged on the sleeve of a shirt hanging in her closet that her mother had bought her for Christmas. She had hadn't worn it since January when she started wearing black, but the shirt really was pretty. It was blue and green with an open neckline and flowing sleeves and was made from a filmy fabric that was so see-through she wore a camisole under it. She fingered the thin fabric and then pulled it off the hanger.

Something behind Ashley, not a sound because her stereo was pounding—more like a feeling—made her turn. The wind must have—

Suddenly nothing was right in her room. It was

as if she were suddenly in one of those creepy fun houses where everything was wrong. Crazy. Crooked walls. Weird lights.

There was someone there. A stranger in a black ski mask.

He rushed toward her. Ashley opened her mouth to scream, but the sound barely got out before he was on top of her, covering her mouth with his hand. *And how would her mother have heard her anyway with the CD blasting and her door closed*, she thought with terrifying clarity.

The intruder, now behind her, his arms wrapped around her pinning her arms down, was wearing rubber gloves like the ones her mother kept in the car for crime scenes. They had that funny latex smell.

Ashley was so scared that for a split second, she was unable to react. Then she got pissed. If this man thought he was going to rob them— She shoved her elbow backward as hard as she could, surprising him, she thought, and he grunted with pain.

But he still had ahold of her.

Ashley threw her elbow again, but he had twisted his body, still keeping an iron grip on her. She missed. He was trying to cover her face with a rag or something that smelled funny, but she wasn't going to let him do it. The beat of the KORN song pounded in her head. She could feel it against her skin the way she could feel the man's hands on her. The song was almost over. There would be a lull on the CD between it and the next song. If she could get her mouth open and scream then . . .

The song ended and the thrum of the electric guitar began in the background, again . . .

Ashley kicked and swung her arms and threw her head back, smacking him in the chin or nose, or something.

He yelped and she twisted in his arms. His hand slid off her mouth and she tried to scream but her voice wasn't nearly as loud as she had thought it would be.

The minute the music had started, Claire had been tempted to march down the hall, go into Ashley's room and rip the electrical plug to the CD player from the wall. But she had the entire kitchen cabinet emptied now. She had sponged out the spilled, dried soap, tossed out the old ant traps and was starting to put the cleaners back just the way she liked them. She placed kitchen products on the right—dish soap, dishwasher tablets, disinfectant spray for the countertops, cleaner for the stainless steel refrigerator. All the other cleaners went on the left—three bottles full of window spray, bathroom bleach spray, air and rug deodorizer.

The thumping cadence of the punk rock music made Claire's headache even worse. Now she could feel every beat of her heart in the throbbing in her temples. It was synchronized to the beat of a song that she couldn't understand the words the singer was screeching. Ashley said it wasn't punk rock. Claire didn't know what the heck she called it. Didn't care. There would be none of it in her father's strict Mormon household; she would guarantee Miss Ashley that.

A sob rose in Claire's throat and she swallowed it. With Ashley gone, what was she going to do?

The song blasting from down the hall blessedly ended, but another began. Just as the guitars and drums were beginning to thump again, Claire thought she heard a sound that didn't seem to go with the music. Seated on the hardwood floor in front of the sink, she turned around and looked over her shoulder. She couldn't see the hallway from this vantage point. Had Ashley come out of her room?

She waited. When she heard nothing but the music again, she turned back to the bottles still on the floor beside her. Two bottles of air freshener, left side. Dishwasher additive to keep glasses from getting streaky, right side.

What sounded like a muffled thump from the back of the house made Claire glance over her shoulder again, a little squirt bottle in her hand. What was Ashley doing? Moving furniture? Sliding dressers and the bed in front of the door so her mother couldn't get in, maybe?

When Ashley was five, she had tried to paint her toenails while her mother and father were busy with one of their arguments. When she had gotten red polish on the tiles of the bathroom door, she'd tried to nail the door shut from the inside so Claire wouldn't be able to get in and see the mess she had made. And had been successful. What she hadn't considered was how she was going to get out of the bathroom once the door was nailed shut. Claire and Tim had had to take the door off the hinges to reach Ashley and send her to her room for a time-out.

Claire smiled to herself. Life had been so easy then and she just hadn't known it.

* * *

The next song was a long one, Ashley knew. Almost four minutes. The intruder was getting angry now. He'd pinched her. She'd knocked him in the teeth with her head again and the square piece of gauze he'd been trying to cover her nose and mouth with had flown out of his hand.

She knew, now, that this man was not a burglar. She'd probably known from the moment she turned and saw him. She knew who he was . . . he was the killer.

Funny thing was, that realization didn't make her any more scared than she already was. Maybe because a person could only be so terrified. Maybe because emotions could only run so high and then you just ran out of feeling. After that, all you had was instinct and Ashley's instinct was to fight. If he was going to kill her, she was going to make him do it right here. She wasn't going to let him carry her out of her room alive, if she could help it.

The intruder got one arm wrapped securely around her shoulders, his hand on her mouth and he began to drag her toward where the white gauze lay on the end of her bed. When dragging her heels did nothing to slow him down, she buckled her knees, dropping all of her weight, and let herself fall to the floor. Miraculously, she took him with her. As she went down, she grabbed the edge of the sheet, hoping to lose the white gauze, at least momentarily, in the tangle of bedsheets and the blanket. She didn't know what was on the gauze, but she knew it had to be the way the son of a bitch was knocking the women out.

On the carpeted floor, Ashley tried to roll away.

She flailed her arms, knocking his hand away from her mouth. This time she let loose a bloodcurdling scream that she prayed would drown out KORN's lead singer. "Mommy!"

Chapter Fourteen

Ashley's scream was the fabric of every mother's nightmare—a cry that penetrates your very soul.

Claire had only heard that earth-shattering cry once before, and that had been when Ashley was eight and had fallen through the glass panel of a storm door at a friend's house.

Claire was up off the floor in a split second, racing down the hall. "Ashley!" Claire cried, afraid of what she might find. Blood? Had she fallen and hurt herself trying to move furniture, or, God forbid, had she done what perfectly normal teenagers do every day—tried to take her own life?

Claire grabbed the doorknob to the bedroom, hearing the pounding of the loathsome rock music. It seemed as if it took an eternity for the door to swing open. And then Claire realized *this* was the nightmare too horrible even to remember when you woke. The kind that left you bathed in sweat, shaking in your bed, unable to recall.

A masked man held Ashley down on the bed. Claire's little girl, dressed in gym shorts and a yellow SpongeBob T-shirt, was fighting him for all she was worth.

Claire's mind seemed to slow until it wasn't moving any faster than her legs.

Her sidearm. She needed her Beretta Cougar. But, out of habit, it was locked in the safe where she kept it when she was home. Away from Ashley, away from any other teenagers who might come to the house.

When Claire burst into the room, she startled the intruder who sat straddling Ashley on the bed. Trying to rape her? He pulled his hand from Ashley's mouth and the teen screamed.

"He's got a knife!"

Claire didn't have time to think. She hurled herself over the pile of dirty clothes on the floor, onto the bed. "Run, Ashley! Run," she screamed. "Get out of the house! Out the front!"

The man in the bed struggled under Claire's weight. He swung a fist and clipped her hard in the chin, so hard that her head snapped back and her teeth rattled.

Claire jerked her head forward, slamming into his face with her forehead as Ashley wriggled under him. He howled in pain and anger as he tried to grab the back of Ashley's T-shirt. She squirmed forward, twisting until she was on her belly, only her legs pinned, her hands on the carpet.

"Let go! Let go of my mother!" Ashley shrieked as she bucked and kicked him.

"Ashley, go!" On her knees on the bed beside

her daughter, Claire raised both hands and tackled the masked man, knocking him backward off Ashley.

The teen slithered to the floor, crawled over her pile of clothes, and scrambled for the open door. "Mom!"

"Go! Go!" Claire reached out, trying to grab the man's mask off his face but he caught her off guard with a knee to her stomach. She groaned, closing her eyes as spasms of pain sent swirls of bright light through her already pounding head.

Ashley raced down the hall, panting hard, shaking so badly that she could barely see where she was going. "Where's the phone! Where's the phone?" she screamed.

"Run!" her mother shouted from the bedroom.

Ashley's bare feet hit the cool, smooth wooden floor of the kitchen. All of her senses seemed to be heightened. She could smell the delicious scent of her mother's marinara that had cooked in the kitchen. She could hear the whoosh of water as it filled the ice trays in the automatic ice maker in the refrigerator freezer behind her. She looked around wildly.

The phone wasn't on its charger on the wall, of course. It never was. Then she spied it on the counter and dove for it. She didn't see the bottles of cleaner on the floor in front of the sink and she tripped over them, falling forward. She caught herself with both hands before her chin struck the counter and with her cheek pressed to the countertop, she reached for the phone. Hitting the *on* button, she punched 911 as she righted herself. She listened for the call to go through as she jerked open the closest drawer, looking for a weapon. A knife, that hammer her mother used to beat chicken breasts, anything . . .

There was no sound on the phone. Just dead air. "Come on. Come on," she muttered.

She heard a loud bang from down the hall. It sounded as if her mother and the man had fallen off the bed and onto the floor. They'd knocked the nightstand over, apparently, because the music stopped.

Still dead air on the phone and now it was all the more ominous, now that the house was devoid of the rock music, quiet except for her own breathing, the pounding of her heart in her ears and the sounds coming from down the hall.

Ashley closed her fingers over a knife in the drawer, slapped it onto the counter and punched the power button on the phone off, then on again. Frantically, she punched 911 once more and reached for the knife. "Come on, come on," she mumbled, tears running down her face.

When the call didn't go through again, she knew he had cut the lines. They did it all the time in movies; apparently bad guys really did do it.

She dropped the phone, closed her fingers over the handle of the knife and jumped over the bottles on the floor, spilling something. The knife wasn't as big as the butcher knife she would have liked, but it had a nice serrated edge.

Trying to catch her breath, rubbing her eyes with the back of one hand, Ashley ran across the kitchen floor. Something deep inside her told her she had to keep moving; she couldn't stay here in the kitchen where he would see her the minute he reached the end of the hall.

Her mother had told her to run. Out the front

door. All she had to do was go the other way—through the living room. But how could she? How could she leave her mother with the man with that knife doctors used to operate on people?

There were still sounds of struggle coming from down the hall, but as Ashley cut through the kitchen to the dark dining room, she heard her mother give a strangled cry and then suddenly she didn't hear her again.

A sob wracked Ashley's body, and she covered her mouth with her hand to keep the man from hearing her. She refused to allow herself to think what the silence might mean. She stood still, listening to the deafening stillness down the hall, and her own pounding heart.

"Ashley?"

A voice called her name, only it wasn't her mother's voice. It was *his*. And she knew that voice . . . knew him. She just couldn't place it.

"Ashley?" He was panting as she heard him come out of the bedroom, down the hall toward the front of the house. There was no sound from the bedroom or from her mother.

Don't let her be dead. Don't let her be dead, she prayed frantically as she clutched the knife.

"Ashley, where are you?"

She ducked down behind her mother's birchwood dining table. She'd bought it shortly after the divorce and had it shipped from out west. It was one of her prized possessions. Ashley thought it was ugly.

"Ash," came the man's voice, almost gently. "Where are you, hon?"

She knew he was at the head of the hall, even though she couldn't see him.

"Ashley? Come now. I don't have time for games," he warned, sounding like a kindergarten teacher.

He was now in the space between the kitchen and living room, effectively blocking Ashley and the front door. She couldn't go that way. But if he would just step into the kitchen, maybe go around the corner toward the laundry room, she could slip into the hall. She could go to her mother.

"Ashley?"

That's it, you sick bastard, Ashley mouthed silently as she listened to his voice grow more distant. *Look in the laundry room.*

"Ash?"

She took a quick breath and at the moment she thought he had stepped around the refrigerator, she dashed forward, around the table, around the chair, through the doorway and down the hall. Quiet in her bare feet. Quiet as a mouse. As a mouse carrying a knife.

Ashley stepped into her bedroom and almost tripped over her mother. She had to cover her mouth to keep from crying out. Her mother was unconscious, laid out on the floor. Dead? No, no, she didn't think so. Just passed out. She tried to listen to the man's voice as he called her again, trying to judge where he was as she leaned over her mother, trying to assess what was wrong.

No blood. She wasn't bleeding. Of course not. Because this man didn't kill women right away. He kidnapped them. Then he killed them, sometimes more than a day later, according to the newspapers.

"Ashley, I know you're in here because both doors are locked from the inside," the man called, rattling the dead bolt on the front door. "Now where could you be?"

Ashley fell to her knees and laid the knife on the carpet beside her mother's head. Hair covered her face, hair the same color as Ashley's. "Mom? Mom?" She brushed the hair from her face and then shook her hard.

She didn't respond.

Ashley spotted the gauze pad on the floor beside her mother. He had knocked her out with some kind of poison or something.

"Ashley, we can make this easy, or we can make this hard. Now, I know you're worried about your mother, but she's all right. Really she is. And you and I, maybe we could make a bargain. Hmmm?"

He had cut through the dining room and was now standing at the head of the hall. Ashley glanced over her shoulder at the window. The sill was high, but she could use the nightstand that had fallen over to boost herself up and over into the flower bed outside.

"Ashley?"

His voice was suddenly closer. He was coming back down the hall. Panic rose in Ashley's throat and for a moment she thought she would barf. No time to get out the window now. He was ten steps from her. Eight.

The closet? No. He'd look there. Under the bed? She'd never fit. Too much crap under there.

"Sweetheart," he crooned, his voice taking on a frightening edge. "You don't want to make me angry."

Her gaze fell on the heap of clothes beside the bed. When she was little, she and her mother had played hide-and-seek and her mother had been good at it. She'd taught Ashley all the best places to hide, such as behind the curtains up inside the window . . . and under a pile of clothes.

Ashley spun around on her hands and knees and backed up, wiggling under the clothes. The bath sheet on top was perfect. He wouldn't see her. He'd never think to look here.

"Ash—"

She spotted the knife beside her mother's head and her stomach lurched. She thrust her hand out, quick as lightning, grasped the knife handle, and pulled it under a pair of green sweatpants that was hiding her arm.

"Now, now, you're trying my patience," the man in the mask called. "Where did you go?"

Ashley tried not to breathe, afraid he would hear her. Her heart was pounding in her chest and she had an itch at her ankle, but she remained perfectly still, taking shallow breaths. She thought of every bad word she had ever heard that she could call him as she waited. He was in the doorway of the bedroom now, looking right at her. Not seeing her.

He stood there for a minute that seemed like a whole day in Biology class, then backed up and went farther down the hall toward the spare room, her mother's room and the bathroom.

Please wake up, Mom. Please wake up, Ashley prayed fervently. She wanted to reach out and shake her, but he was so close there in the hall that she didn't dare.

The Bloodsucker hesitated in the doorway of a dark room, then reached over and flipped on the wall switch. It was a bedroom that obviously was not used. He stepped in and opened the closet:

coats, suitcases, too small for a girl Ashley's size to hide. He peeked under the bed, gripping the warm handle of the scalpel. Nothing there but some clear plastic boxes with more clothes. Women liked clothes. He backed out the door, shut off the light, and closed the door.

Taking his time, he continued down the hall. It was true that the evening had taken an unexpected turn, but he was still in control.

Ashley couldn't get away from him. She was right here and there was no need for him to panic. She was just a little girl, really, in an adult woman's body. She wasn't as smart as he was, couldn't possibly be. She couldn't outwit him. This was just a game. And a fun one at that. One that would become even more fun once he and Ashley could be together in the barn.

"Ashley," he sang. "Come out, come out, wherever you are." He pushed open the bathroom door, flipped on the light. The tropical fish shower curtain was open. No place to hide. The bathroom smelled good, like baby powder and shampoo and hair spray. He lifted a towel hanging on the rack and brought it to his nose, inhaling. He knew Ashley would smell good, too. The way he remembered his mother smelling.

He let go of the sweet-smelling towel, flipped off the light, closed the door and moved down the hall to the last door. Claire Bear's bedroom. Inside the dark room, he hesitated. It felt unoccupied, but she had to be here. Where else could she have gone when both doors were locked?

He listened to the stillness. The quiet was much better than that awful music Ashley had been playing when he went into her bedroom. They would

have to talk about her choice of music and he
would cite the statistics on crimes committed by
teens who listened to such violent lyrics. He was
surprised a police officer would allow her daughter to listen to such garbage. He flipped on the
overhead light below the ceiling fan with a sigh.
The music was just another example of Claire
Bear's poor parenting skills.

The Bloodsucker stood in the doorway, the
scalpel at his side, and studied the room. It wasn't
overly feminine. No ruffles, bows or flowered wallpaper. It had kind of a Southwestern look—like
maybe one of the interior decorating shows he'd
seen about a house in New Mexico. The walls were
painted a pale, earthy sand color and there was a
geometric patterned, Indian-looking blanket on
the bed. The lamps on the nightstands were big
clay jars, and there were some Indian prints on the
walls; Navajo, he guessed. He had seen a show on
the Discovery Channel about the patterns in
Navajo art.

His gaze flickered to the windows; the curtains
were drawn and the windows were shut. He passed
the closet, which was open. He drew his fingers
over several dry-cleaning bags hanging there.
Uniforms. Shoes lined neatly on the floor. He
pushed back a dress and spotted the safe. He wondered what was inside, but it was only a passing interest. He was not a thief.

"Ashley," he called softly, stepping back. There
was no master bedroom bath. Claire Bear and her
daughter shared a bathroom. How frugal.

He took a couple of steps back, returning to the
doorway. He was beginning to get a little nervous
now. Where was she? He couldn't stay in the house

much longer. It wasn't safe. Too many things could go wrong.

His gaze flitted to a mirror over the dresser. He studied the man in the ski mask. The man smiled back. He liked the mask. Liked the feel of it against his skin. The power it gave him.

He shut out the light, closed the door quietly and listened. Not a sound. Where was she? Where was she? He trembled. He wanted Ashley. He wanted her so badly.

He slipped down the hall and stopped in the doorway of the teen's bedroom. What a mess; clothes everywhere, a trash can spilling over onto the floor, books in piles on every surface. And the dark purple walls with the posters were hideous.

His gazed shifted to the open window and he felt sick in the pit of his stomach. He looked over his shoulder, then at the window again. A light evening breeze made the purple and black curtain ripple. Had Ashley sneaked back down the hall when he'd gone to the front of the house and climbed out the window?

Claire, on the floor at his feet, twitched, startling him. She was waking up. They never woke up this quickly, but he never had the gauze that was soaked with chloroform out for so long, either.

His heart rate increased as he struggled in indecision. He had the mask on. Neither of them had seen him. Did he just run? He wouldn't get caught. Especially not with Captain Kirk taking over tomorrow. He could just chalk this one up to experience.

Then he looked at Claire on the floor in front of him, her beautiful hair spread across the dark, ugly carpet. She was so lovely. She was not Ashley, but she was so lovely. And smart . . . though not as smart as him. She would make a good companion, if only for a little while.

Claire's foot jerked, forcing him into action. He had dropped his backpack somewhere in the struggle. He spotted it at the end of the bed, grabbed it and dropped to his knees. Tucking the scalpel carefully into its plastic sheath, he put it in the front pocket and pulled out the duct tape. It worked better than rope and was faster. He put her ankles together, taped them and then taped her wrists together.

He was upset with himself that he had been so foolish to let Ashley get away. She was probably out in the yard in the dark, poor thing, scared out of her wits. Crying. Huddled behind a bush, bare-foot, and unable to get help for her mother. He wished he had time to look for her. He could take them both back to the barn.

That thought pushed his fears aside, filling him with anticipation again. He knew he didn't have time to look for Ashley. But this would all just add to the drama, wouldn't it?

With Claire Bear taped, he slipped on his back-pack. He debated whether or not to pull off the mask. He didn't really need it now, but he liked it. He'd take it off at the car, before he drove away. He would never want to impede his vision with such a thing.

The Bloodsucker leaned over Claire Bear and lifted her easily into his arms. He could tell she was beginning to come out of it, but when he got her to the car, he'd dose her up again. He kept an extra baggie in the car for just this kind of emergency.

He glanced at the open bedroom window, trying to figure out how to climb back through it with the police chief in his arms. Then he laughed aloud at himself, turned and headed down the hall. Why did he need a window? He'd walk out the front door.

Once Ashley heard the front door close, she waited a full five minutes before moving. She counted as the seconds ticked by, refusing to think about all the bad things that could happen next. Even though she wanted to jump up and run after the man who had taken her mother, she knew that would be stupid at this point. She had to get help. But first, she had to make sure she was safe. What if the creep had walked around the back of the house and was looking in the window right now? She hadn't heard a car start outside. How had he gotten away?

But she wasn't really sure she would hear anything right now, her heart was beating so loud.

At last the five minutes were up and Ashley crept out from under the clothes, half expecting the masked man to pounce on her. He didn't. The room was empty, but she ran for the light switch and flipped it off anyway, afraid he might see her through the window and shoot or something.

Still clutching the kitchen knife, she ran for the window, slammed it shut, and locked it. It wouldn't keep bullets out or Freddy Kruger with an axe, but it would keep a man in a mask out who you were dumb enough to invite in because you had to have a smoke to piss off your mother.

Ashley went to the doorway of her bedroom,

stopped, and listened to the house, listened for any sign he might still be around. She heard just the usual, familiar sounds a house made: the ceiling fans whirring, the drip at the kitchen sink, the frogs croaking in the woods that were loud enough this time of year to even hear inside if you listened carefully. And there was a cricket somewhere in the living room, chirping. Her mother had tried to find it last night and been unsuccessful, and Ashley had secretly been pleased. She didn't like it when her mother squished crickets. Thinking back now, she felt guilty about it. It was kind of childish taking pleasure from such little triumphs, especially now if—

She stopped her thoughts right there and then. If she let herself consider the ifs, she'd dissolve in a helpless puddle right here on the carpet and he would win. And she wasn't going to let him win. She wasn't going to let him kill her mother. Her mother had saved her life and now she was going to save hers.

Ashley took a breath and walked out into the hallway. She listened, then crept in the direction of the living room. She checked the door. Shut. She ran for it and clicked the dead bolt. Then, she walked through the kitchen, toward the laundry room. She caught the scent of her mother's marinara, and swallowed the lump in her throat.

No time for thinking now. Time for action, she told herself.

The back door in the laundry room was locked. She went back to the kitchen and thought for a moment. It was more than two miles to their closest neighbor and the phone was out. She'd have to run there. But what if the guy was outside? Or waiting for her on the road? What if he came after her and tried to run her over with his car? Every bad horror movie she had ever seen flashed through her head.

Then she thought of something. The cell phone! Her mother's cell phone!

But where was it?

She raced down the hallway and into the bedroom. She turned on the light, realized how stupid it was to still be carrying the knife and dropped it on the bed. "Where is it? Where is it?" she muttered out loud.

Not on the dresser. Not on the nightstand. "Mom," Ashley groaned. "Where did you leave it this time? Not at work. Please not at work."

She jerked open a couple of drawers, but the cell phone wasn't there either. Her mother was too neat for that, anyway, too organized. It wasn't in the bedroom.

She ran back down the hall to the kitchen counter. Surely she would have seen the phone if it had been in its charger on the counter, but—not there either. "Damn it!" she shouted in frustration.

The police car?

She looked at the door. That would mean going outside and suddenly she was terrified again.

But what were her choices? The minutes were ticking by. She had to get help.

She ran barefoot for the front door, flipped on the porch light, twisted the dead bolt and threw it open. There was no one there. The yard was quiet. Nothing there but the police cruiser and an old pickup alongside the house that wasn't even tagged anymore.

Ashley stepped out onto the cool cement porch,

then remembered the keys on her mother's dresser. Of course, the cruiser would be locked.

She ran back down the hall, snatched up the keys and went back out the door before she had time to let herself get scared again. By the light of the security lamp in the yard, she fumbled with the keys, found the right one and unlocked the door. She jumped in and clicked the switch on the door to lock herself safely inside. Then she turned the light on overhead. There were manila envelopes on the seat with photos inside. She dumped them onto the floor and when the pictures fell out, she instinctively looked down. They were photos of the women the killer had kidnapped. Photos of the dead women. A sob rose in her throat.

"Got to be tough," she told herself aloud as she knocked the rest of the envelopes on the floor, looking for the phone. "Got to be tough like Mom. I know, you don't want to be her, or anything like her, but right now, Ash . . ."

The phone wasn't there. It just wasn't. She checked the glove compartment. Under the seat.

"Damn it!" She slapped both hands on the steering wheel. Then looked up, hands still on the steering wheel.

She didn't know how to drive . . .

She grabbed the key ring off the seat beside her, hand shaking, and inserted the key. It slipped right in.

She took a deep breath and turned the key. It started right up.

"Come on," she told herself. "You wanted to take driver's ed. This will be a good start."

She put her foot on the brake, pulled the shift toward her the way she had seen her mother do a million times and watched until the little "D" was lit up.

"Here we go," she muttered. She twisted the knob on the end of the signal thingy and the headlights came on, filling the yard with even more light, pushing back the darkness. She eased her foot off the brake and the car crept forward. Her mother usually backed up and then pulled out, but she didn't want to test her backing up skills. She didn't really want to test her driving forward skills, either, but she didn't see any other choice.

The car slowly went around in a circle. One tire hit the sidewalk and she cringed, thinking of the poor little plants in the flower bed she had probably crushed. At last she was moving down the driveway, but the car was going so slow that she could have pushed it faster.

"Gas," she said aloud. She pushed on the pedal and the car shot forward, scaring her. She pulled her foot off and it slowed right down.

"Okay, okay." She pressed the gas pedal again, only evenly this time. The car sped up slowly until she was going twenty-five. Fast for the dirt driveway. At the end, she let her foot up and eased down on the brake. There were no cars coming in either direction.

The neighbors were to the right, two miles, around a sharp curve. Town was five miles to the left. The neighbors were closer, but it was around that curve and she wasn't sure how good she would be at steering. And what if they wouldn't answer the door? They were old; they might not hear her.

She gazed into the darkness in the direction of

town and made her decision. She'd go to the police station.

She buckled her seat belt, took a deep breath, eased off the brake, turned the car, and pushed the gas pedal as it came around. No problem. She speeded up. Before she knew it, she was going forty miles an hour and the telephone poles were whipping by her. Gripping the wheel, her gaze strayed to the switches on the console between the front seats. She knew what most of them were for.

Without hesitating, she hit one button, then the one beside it. The siren on top of the car screamed, and the blue lights flashed. Smiling to herself, she pushed the car up to forty-five.

Chapter Fifteen

Claire woke slowly. Her mind was fuzzy and she was disoriented. She'd had the most bizarre dream . . .

As she became more alert, even before she managed to open her eyes, she realized it hadn't been a dream. Her head hurt like hell and she was slightly nauseated. But that wasn't her biggest problem right now. The fact that her ankles and wrists were tied together was.

She took a moment before she opened her eyes. She knew he was there. He made no sound, but she could feel him. She could also tell that she was in large room, one that smelled of hay. No animals, but it smelled like a barn. Fighting the nausea, she thought back over the list of names of possible suspects, trying to force her mind to begin functioning again. Mayor Tugman had a barn on the rear of his property, behind the old Victorian house he'd inherited. But it was not Morris who watched her now. And Patrolman

McCormick's parents had a chicken farm west of Albany Beach. Though she'd never been out there, she knew they must have barns. But the man she had wrestled in her daughter's bedroom wasn't Ryan. This man was slightly less muscular. More slender.

"I see you're beginning to wake up," came a male voice from in front of her. She could tell he was sitting, too. But still she didn't open her eyes. Sensory overload. She had to stay in control. She had to, if she was going to remain alive long enough to get away.

"Where's Ashley?" she asked, her voice surprisingly strong, considering the circumstances. She could tell now that she was tied to a hard chair at her waist, and her ankles were not only tied . . . no, taped if he was sticking to his MO, to each other but also to the chair.

"Don't worry about her," he said in a voice that she now knew would haunt her the rest of her life. However short or long that might be. "She—"

"Damn it, Alan! Where the hell is my daughter?"

She opened her eyes to see the hospital phlebotomist seated on the bench of an old wooden picnic table about eight feet from her. He was still wearing the stupid ski mask, but she knew it was him. She'd marked his name with a red marker only this morning.

The table he sat at was the kind of table her grandparents had always had, the kind with the benches attached. For a moment, he just stared at her.

She was so angry that if she'd had her Cougar right now, she could have shot him and killed him. Justice and her oath be damned. But, she was also scared . . . not for herself, but Ashley. Had she gotten away? The last thing she remembered was Ashley running out the bedroom door.

"Where is she?" she whispered. She tried to move her feet slightly, then her hands, just to analyze her situation. It wasn't good. She could now see that she was duct-taped to a plastic deck chair that had been covered in a sheet of plastic. She tried not to think about the purpose of the plastic.

The Bloodsucker stared at Claire Bear in disbelief. How did she know who he was? *How?* She'd been unconscious since the fight in Ashley's bedroom, and he'd not yet removed the mask.

He was disappointed that she knew who he was. A little hurt. He felt silly.

He grabbed the bottom of the mask and pulled it over his head to reveal his face. The thing was beginning to get hot and itchy anyway.

He shifted his gaze slowly to look at Claire Bear as he smoothed his close-cut hair; he needed a haircut. She was staring right at him and he knew immediately that she would be different than the others. It was all he could do not to look away. He was glad she was tied up. She scared him just a little, the way she looked at him. Granny had looked at him that way sometimes.

"Tell me where she is," the police chief demanded from between clenched teeth. She didn't seem afraid so much as angry.

"What if I don't want to?"

She looked away, then back at him. "She's my little girl," she said quietly. "Please, Alan."

He didn't like her using his name the way he had liked it when the other women had. Claire's voice was accusing, somehow. Ugly.

He got up from the back bench on the picnic table and walked around, glancing at the tray all set up and ready for Claire. She was a little scary now, but he knew that soon she wouldn't be. Not after the bleeding started.

He took a step toward her and she tipped her head back and screamed, "Fire!" so loud that he covered his ears.

"Don't do that," he yelled. "There's no one around here to hear you, but it hurts my ears."

To his surprise she tilted her head forward again and didn't scream. Now she was trying to twist her hands and loosen the duct tape. The plastic that protected the chair from blood crackled beneath her.

"You won't get away with this," she said.

He smiled, grabbing the duct tape off the table. He hadn't suited up yet, so he had to be careful. "I have."

"Nope. I already knew it was you, Alan. It makes perfect sense; a phlebotomist obsessed with blood. I feel like an idiot that I didn't know sooner." She was quiet for a second, but when he didn't say anything, she went on. "You were watching us from outside the house, weren't you? Didn't you see me on the phone? I was talking to Captain Gallagher. I told him it was you."

"You lie." He smiled. Now that he was up and moving, he wasn't afraid anymore. He knew who was in control here. He was. "You lie because if you had really told Captain Gallagher it was me, he'd be here by now." He pulled a strip of tape away from the roll. "He and his backup cars, and canine units and maybe even a helicopter with a searchlight." He made the roll of duct tape fly in the air

the way he had seen a police search helicopter maneuver in a movie he saw the other night.

She shook her head. "We were waiting until tomorrow. So we could all confer and then come to
the hospital to arrest you there."

He watched her. He knew Claire Bear might try
to trick him so he had to be careful. Granny had
been crafty, too. "I don't believe you."

She somehow managed to shrug. "Just don't say
I didn't tell you so when the canine units arrive. Of
course, if you told me where Ashley is, I might be
able to help you out."

He frowned. "I have no intentions of getting
caught, Claire Bear. I'm not one of *those*." He pulled
the tape out a little farther and began to tape her
forearms together. She wriggled a little, but not that
much. He had done a good job with the taping. His
practice was improving his technique.

"You called me Claire Bear, Alan," she said, giving up the struggle. Realizing she was just wasting
energy she would need later. "Why did you call me
that?"

He lifted his shoulder, feeling a little silly again.
"It's just what I call you," he said softly.

"Well, don't," she snapped.

He yanked hard on the tape, tearing it, hurting
her, but she didn't cry out. He walked back to the
table, dropped the roll of duct tape and reached
for the scalpel. When he walked back to her, she
didn't scream in fear the way the others had. She
didn't even cry.

"Don't do this, Alan," she said. "You have no
reason to do this to me. To Ashley."

"I didn't hurt Ashley." The minute he said it, he
wished he hadn't.

Still, she didn't take her gaze off him. "I've always been nice to you, haven't I? I was never like those other women who maybe said something hurtful. Maybe they turned you down when you just wanted to go out, and maybe get to know them better."

"You don't understand, do you?" he shouted, hearing the buzzing in his head. Now it wasn't just Granny's buzzing. It was hers. It was Claire Bear's.

He lowered the scalpel and made a careful incision.

"Where is she?" Graham banged both palms loudly on the glass wall the night dispatcher sat behind. He probably needed to calm down or he'd end up in a cell in the basement. What good would he do Claire there? "Where is Ashley? I want to see her this minute," he demanded, so angry, so scared, that he couldn't quite catch his breath.

"I'm sorry, Councilman, but—"

At that moment, by luck, Detective Robinson passed on the other side of the glass room. When he spotted Graham and realized what was happening, he signaled to the dispatcher to let Graham in. The door alarm buzzed and Graham twisted the knob, afraid if he wasn't fast enough, he might not get into the back of the police station before the door locked again.

"Detective Robinson," Graham called, sprinting down the hall. "Where's Ashley?"

The detective halted outside the break room. The door was closed. "How'd you hear?"

"Neighbor has a police scanner. She in here?" He laid his hand on the door to the break room.

Robinson muttered under his breath. "Great, another hour and everyone in the state will know. I told them to stay off the radios." He looked at Graham. "She's inside, but I don't know if you should talk to her yet. She's pretty shook up."

"He kidnapped Claire from the house? How'd Ashley get away? How'd she get here?"

Robinson's plump mouth turned up in a half smile. "Chief's got a pretty smart cookie here," he said affectionately. "Phone lines had been cut, no cell phone. She took the police cruiser. Taught herself to drive on the way into town. Lights and all."

Graham smiled grimly, mostly because he knew how proud Claire would be of her daughter. He just hoped she would live to hear the story. "Is this the guy?"

Robinson grimaced. "MO is nothing like his previous hits. He came into the house through a window." He hesitated. "But Ashley says he had a scalpel."

Graham tried not to think about Claire with a madman with a scalpel. He tried not to think about the women found in the Dumpsters. "Let me see Ashley, Detective. Let me talk to her. She might be able to tell me something—"

"Robinson," a man bellowed from down the hall. "I've got troopers on Claire's property. Anything they need to know before they go in that I don't know about? Dog? Booby traps?"

Graham saw Captain Kurt Gallagher coming down the hall. He'd dressed quickly, too, but had taken the extra minute to comb his bed head.

"What the hell is he doing here?" Gallagher

barked when he saw Graham. "There are no *visitors.*"

Graham felt his hackles go up. "Ashley shouldn't be alone," he said.

"And she won't be." He walked up to them. "I'll be in with her."

"But she knows me. We have a rapport," Graham argued.

Gallagher frowned. "She knows, me, buddy. Claire and I dated—"

"Dated. As in the past tense," Graham interrupted, trying hard not to lose his temper. "You're history, and you and I both know it."

Robinson backed up. "Look, fellows—"

"Now let me in to talk with Ashley. Let me see for myself that she's all right and then maybe I can help you figure out where he took her."

"Do I need to call an officer back here to escort you out, Councilman?"

"Captain," Robinson said quietly. "He might have a point. Ashley's been seeing a lot of the Councilman lately, and as best I can tell, no offense intended, but you're not one of Ashley's favorite people anymore."

"What the hell do I care—" Gallagher cut himself off and glanced away.

"Look," Graham said quietly, not caring if Robinson heard. "You don't want to get in a pissing contest with me over this." He met the state policeman's dark gaze. "You just don't," he warned.

Gallagher threw up his hand. "What the hell. Let him in. How can it hurt? Right now, we have nothing. A man with a black mask who appeared out of thin air. For all we've gotten out of the kid so far, it could have been one of the crazy dish-washer's aliens who took her."

Claire held her breath so long that she made herself dizzy, then exhaled in relief. She almost laughed. Alan hadn't cut her. He hadn't cut her. He was just cutting the duct tape around her wrists to free them, now that her arms were bound to-gether just below her elbows.

But he was just getting ready to cut her and she had to do something fast.

"Alan," she said, looking up at him as he tore the tape off her wrists. It smarted, but she ignored the pain. "Alan, tell me why you're doing this. Tell me why you need these women. I just want to un-derstand."

He balled the tape up in his hand, looking down at her. "You're very pretty," he said. He reached out tentatively and brushed her hair with the back of his hand.

"Do I remind you of someone?" she whispered.

He looked away and then when he looked back, his eyes were watery. "Some people don't deserve children. I'm very disappointed in you. Ashley shouldn't be sent to her father's. It's wrong to send her away." His voice caught in his throat with the last words.

Claire's mind was racing. Nothing he was saying was making any sense, but then, he was crazy so what made her think he would? She watched him walk back to the picnic table, throw away the tape and begin to don a plastic jumpsuit. "Is that what happened to you, Alan? Did someone send you away?"

"I don't want to talk about this." He shook his head. "You, of all people, wouldn't understand."

"But I want to, Alan. I want to. I want to understand so that . . . so that I can be a better mother to Ashley. And . . ." She wasn't sure where to go next with this conversation, but any direction was better than standing still. "And I wasn't really going to send her away."

He looked up from slipping plastic covers over his sneakers. "You weren't?"

She shook her head. "Of course not. That's just the kind of thing parents say to scare their children into behaving. I would never send Ashley away, not even to her father." When she said that, she remembered a conversation she'd had years ago with someone. She remembered that Alan had been raised by his grandmother on an old farm outside of town. It was probably where they were right now. She had never heard what happened to his parents; no one had ever said. "But that happened to you, didn't it?" she said, taking a chance.

"I said I don't want to talk about it." He covered his head with a plastic shower cap.

"Tell me, Alan," she whispered trying to wrack her brain, trying to remember all the things she'd read about men like him. "Then you can cut me. Then you can do what you need to with me."

He looked up, obviously confused. "I can?"

"Look, I don't really understand about the blood," she said, flying by the seat of her pants. "But I understand wants. Desires. Needs. And it is the blood of blond-haired blue-eyed women that you need, isn't it?"

He nodded slowly.

She waited.

"My mother left me," he said so quietly that she wasn't even certain what he had said.

"Your mother?" she breathed. He nodded.

"She left you here, didn't she?"

He nodded.

"With your grandmother?"

He flinched and looked away.

"And your mother shouldn't have left you here, should she?" Claire suddenly had an awful feeling. She had read time and time again that serial killers had often been abused as children: sexually, verbally and physically.

He hung his head for a moment, then looked up. "Would you like to see her picture? My mother's?"

What I'd really like to do is get the hell out of here, Claire thought. But she forced herself to focus on Alan again, trying desperately to recall everything she'd read about these killers. "I would," she said, smiling.

"I've never shown anyone before." He unzipped the plastic jumpsuit and slipped his hand into the breast pocket of his long sleeved navy T-shirt. He walked closer, holding out a small, tattered photograph of a woman.

She was so young that a lump rose in Claire's throat. She looked so much like Ashley with her hair blond again that it pained her. But she couldn't think about Ashley right now. She had to believe she had gotten away from Alan as he had hinted. She had to believe that Ashley was getting help at this very moment.

"So this is your mother?" Claire asked, smiling at what was obviously a school picture. From the style of her clothing, it looked like the photo had been taken in the early sixties. She appeared poor and uneducated, if it was possible to see that in a fif-teen- or sixteen-year-old's eyes. "Alan, she's so beau-tiful." She looked up at him, trying not to see the monster he obviously was. "And you have her eyes."

He pressed his lips together, studying the photo himself for a moment before he put it back in his pocket.

"What happened to your mother?" she asked. "Why did you have to come here to live with your grandmother?"

"I don't really know," he answered after a mo-ment. "I guess she couldn't take care of me so she left me with my father's mother."

"Cora Bradford," she offered.

"Don't say her name," he exploded, reaching out and striking her hard across the face. "We don't ever say her name!"

He hit Claire so hard that she felt as if her head might snap off her shoulders. She closed her eyes, fighting the tears. "I'm sorry," she whispered, turn-ing back to him, opening her eyes.

He walked back to the table and picked up the scalpel.

Claire's heart gave a trip. *And things seemed to have been going so well for a few minutes.* "So . . . so your mother left you here," she said, trying to keep her voice steady despite how scared she was. "Did you ever hear from her?"

"No. She just left. I don't know. Went to Califor-nia and became a movie star, maybe." He looked at her. "She wanted to be a movie star."

"I like movies," Claire said.

He smiled hesitantly. "Me, too."

"But she could have just died a drunken drug addict whore in Baltimore, too," he snapped.

She waited, not sure how he wanted her to respond.

"That was what Granny said happened, but I never knew if I could believe her because she said a lot of things."

"She lied a lot, didn't she?" Claire pressed.

He nodded, studying the scalpel in his hand, watching the way the light from the camp lantern he'd placed on the picnic table reflected off the blade.

"How old were you when you came here to live?" she asked as he walked slowly toward her.

"Four."

"And you never saw your mother again?"

He shook his head.

"I'm sorry, Alan."

He lifted his head, meeting her gaze. "I almost think you are." He grabbed one of her wrists. "Now we have to get started."

Claire watched stunned as he lowered the scalpel and with the precision of a well-trained hand, split the pale flesh at her wrist. It barely even hurt. And then the blood began to flow in earnest.

Graham opened the door and walked in, making an effort to appear calm. Ashley was seated cross-legged the end of a beat-up couch, barefoot in a pair of shorts and a T-shirt.

"Hey," Graham called.

She looked up.

"Heard you got caught taking your mom's wheels for a spin." He shook his head. "Can't wait to hear the explosion over that one."

Ashley wiped at her teary eyes, but smiled at the

same time. "Can you hear her, now? I'll be on restriction until I'm a grandmother."

"Bet the flashing lights were cool, though." He sat beside her on the couch. "So, you have any idea how we can figure out who the man was?"

She looked at him. "You're asking what *I* think?" She touched her chest with a pointed finger.

He shrugged. "Everyone body else out there is just guessing. No reason why you can't, too. Someone is bound to be right."

Ashley looked down at the floor. "It's him, isn't it?"

He saw no reason to lie. "Probably."

"So . . . didn't the police have some suspects?" she asked. "I mean, I know she thought it was Chain, which it wasn't. But he wasn't the only one she suspected, was he?"

Graham tried to calm his pounding heart. He needed some blood flow to his brain. Needed to think. "You get a look at this guy at all?"

She shook her head. "He was wearing a mask."

"No tattoos? Anything like that?"

Again, she shook her head. "Khaki pants. A long sleeve navy blue T-shirt. Just a guy."

"Did he speak to you?"

She nodded.

"But you didn't recognize his voice?"

"No," she said. Then she hesitated. "Well, kind of. Like I know I've heard his voice before, but I couldn't place it."

The door opened and Patrolman McCormick, dressed in civilian clothes, walked in. Graham was relieved to see him. It was a name to cross off the list.

"I brought you a Coke," he told Ashley. "You want something to eat?"

"No. Thanks." She accepted the soda.

"I'm going to go out to your house if you think you're okay here," McCormick said, hands stuffed into his jean pockets. He wasn't the tough cop Graham had seen before. He seemed like a concerned friend right now.

"I'm all right. I just want you to find my mother." She wiped her nose with the back of her hand. "Before . . ." She didn't finish the thought that was on everyone's mind.

Graham rubbed her shoulder, then let his hand fall. Ashley was holding up well, but he didn't want to push it. If he showed too much emotion, he was afraid she would lose control of hers and right now both of them needed to focus. "I'll stay here with her."

"We sent a car for her grandparents. They'll be here soon. They can take her home to their place."

"I'm not going to Grandma and Grampa's," Ashley said firmly. She popped the tab on the soda can. "I'm staying here. I have to stay here and help you."

"Look, Ashley," McCormick began. "The best thing you can do for your mother right now is—"

"I'm the only one who saw him," she cut in stubbornly. "I'm the best chance you have."

The strength of the teenager's conviction obviously took the officer by surprise. He didn't know what to say.

"I'll handle this," Graham told McCormick, holding up his hand.

"Right. Well . . ." McCormick backed out the door, passing Gallagher, who was on his way into the break room.

"We've got state troopers in the house, Ashley. Now if you could go over with me what happened again, just so I'm sure I have all the details." Gallagher pulled up a chair at the table in the center of the room and slipped a pen from the pocket of his wrinkled oxford shirt. "Maybe we can piece this all together."

"Have you started picking up the suspects on Claire's list?" Graham asked, impatient because there seemed to be a lot of mulling around going on in the station, but not a lot of action.

"We're sending out cars shortly, but—"

"He's got her now, Gallagher." Graham rose, gesturing at the floor with his finger. "That means she's still alive. He never kills them right off—"

"You want lighten up here, buddy?" Gallagher cut his eyes at Ashley.

Graham looked at the teen, then back at the cop. "What, you're going to pretend what's going on here, isn't?" He turned back to Ashley, the bruise on her cheek had not gone unnoticed. "How did you get away?"

"He came into my room and tried to put that stuff over my face, and then Mom came and she jumped on him and I ran." Her voice was shaky, but she continued. "Then I hid under this big pile of clothes on my bedroom floor until he was gone."

Graham glanced back at Gallagher. "She fought off the killer; she knows what's going on here, and after what she's been through, she deserves to be treated with a little respect."

"We don't use kids—"

"I'd say Ashley is pretty much past being a kid. At least after tonight, she is, wouldn't you say, *buddy*?"

Ashley smirked and looked away.

"Look." Gallagher set down his pen. "We let you in here as a courtesy. To Ashley. To Claire. You were never a part of the investigation and you aren't now. So, you can either sit here quietly and be supportive of this young lady or you can—"

"Have you seen her new list?" Graham broke in. "The one from this week, since she's been investigating hospital employees?"

Gallagher spoke as if it pained him. "We briefly discussed her hospital investigation earlier this evening,"

"But she didn't give you any names?" Graham thought for a moment. "You look in her office for this week's notes? She keeps them on yellow legal pads." He used his hands to show the police captain the size of the notepads.

"Already been in there. Old stuff."

"And there were pictures in her cruiser." Ashley wrinkled her nose. "Pretty gross."

Graham smiled sympathetically. "Did your mom bring her briefcase home this weekend?"

"Sure. I guess." Ashley shrugged.

"I bet the notes are in there," Graham told Gallagher as he got out of his seat. "Come on, Ash." He jerked his head in the direction of the door.

"Where the hell do you think you're going?"

Ashley was already off the couch. She set her Coke can on the table beside Gallagher's notebook as she passed him. "We're going back to my house. Graham knows how my mom's sick mind works. If he and I both look at her notes, maybe we can help figure out who she might have thought it was."

Graham held the door open for her. "You know, it's got to be a hospital employee. She got too close and he went after her."

Captain Gallagher rose from the chair. "Ashley, you can't go with him. And you." He pointed to Graham. "I want you out of here, buddy."

"Going," Graham said, lifting his hand in a wave.

"You know, I don't have to let you into her house," Gallagher called, following them down the hall.

"I know you don't." Graham glanced over his shoulder as he waited for Ashley to catch up to him. "But that would be stupid, wouldn't it, Captain? Because what we all want here, is to get Claire back alive."

Chapter Sixteen

"Claire? Can you hear me?"

She woke slowly, drifting in that place between sleep and consciousness that was soft and warm and pleasant. That place where you felt like you were floating.

"Claire?"

She could feel Alan holding one of her wrists, applying pressure. He rubbed her shoulder as if he were a concerned friend. "I'm sorry. That's never happened before."

Recollections of the last few hours floated through her head. She was hoping she was dreaming. That happened sometimes; she'd wake in a dream to find that she was still dreaming. But, as she lifted her weighted eyelids and connected with the voice, she knew there was no such luck in this case.

"There you go, that's right. Don't leave. Not yet. Gosh, I'm really sorry," he said anxiously. "I never make them that deep. I don't . . . know . . . what happened."

She tried to focus on Alan's face, thinking how bizarre his words were. He was apologizing, for God's sake. He had intended to slit both her wrists, but apparently the first cut had been deeper than he intended. She'd passed out. Maybe from blood loss, but more likely her fear mixed with her quick drop in blood pressure had done it.

"Alan," she whispered.

"That's right. That's right. I'm right here." He rubbed her hands between his gloved ones.

The concern for her in his voice surprised her. The last thing she remembered was him screaming at her like a madman. Calling her Granny, or calling to his grandmother. Alan was a complicated man and the circumstances that had led him to this place in his life were probably complex enough to fill a psychiatrist's best-selling book. Somewhere in that complexity maybe there was a way to save her own life.

"You don't want me to go?" she said, fluttering her eyelashes, purposely pretending to be drowsier than she really was.

"No." He sounded like a little boy. The madman she had seen a short time ago was gone. "Don't go yet."

She remembered what the FBI agents had said about these killers fulfilling fantasies. She still didn't know what his fantasy was, but she knew that the profiler had been right about his wanting to form relationships with the blond women before he killed them. She was no psychologist, but she could guess it was his relationship with his teenage mother that he was trying to reproduce. A relationship he had fantasized about, but that had never truly occurred because she had abandoned him when he was still so young.

She also recognized that when he had cut her, a few minutes ago—an hour ago—she didn't know how much time had passed—he'd been angry with his grandmother and probably his mother, too. It had to be an emotion he'd long been repressing. He was one sick cookie.

"Alan, I think you let me bleed too long," she whispered, a plan forming in her head as she watched him through a veil of lashes. The plan had no real direction yet, but she didn't let that small detail stop her.

"I know. I know. It doesn't look like that much, though." He kicked the sawdust, stained with her blood, with his shoe that was covered in a plastic bootie. "I'm usually more careful than this. I don't usually make mistakes, but I guess I'm tired." He brushed his forehead with the back of his hand, still holding a white hand towel stained red. He'd been using it to staunch her blood flow, apparently.

"You've been working long hours at the hospital," she said. "I understand you're an exceptional employee, from what your supervisors say." She rolled her head back, opening her eyes a little farther. Her neck hurt like hell, more than her wrists, and she really needed to sit up and stretch, but this wasn't the time to be wussing out. She had to play the game—a game she didn't know any of the rules to—and play it well if she was going to walk out of here. If she wasn't going to end up in a Dumpster on the boardwalk.

"Mr. McGary said that?" Alan's voice was a mixture of wonder and pride.

She nodded, letting her eyes drift shut again.

"Claire? Wait—don't go back to sleep."

"Alan, I'm really tired. I . . ." She hesitated long enough to make him lean closer with apprehension. If her hands had been free, she could have strangled him.

"Claire?"

"Maybe if we talk," she said. "Maybe that will keep me awake."

"Yes, yes, we can talk. It's what I like to do, really. Talk with my guests."

"Is that why you bring the women here, Alan? To talk to you?"

"Sure. I just want to talk. Would you like a drink of water? I have some bottled water." He pointed to the picnic table that had been set very precisely with all the items he deemed necessary to bleed a woman to death.

She wanted to refuse the water, out of pride, but she knew that was silly. She had lost blood, how much she didn't know, but she was light-headed. Hydration might be important. "I am thirsty . . . do you have any juice, Alan?"

"Orange juice, yes. In the kitchen." He pointed beyond the ring of light that had become her world. Then he looked back, hesitating. "But I can't leave you. That would be silly."

She half smiled and let her head roll forward. "Think I'll run away?" She tried to make it sound like she was teasing.

Honestly, she didn't know what she would do if he did leave her alone. She was duct-taped to a chair, for God's sake. She'd have to get her forearms loose first, to get herself out of the chair, and the tape was pretty tight. But it was also very warm tonight and she was sweating. The adhesive might loosen up with the dampness, if she was lucky.

He stood where he was, obviously contemplating what to do. She could tell he wanted desperately to please her, even for her to like him; he also didn't want to risk *losing* her. She held her breath, praying.

"I'm sorry," he said as he finally exhaled. "I just can't leave you."

She closed her eyes for a second, fighting a flutter of panic. She couldn't allow such a small defeat to overwhelm her. "Some water would be nice, then," she said.

He picked up a bottle from the picnic table, twisted off the lid, and brought it to her. He tipped it and she drank several mouthfuls. A little slid out of the corner of her mouth and she moved her head slightly, hoping it might drip on her forearms and the tape.

"Some more?" he asked.

She shook her head. When he turned his back to return the bottle to the table, to the exact place where he'd found it, she let some water trickle out of her mouth. It ran down her arm and pooled at the tape.

"What do you like to talk about?" Claire asked.

"I don't know." He walked around to the far side of the table and sat down, resting his elbows on the table.

"Well, what did you talk about with Marissa and Brandy? The others?"

"I said I don't want to talk about them." His face grew stony. "We don't talk about them. Now they're gone. They were here with me, but now they're gone."

They're gone, all right, disposed of, the way all women deserve, Claire thought. But she knew that dwelling on that subject wasn't going to get her anywhere. Right now, she just needed to get him to talk. About anything. She needed a chance to work on the tape. "You said you like movies." She closed her eyes again, keeping her voice low and weak.

"I do."

"What have you seen this summer? That action movie with the guy whose name sounds like gasoline, or something?"

"I don't go to the movies. I like TV," Alan told her. "Movies, documentaries. I have a satellite dish so I get a hundred ninety-six stations."

"I like old movies. Ashley and I—" She let her voice catch in her throat, which wasn't hard to do right now, and she closed her eyes and was quiet.

"You and Ashley, yes?" Alan said, nervous again. He was falling for it.

"Is she all right, Alan?" she whispered. "I think I would feel better, stronger, if I knew she was all right."

"She's fine, I'm sure," he said quickly. "She climbed out her window and ran away. I'm certain she's fine. I mean, I know she's upset, but . . ."

Claire pressed her lips together, saying a prayer of thanks to God. If she didn't get out of this, at least Ashley was safe.

"Claire?"

She lifted her head and opened her eyes. "Did you watch a lot of movies when you were a boy?" she asked, trying to steer the conversation back toward the root of his psychosis. Obviously it had to do with his mother abandoning him, but there had to be more. "Is that what your grandmother and you did together? I used to love it when—"

"What we did together," he snapped angrily. Talk about a Jekyll and Hyde trick. One minute he was soft-spoken and kind, the next, a man with frightening rage. "We never *did* anything together. She hardly ever let me watch TV and then it was only to see those crazy TV evangelists."

"So she was a religious woman."

"Claimed to be," he scoffed. "Cora's father was some kind of preacher in Arkansas or something. Bunch of damned superstitious hillbillies."

"Superstitious?" She opened her eyes a little farther, watching him carefully. "What do you mean?"

"It doesn't matter," he said softly, staring at his arms crossed in front of him. "It doesn't matter," he repeated.

She watched him scratch his forearm. She'd pushed a button again; she just wasn't sure what button or where it was taking her. She backed off to give him time to recuperate. "Tell me what your favorite shows on TV are."

"I like the movie marathons." He rubbed the other forearm through the plastic jumpsuit.

"Me, too. Which ones?"

"Last week was bank robber week on TNT." He grew more animated. "You see any of those?"

"I think I might have caught the tail end of *Bonnie and Clyde*," she lied. Actually, she'd been flipping through the channels trying to find out if it was going to rain the following day and had seen the movie go by on the screen.

"I saw that one! There was one on Patty Hearst, too. Did you realize that she didn't wear a mask when she walked into that bank?"

She tried to slide her arms back and forth a couple of times, hoping he was too preoccupied with the conversation and his itchy arms to notice. "Guess I didn't really think about it."

He was quiet for a minute as he rested his chin on his forearm. He did look tired. Beyond tired—exhausted. Like a man whose demons were keeping him awake at night.

"What other movie marathons have you seen?" she asked.

"Umm . . . one about vampires."

The minute he said it, she thought of Brandy and the bite on her neck. Had he gotten the idea off the television? And the mask he had worn into her house . . . was Patty Hearst responsible? It was so incredibly bizarre a thought, that it was quite possible.

"What else?"

"I don't know. Don't remember." He rubbed his arm viciously.

She lifted her head, bringing it upright and as she did it, she tried to slide one arm forward as hard but as slowly as she could. She could have sworn it shifted slightly. "What's the matter, Alan? Get into some poison ivy or something?"

He closed his eyes for a second, and she couldn't help think what a nice-looking thirty-three-year-old man he was. How ordinary in appearance. It was hard to believe, looking at him, that he worked in the hospital day after day, providing excellent, compassionate health care, *and* killed seven women . . . was shooting for eight.

"Yeah," he said, rising suddenly to pace. "It must be poison ivy."

Concerned that he had become agitated again, Claire let her head roll back and she closed her eyes. A full minute passed before he seemed to notice. "Claire?" he said. "Claire, I thought you said you wanted to talk. I thought you said that you felt like talking."

She lifted her eyelids halfway. "Sorry, I'm just a little sleepy."

He walked over, his face lined with concern as he checked out her wrist wound. The more deeply cut one had begun to bleed pretty heavily again. She'd probably done it, sliding her arms back and forth. The sight of the blood pooling on the plastic shower curtain he had considerately placed across her lap made her suddenly woozy, and she was forced to close her eyes in earnest, this time to stop the barn from spinning around her.

"Claire." He ran back to the picnic table and brought the white towel, now stained with red blood, to hold against her wrist. "Let's talk."

"Okay," she breathed, kind of wishing for a break at this point. Now that she knew Ashley was safe, her determination to get away didn't feel quite so strong. But a part of her mind knew that was just the blood loss talking, and the lull in adrenaline. She wanted to live for Ashley. She wanted to live to put this sick bastard in jail. "Tell me about the other women," she said.

"I don't really want to talk about that."

"Okay," she whispered and closed her eyes again.

"But . . . but we can if you want. I mean, what harm can it do now, right?"

She smiled, her eyes closed.

"What do you want to know?" He released the pressure on her wrist. "You want some more water?"

"Water would be good." The minute he turned his back, she shifted both arms. The tape wasn't really loosening, but the adhesive wasn't sticking to her skin the way it had been. There was definitely more give. "Did you find them all at the hospital, Alan?"

He came back toward her with the water bottle. Nodded. "Everyone except Phoebe. She was a mistake. I thought she was Marcy that night, but you knew that, didn't you? You already figured that out. Here, drink."

She took a couple of sips, feeling a certain amount of pride in the fact that she had concluded that Phoebe Matthews had never been his target. "Can I ask why you killed them?" She bent her head to drink again, figuring what the hell, he might just tell her.

"I . . . I didn't kill them. They just died."

"When they bled to death," she bit out before she could stop herself.

He was quiet for a minute. "That wasn't a very nice thing to say."

She didn't answer.

"And I didn't want . . . I don't want to hurt anyone. I really feel bad about Marissa and Brandy."

"What do you mean?" She studied his face. "Oh,

you mean the way you hit them?" She hesitated. "Like you hit me?"

"I'm sorry." He lowered his head, shaking it in shame.

"Alan, did someone hit you when you were a child?"

He turned away from her, taking the water bottle with him. "Granny was more creative than applying a switch to a boy's backside."

His bitterness and pain were undeniable and against her will, her heart went out to him. She knew it was crazy, she knew child abuse was no excuse to grow up to be a woman killer, but the idea of any child being abused always upset her. "I'm sorry," she said. And despite her hatred of him, she was.

"Yeah, well. That's the way the cookie crumbles sometimes, doesn't it?"

"Tell me some more about your mother." Claire watched him return to the picnic table and sink onto the bench. "Did she know your—that you were being abused?"

"I told you," he said, his tone tense again. He rested his forehead on his hand. His voice was muffled because his head was down. "She never came back. She never knew crap. She left me here with that . . . that . . ."

He didn't finish his sentence and Claire was quiet for a minute. They were both quiet. She could see now that his eyes were drifting shut. He was worn out, perhaps not just from the physical strain of the long day, but maybe from the emotional stress she had pushed on him.

With a little surge of adrenaline, Claire slid her arms back and forth again.

*   *   *

"What the hell are they doing?" Graham asked as he and Ashley cut across the front yard that was filled with both Albany Beach and state police cars. There were dogs, too. Two of them, barking wildly on the end of their master's leashes.

"Checking tire tracks," Gallagher explained, following them toward the house. "Just on the outside chance he'd driven up the lane."

"I told you, there was no car here," Ashley argued.

"I know. We check anyway." The captain hooked his thumb in the direction of the woods. "Dogs followed a scent through the woods to an old logging road. He had a car parked there. Trail gets lost once he hits the pavement, though."

On the front porch, Graham stepped back to let Ashley pass. Every light in the house was on and there were police officers in uniforms and civilian clothes taking fingerprints and photographs.

"Found her briefcase, Captain," McCormick called from the dining room. "Want me to open it?"

"Come on," Graham told Ashley. "Let's see what we can make of your mother's scribbling."

Chapter Seventeen

Claire watched through her lashes as Alan rested his head on his folded arms on the picnic table and let his eyes drift shut. "Just five minutes," he murmured, speaking as much to himself as to her. He thought she had passed out again.

Truthfully, she was close to it. While his attention had stopped the heavy flow of blood from her left wrist, it was oozing enough to continue to puddle in her lap on the plastic. She was beginning to become concerned that she might pass out again. Her head was so woozy that she was having trouble keeping her thoughts together.

As she worked her arms back and forth, ignoring the pain the friction of the tape was causing, she tried to stay mentally active. She studied the old barn, thinking it would have been a wonderful place to play as a little boy, had it not been for the grandmother and the abuse, which she could only imagine Alan had suffered. How difficult for a child to be born to a young, uneducated mother, then abandoned with an abusive relative. How could he have not grown up warped in some way?

But he was smart. That was obvious by how his crimes had played out. It was also obvious from the set-up here in the barn.

She continued to work her arms back and forth, and she studied what she could see in the ring of light from the lantern. Alan had covered the dirt floor of the barn with sawdust, to be able to easily dispose of any blood that fell, obviously. It could be raked up, burned. The makeshift wall around the chair, covered in plastic sheeting, was clever, too. It would stop any blood spatter, and afterward, it too, could be burned, destroying any evidence. The only blood trace that might possibly be left behind would be on the scalpel, but maybe, if a person boiled it, or sent it through a disinfecting machine, the evidence would be gone. Better yet, a person could easily dispose of a bloody scalpel in any of those red boxes in the hospital.

She glanced at Alan whose shoulders were now rising and falling rhythmically. The plastic cap that covered his head had shifted and now a tuft of neatly trimmed brown hair was exposed. She gazed down at the damp, dark sawdust at her feet as she continued to work the tape around her forearms.

She wondered if this was all Alan did with the blood . . . let it drip onto the floor. She didn't know what the other possibilities were . . . saving it, cooking with it. She thought of his vampire movies. Drinking it? She was curious, but not enough so to want to wake him and ask him.

She smiled grimly at her own sick humor.

And why was he fixated on the blood? Had he

seen a terrible accident as a child and been marred by the sight of blood? In one of the reports on psychotics she had read, there had been a case of a man who had been repulsed by the sight of his mother's menstrual blood as a young, schizophrenic teen and had gone on a killing spree at eighteen, trying to rid the world of all the women in his household and their blood. He'd killed two teenage sisters and his mother before committing suicide.

A wave of dizziness and nausea passed over Claire and she closed her eyes, trying to will the earth and the barn to stop rotating on its axis, at least for a few minutes. Her arms were definitely looser now; she could feel the tape riding up and down on her sweaty arms that had been removed of all their hair with adhesive. Her left wrist had also begun to bleed in earnest again, probably because of her movement.

She glanced at Alan again. He was sound asleep.

Please, please God, she mouthed silently. *I know you hate bargaining Methodists, but please get me through this and I swear I'll stop skipping Sunday morning service. Please just let me live long enough to get that tattoo off Ashley's butt.*

She smiled to herself at the thought of her daughter. She was still pretty angry about the tattoo, but who couldn't love a fifteen-year-old who had fought Alan the way Ashley had? How could you not love a girl with the good sense to run when her mother told her to?

Claire stopped moving her arms for a second, enjoying the peaceful lull. She was so tired that a quick nap seemed like a good idea. Maybe a few minutes of rest would give her the energy she would need to get herself out of here . . .

Claire felt her eyelids close and she sat there for a minute, head hung loosely forward. Then she jerked her head up. "Come on," she told herself under her breath. "You've got to get out of here. Ashley needs a mother. She still needs you."

Taking a deep breath, ignoring the pain that burned along her forearms, Claire gave her right arm a good shove. Her left arm shot back, popping herself in the boob, and it smarted so badly that she had to clamp her mouth shut to keep from crying out.

She ripped her arms loose and looked down through tears to see a wide loop of silver duct tape around her wrist.

Oh, God, oh, God, thank you, she screamed inside her head. And who said there were no more miracles? Her arms were free. Now she just had to get the tape off her bare ankles. She went to lean forward, letting the plastic sheet on her lap drift to the floor. She froze as it made a crackling sound as it hit the floor, but Alan didn't stir.

The tape around her waist prevented her from reaching her ankles . . . that and the wooziness that was back again. She felt like she was drunk, only she hadn't had the pleasure of even a nip of vodka.

Okay, okay, she told herself, keeping one eye on Alan. Keep your head up. Get the tape off from around your waist, then tackle the feet. She dug the edge of the tape on the left side of her stomach, trying to cradle her bleeding wrist against her chest. The tape started to pull away from itself but it made such a loud sound that she froze at once.

Alan lifted his head, turned it and laid it down again, eyes still closed.

Claire breathed again. Okay, so tearing the tape wasn't going to work. She looked down at the way he had taped her into the chair, fighting the dizziness. The tape was around her T-shirt, not her skin. The easiest, quietest solution was to wiggle out of the gray police academy shirt.

But she didn't have anything on under it . . .

Realizing what a ridiculous thought that was, she rolled her eyes. Then regretted it. Just the simple motion made her dizzy again.

OK, off with the shirt, she told herself. *Strip for him, baby.*

She took one last look at Alan. From this point out, it would be obvious what she was doing. If he woke, he'd catch her. He'd pick up that shiny scalpel placed just so on the plastic lunch counter tray, and he'd kill her.

Claire shook her hand, letting the loop of tape fall to the damp ground, and then began to pull her arms inside the T-shirt. It was tricky with the tape and the chair and there was very little room to maneuver, but she was soon resting against her shirt, topless. She closed her eyes for a minute, catching her breath. She was sweating hard. Now, all she had left was her feet and then she'd be free.

Surprisingly, the feet were the easiest of all. Alan hadn't been as careful as he should have been. But why did he need to tape her feet tightly to the chair? She hadn't had a way to reach them.

Claire dug at the tape, with her left hand, where it had adhered to her bare skin, and in less than five minutes she was sitting in the chair, free.

Now what? she thought, a little shocked that she didn't just spring up. But she knew she had to plan carefully. One sound and he would wake and in her weak state she'd be no match for Alan in a wrestling match. Not this time.

Claire rose slowly, and when she shifted her full weight to her feet, pain shot through them. She wobbled, but she didn't fall. Holding her left wrist against her bare breast, she slid one foot forward. The sawdust, damp and clumpy with her blood, felt gross under her bare feet. She slid the other one forward.

The barn was spinning around her. She felt like she was going to be sick. She took another sliding step, easing forward toward the picnic table where Alan slept, her gaze fixed on the only decent weapon in sight, the scalpel he had used to cut her.

Time seemed to drag. You would have thought she was running a marathon.

She lifted her foot and brought it down, realizing a second too late that she had stepped on the plastic sheeting that had been on her lap. The crackle was earth-shattering.

Alan stirred.

She halted. Held her breath.

After a moment she carefully slid one foot and then the other left, circumnavigating the bloody plastic. Another three feet and she would be there. She thrust her right hand out in anticipation of the feel of the cool steel at her fingertips.

Another foot. She stretched, swallowing the nausea that rose in her throat. Her fingers closed over the scalpel's handle.

"You shouldn't have done that."

Claire's head snapped up just in time to see Alan lunge at her across the wooden picnic table. She slashed at him and the sharp tip of the weapon caught the sleeve of his jumpsuit and shirt and tore a long, clean slice. The plastic and fabric fell away revealing hideous red scarring up and down his entire forearm.

Claire tried to pull back, but she was so weak. Her reflexes weren't fast enough and when Alan swung his other arm, he clipped her elbow and the scalpel fell on the picnic table between them. She screamed with every ounce of strength she had left and instead of trying to pull back, in a last ditch effort to save her life, she threw herself forward on top of him.

"Where is it? Where is it?" Graham said, growing more frantic by the moment as the clock on the dining room wall seemed to tick louder and louder.

For two hours he and Ashley and Captain Gallagher had been pouring over Claire's notes. There were three folders of information she had gathered on more than seventy hospital employees. There were pages of basic personal and professional information on each person. But there were also little cryptic notes written in the margins. Doodles.

Graham lifted his head from the legal pad he was looking at for the second time. Ashley sat across from him, her head cradled in her arm as she flipped through another pad of paper.

"You should let me call your grandmother back," he said quietly to her. "You should go home with her and get some sleep."

Ashley shook her head, stoically. "It's here," she

said, not lifting her gaze from the paper as she flipped the page. "We just have to find it."

Graham glanced at Gallagher seated to his right at the head of the table. Gallagher looked up.

"Can you just start paying a visit to the men on this list?"

"All of them?" Gallagher asked. "What, send patrol cars around? Knock on doors, wake people up and ask if they happen to have the town's police chief held prisoner?"

Graham didn't appreciate the cop's sarcasm, but he got the point. And as much as he hated to admit, Gallagher was right. For right now, this was the best they could do. He hesitated and then lowered his head over the pad of paper in front of him again. "Come on, Claire," he said under his breath. "Talk to me."

Claire screamed as she threw herself almost into Alan's arms, taking him completely by surprise. Her arms felt like lead. Nothing seemed real as she struggled with him, trying to prevent him from reaching the scalpel that was just to the side of her left knee.

"No," Alan cried. "It's not supposed to be this way."

Her bare chest pressed against his, her head almost on his shoulders, locked with him in a bizarre lover's embrace, Claire managed to get her right hand up. She shoved the heel of her hand against his face and her fingernail snagged on the lower rim of his eye socket. Alan howled in pain as she tried to gouge out the eye, still holding him just out of reach of the scalpel on the table.

Her left wrist was bleeding profusely and the arm seemed almost lifeless, but there . . . right there next to her knee was the scalpel.

With every last bit of strength and determination she possessed, she shoved her right arm down and across her body, grabbed the scalpel and wheeled it upward. She meant to hit his chest, but he drew back at the last instant, her arm continued to travel upward, her wrist turned, and the tip of the razor-sharp scalpel found soft flesh at the base of his neck. Instinctively, Claire drew the instrument sideways, effectively slitting his throat.

Alan's eyes went wide as he tumbled backward off the table, pulling Claire down with him.

There was blood everywhere, and she drew back in repulsion as his head hit the dirt floor and gave a little bounce. Still clutching the bloody scalpel, she had landed straddling him and she now scrambled to get off him.

She fell to his left and frantically tried to push away from him, her left arm hanging at her side.

Alan made no attempt to come after her. In fact, he didn't move and after a moment, she pulled herself up on her knees, passing the scalpel to her right hand. If he came after her, she'd cut him again.

Alan lay on his back, staring up.

For a second, Claire thought he was dead. Then she saw his chest rise slowly. Fall. He never moved a muscle, but shifted his gaze to meet hers. His eyes filled with tears. "I'm bleeding," he gurgled.

Bleeding out was the truth of the matter. Blood was gushing from his neck. She'd hit his jugular.

"I'm bleeding," he repeated in horror as he lifted his hand to cover the gaping wound on his throat. "Please don't let me *bleed* to death. Anything but that."

Claire stared down at him, her eyes filling with tears.

She knew she needed to run. Out of the barn. To the house. To the car she knew must be parked just outside.

Instead, still clutching the scalpel, she rose and grabbed the white towel off the picnic table and dropped to her knees again beside Alan. The pool of dark, wet blood beneath him was growing wider by the moment.

"I'm bleeding," he moaned, tears running down his cheeks. "Please don't let her do it." He was rocking his body. "Please don't let her kill me this way."

He was so weak he could barely move, yet he continued to jiggle like a child.

She set the scalpel down, knowing she had nothing further to fear from Alan Bradford, and she pressed the towel to his neck. "Don't let who?" she asked.

"Granny." He fixed his gaze on her. He had such a frightened look on his face that she had to choke back a sob. "She cut me. Here." He raised his arm, then let it fall.

She looked down at the awful red and white lumpy scars running the length of his forearm that she had revealed when she cut his sleeve. "She did this to you?" Claire whispered.

He nodded.

She bit back her tears. "Why?" she breathed.

"Blood has ill humors."

"What?" She leaned forward, needing for some reason, to hear. To understand.

"She always said that blood had ill humors. Bleeding was a way to rid the body of evil spirits, of sickness." His breathing had turned ragged. His eyelids were beginning to flutter. "Of evil."

She pressed her lips together, fighting her own emotions. He was pathetic. "She bled you, Alan?"

He closed his eyes, then opened them in affirmation. "She didn't understand blood, but I do. I understand the power of it."

He bled women for their *power?*

"She . . . she never wanted me." He was rambling now, his eyes drifting shut again.

Claire couldn't stop the bleeding. The towel was soaked. Useless. She was covered in his blood.

"I was a burden to her. A *bloodsucker* who lived off the goodwill of others. Who lived off her. That's what she called me. The Bloodsucker. *Stupid. Worthless,*" he muttered as if still hearing her accusations in his head.

Claire closed her eyes for a moment. "Alan, I have to ask you something." She took a breath, not knowing why she had to know, but she did. "Their blood. Did you ever do anything with their blood? Save it?" She hesitated. "Drink it?"

He managed to make a face of repulsion. "No. Of course not. What kind of monster do you think I am?"

She was afraid to answer. Instead, she rubbed his shoulder. "Alan, what your grandmother did was wrong. It was criminal."

"Lousy, worthless bloodsucker," he mouthed.

"Alan, you were just a little boy," Claire argued, pushing his hair away from his eyes. "It wasn't your fault your mother left you there. It wasn't your fault your grandmother had to take care of you."

"Not my fault," he murmured.

He was going fast now. Claire knew she couldn't just sit here and watch him die. She glanced up at the barn around her, then looked down at him. "Alan, I need to get to a phone so I can call an ambulance. So someone can help you. Is there a phone in the house?"

"No!" His eyes flew open and one hand flopped as he tried to reach up to her. They were on the very edge of the circle of lamplight and his face was partly in shadows. "Please don't leave me," he begged, sobbing. "Don't let me lie here and bleed to death, alone. She left me to bleed to death alone in my room." He squeezed his eyes shut, fighting the sob that wracked his body.

Claire didn't know what to do. She hated to leave someone in such mental agony, but if there was any chance at saving his life, she had to get help. She left the soaked towel on his neck and picked up his hand as she rose to a crouch. "I'll just run into your house, call 911, and then come right back to you. I swear I will. I'll stay right here with you until the ambulance comes."

He rolled his head from side to side, his eyes closing, tears running down his face. "Don't let me bleed to death," he mumbled. "Just kill me now. Kill me now."

"You know I can't do that." She let go of his hand and stood up.

Claire walked out of the circle of light toward the far wall where she found a door. She lifted the latch and stepped out into the warm, humid night. To her left, less than a hundred yards away, was a ramshackle white farmhouse, a light burning on the back porch. The grass tickled her bare feet as she hurried toward the light. She was too weak to run.

Halfway there, a brown mutt, asleep on the porch, lifted his head. Spotting her, he got up, went down the wooden stairs and trotted toward her.

"Hey, boy," she said, trying to judge if he was friendly or not. *Wouldn't that be a hell of a thing*, she thought. *To survive being kidnapped by a serial killer only to be mauled to death by Fido . . .*

But the dog just circled her and then fell into place at her side, her own personal escort.

Claire used the rail to pull herself up the stairs. She was dizzy and light-headed and dangerously close to fainting, but she pushed ahead. She entered the house through a small laundry room. It was pin-neat and smelled of damp plaster and fabric softener. The room emptied into the kitchen which was also neat and looked like something you would see in a movie set in the thirties or forties. Faded, patterned wallpaper, cracked yellowed linoleum. A wooden table with four wooden chairs. The phone was an old dial wall unit on the far side of the room.

Claire lifted the receiver, punched the three digits, ignoring the fact that everything she touched turned bloody. Waiting for the call to go through, she leaned against the wall and slid down until she was seated on the old floor.

"Nine-one-one, what is your emergency?" came a clear, professional voice.

It was Katie Duchet. She'd worked for the county for years as a 911 dispatcher. Claire could hear the New Orleans accent in her perfect diction.

"This is Chief Claire Drummond of the Albany police," she said. It took every bit of energy she could muster to talk loud enough for Katie to hear her.

"Claire?" There was a sound on the other end of the line. "I'm sorry, Chief Drummond. It's just that—"

"I know." She smiled. "Bet you heard a few people are looking for me. Listen, I need some help but can you tell me if my daughter is all right?"

"Ashley's with the councilman, I heard," Katie said. "Now where are you, Chief?"

"I need an EMT bus right away. Ambulance, too. You should probably give the station a buzz. You need to check the exact location of an Alan Bradford. I think it's Picket Road but you should be able to get that info with your enhanced system."

"Already got your location, Chief."

Claire paused, breathing deeply. She was beginning to see twinkling lights, but couldn't check out, not yet. "We'll be in the barn."

"Got, it, Chief. Dispatching now. You want to hold the line until someone gets there?"

It was tempting. After the night she'd had, Katie's friendly voice, any friendly voice sounded good. "No," she said. "I'll be fine until they get here. We're in the barn."

Claire released the phone and dropped it to the floor beside her, the old cord stretched to its limit. Her eyes drifted shut of their own accord.

The dog whined and pushed its wet, cool nose against her cheek, then licked her face. She laughed, opening her eyes. "What? What is it, boy?" She scratched behind his ears.

He whined again.

"I know. Can't take that catnap yet." She paused, gathered her wits as best she could, and then using the dog and the wall for support, pushed herself to her feet.

Forcing one foot in front of the other, she crossed the kitchen and on the way through the laundry room, realizing she was still topless, she grabbed a men's white T-shirt from a neat stack on the dryer. If she flashed the EMTs and ambulance squad she'd never hear the end of it.

Pulling the shirt over her head, she went out the old wooden screen door and down the porch steps. The dog stayed right beside her all the way across the dark lawn to the barn.

"Alan," she called as she walked through the open door. "There's an ambulance on its way. EMTs, too."

She stepped into the circle of light and crouched down beside him. He was looking up at her . . . but his eyes were sightless.

She pulled the blood-soaked towel from his neck. The blood flow had stopped, not because the wound had coagulated, but because his heart had stopped. She tried to get a pulse at his wrist, anyway. Nothing. No rise and fall of his chest, either. She thought about starting CPR as she slumped back against the picnic table, but she knew it was pointless. She didn't have enough energy left in her to sit up again anyway.

A minute or two later—it was hard to tell how much time had passed— Claire heard the wail of a siren. Two. Tears slipped down her cheeks and when she tried to stop them, she just cried harder.

Her back against the picnic table bench, she threw one arm around the brown dog and cried for Alan. Not for the monster he was, but for the little boy he had been.

"Mom. Mom, can you hear me?"

Claire's eyelids felt too heavy to possibly move them. She could hear a siren loud now. And Ashley. Ashley was talking to her.

"Mom, please."

She felt pressure on her hand. Ashley was squeezing her hand so hard that it hurt.

"Honey, you can't do that," a gentle voice warned. She knew the voice. Kevin, the EMT.

"Sorry," Ashley said tearfully.

"Come on, sit beside me, Ash," another voice said. "We'll be at the hospital in a minute.

It was Graham. She didn't have enough energy to smile, but she smiled inside. Graham, her Clark Kent. Graham who was pretty fine in bed, if she recalled correctly. Graham who she was in love with, or at least would be if she could find the time to go out with him. Something told her she'd have the time now.

The sound of a sniffle tugged at Claire's foggy brain. She knew that sniffle. Ashley was crying.

"Ash," she whispered.

"Mom? Mom!" Ashley was at her side again in a second.

Claire mustered up every ounce of energy she had left in her and opened her eyes. "Hey."

"Hey," Ashley breathed. Her eyes were red with tears and her nose was running. "You okay?"

"Peachy." Claire took a deep breath, willing herself to keep her eyes open just another second for her daughter's sake. She could see that she was on a stretcher, in an ambulance. Kevin was leaning over her, checking an IV he'd put in her foot, of all places. "How about you? You okay, Ash?" Claire asked.

"Peachy," she answered, smiling through her tears.

Claire closed her eyes again. "Well, I'm glad you're safe, but that doesn't mean you're off the hook with the tattoo." She could feel herself drifting again. "We'll talk about it later, okay?"

"But we'll talk about it, you and me, right?" Ashley said. "I'll stay here with you and we'll fix it. I don't have to go to Dad's to live."

"You don't have to go to your dad's," Claire murmured.

"Come on," Graham told Ashley, gently. "Your mom's going to be all right. We need to let her rest."

"I love you, Mom," Ashley said, throwing her arms around her mother, her blond hair falling across Claire's cheek.

Claire couldn't hug her daughter in return because both arms were strapped to her sides. Someone was working on a bandage on her right wrist. But she breathed in deeply, inhaling the sweet scent of her daughter's hair. Her skin. "I love you, too, Ash."

Epilogue

One year later

"Hey, sorry I'm late." Claire, dressed in her uniform, walked up to the table in the diner where Graham was already seated, leaned over the table and kissed him on the mouth. "A little problem on the boardwalk. A couple from Pennsylvania went into a fry place, left their beach chairs outside the door, and these kids thought it would be funny if they hid them in the public bathroom. The tourists wanted to file charges." She rolled her eyes, taking a seat across from him on the nagahide bench.

"The crime in this town." Graham shook his head. "Frightening, isn't it?"

She met his gaze across the table, her thoughts tumbling back to the summer before. She still had a couple of raised red scars on her wrist from Alan's scalpel, but they had healed nicely. Others, inside, would take longer . . . maybe a lifetime.

Claire was just thankful to be alive, to have

Ashley and Graham. Despite regrets and remorse, she was thankful she had been able to stop the poor sick son of a bitch before he had murdered any more young women. She regreted never knowing what had set Alan off on his killing spree, but sometimes you just didn't get all the answers. As for her remorse for not catching him sooner, it was just something she'd figured she lug around with her the rest of her life. Nature of the beast, the FBI psychiatrist she had seen a couple of times had explained to her. No law enforcement agent who dealt with a serial killer and survived didn't carry some guilt.

Graham reached across the table and took her hand in his. He didn't seem to notice the raised welts on her wrist. "You talk to that guy? The one who wants to write the book?"

She glanced up, focusing on his face, pushing Alan's from her mind. "Sydney McGregor's husband? Yeah. His name's Marshall King. Nice guy. You can tell he's not from around here, but . . ." She lifted her shoulder.

She knew she should take her hand from Graham's. She was in uniform; public displays of affection were inappropriate for officers on the job. But she just wasn't ready to let him go. Not sure if she would ever be.

After she'd gotten out of the hospital last August, she'd asked Graham to move in with her and Ashley. He'd countered by asking her to marry him. They'd remained at a standoff until Christmas Eve when Ashley had accepted Graham's proposal and the antique platinum engagement ring from him for her mother.

Just thinking about Ashley made her smile. She

was so proud of her and not nearly so worried as she had been the year before. Her daughter's hair had remained blond, the black eyeliner was gone, and she was still dating Chain who would start college in the fall. Ashley was on the right path.

Claire looked down at the sparkling diamonds on her finger. And so was she. The wedding was the first weekend in October—as soon as the tourists went home and work slowed down. She couldn't wait to be married, mostly because she couldn't wait to wake every morning to see Graham in bed beside her.

"You going to let him write the book?" Graham prodded gently.

"No letting him about it. The details of the murders are well-documented; no records are sealed. He's free to write whatever he likes."

Graham tightened his grip on her hand, holding her gaze. "You know what I mean. He wants to interview you in depth. He wants to know what it was like. That would mean having to relive it all, Claire."

She sighed, pulling her hand away to make room for a pert waitress to slide her iced tea and chef's salad across the table in front of her.

"But it might be good for you, you know." He leaned back to make room for his tuna croissant.

"Anything else?" the waitress asked.

"No. Thanks, Sheila." Claire offered a quick smile and waited for her to walk away before she spoke again. "I keep thinking about Alan growing up in that ramshackle farmhouse with that old woman, that . . . that *monster*. I just keep thinking that—"

"Claire, abuse is a factor in creating twisted men

like Alan Bradford, but there are plenty of people who survive abuse; physical, emotional, even sexual, and they do not end up torturing and murdering young women."

She picked up her fork and nudged a piece of hard-boiled egg in her salad bowl with the tines. "I know that. Dr. Greene keeps reminding me. It's just that it was going on right here in our town." She stabbed the egg. "I was growing up right here in Albany Beach, riding my bike to the beach, getting my dad to take me to swim lessons, taking horseback riding lessons and Alan was . . . he was—"

"Claire," he interrupted. "You have such a good heart that I know you can't help thinking these things, but you need to let them go."

"I know." She looked up at him and smiled. Popped the egg into her mouth. "Thanks for listening. How much you charge an hour on your lunch break, Doc?"

"Oh, there's a fee." He grinned lasciviously. "A hefty one, but I plan to wait until my wedding night to collect."

Claire reached for her iced tea, laughing. She could feel her cheeks grow warm. In all these months, she and Graham hadn't made love again. He insisted he was "saving himself for marriage." In a way, it angered her sometimes. She wanted desperately to feel his naked body against hers again. But in another way, it was so romantic. So damned sweet of him.

"Promises, promises," she complained. She looked up. "Yes."

"Yes, what?"

She lowered her voice, leaning over the table.

"Yes, I'll marry you. Yes, I'll hop into bed with you and have hot sex on October 3, and yes, I think I will let Marshall interview me. I think I need the therapy and he's actually going to pay *me* for it."

Graham smiled. "I love you, Chief Drummond." He lifted one eyebrow. "Even if you do scare me a little when you're in that uniform."

She laughed, scooting back in the seat and reaching for her glass. "That's all right. Sometimes, I scare even me."